# Clifford's War
# REDIVIVUS

J. Denison Reed

# J • DENISON REED

# Chapter One

_Breckenridge, Colorado_

**The light blue sedan** drags up the steep incline of the decorative stone driveway and comes to a full stop. Raymond steps out of the car, heads up the front steps of the large home, and turns around to admire the untouched snowy grounds the beautiful home sits on. He breathes out a long, anxious sigh before ringing the doorbell.

"He's here!" Hadley exclaims as she jumps up from her chair, awaiting her father's arrival.

Her mother gasps, startled. She rolls her eyes at her jumpiness and directs her irritation outward.

"Jesus, Hadley. Calm down."

She looks at her steward.

"She acts as though he's been away to war."

"If I may, Ma'am. It _has_ been over a month."

She purses her lips and narrows her eyes at the comment. "And whose fault is that, Spencer?" she retorts.

Spencer holds his tight-lipped smile. "Fair point, Ma'am," he replies.

She makes her way toward the door to join Hadley and her ex-husband.

"Hello Raymond," she says, tucking her blonde hair behind an ear before folding her arms to ward off the cold air that was brought in.

Raymond straightens his posture after hugging their daughter and clears his throat. "Grace. You look well."

She rolls her eyes.

Hadley places her hand in Raymond's as Grace starts the lecture they both know is coming.

"This is your first visit in over a month and first unsupervised visit since our div-"

"I'm well aware, Grace," Raymond says, cutting her off.

Grace exhales sharply through her nose before she continues, "You're only getting this time because I'm allowing it, and I expect constant communication."

Raymond looks down, regretting his interruption. Hadley gives his hand a light squeeze, which he returns while he nods and looks back up to meet his ex-wife's eyes.

She continues. "No drinking, no drugs, and absolutely no gambling while she's under your supervision. Got it?"

"Of course. I would never-"

Grace cuts in, "You already have. You can't say never if you've done it."

Raymond rephrases, "It won't happen again. I promise."

"Good."

She turns and nods to the valet, who takes Hadley's bags to the trunk of Raymond's sedan.

"Meet ya at the car, Sweetpea," he says before following the valet.

Hadley huffs and folds her arms. "You don't have to be so mean to him, Mom."

Grace cups her daughter's face gently and smiles.

"I need him to understand that you're my top priority, and he needs to earn his time with you. I'm aware you love your father, but he has been very irresponsible, and I worry. He needs to know that. Your time is not a right; it's a privilege, Hadley, and that goes for everyone, not just your father."

Hadley nods, saying, "I get it, Mom, but try to be nicer about it? Please? He's trying."

Grace sighs. "I suppose. It does seem he's been getting better."

Hadley hugs her mother, squeezing her tightly. The top of her head is resting just under Grace's chin.

Grace kisses the top of Hadley's head and swallows the lump trying to form in her throat.

"Here," Grace takes Hadley's arm to stand on the front porch. "Let me get a picture of you to hold me over until you get back."

Hadley laughs and strikes a pose for her mother before running to her father.

Grace stands in the doorway, watching Raymond help the valet load the luggage into the trunk. Hadley's shiny, forest green plastic shell luggage is taking up most of the space.

During his conversation with the valet, Raymond glances up at Grace with a smile. She feels her own smile growing as she watches him swoop their daughter in a swinging embrace. Something he's done since she was a toddler.

Grace takes no pride in having kept father and daughter apart for so long, but Raymond put their family in danger with his reckless behavior too many times. Her lawyers made sure she had full-custody.

Raymond helps Hadley into the car and shuts the door.

He walks back up to Grace. "Here's all the information on the lodge," and hands her a slip of paper.

Nostalgia briefly surprises Grace. Texting under the circumstances would have been suitable, but she knows a hand-written note is classic Raymond; something she had once loved most about him.

She sets her jaw, focusing on the present rather than allowing her melancholy to take her down memory lane.

She looks up to see the sun heading west in the mid-afternoon sky. "How long of a drive do you have?"

"It's only 90 minutes north of here. Most of the roads are fine, but there may be some icier ones the closer we get. I'll take it slow. Give us about two hours and I'll have her call you directly from the room."

Grace narrows her eyes to hide her growing apprehension the closer he gets to driving Hadley away.

"I'll take good care of her. I promise."

"You'd better."

Raymond looks away, deciding to ignore the veiled threat.

Grace looks past Raymond and waves and blows a kiss to her daughter.

Hadley smiles and blows a kiss back.

Grace steps back into the house and turns toward him. "Raymond," she pauses, getting his attention before continuing, "be safe," she says, closing the door.

Spencer watches his employer fight her tears as she shivers from the cold air. He's glad he thought to grab her shawl. She thanks him as he drapes it over her shoulders.

"I took the liberty of starting a fire in the sitting room, Ma'am."

"Lovely, Spencer. Thank you."

He tucks a cashmere throw blanket around her legs. "I have a cup of chamomile tea for you," he says as he moves to the silver tray on a credenza.

"You are too good to me, Spencer."

Spencer nods. "I know, Ma'am."

She chuckles at his blunt response.

With a stiff nod, Spencer proceeds out of the room and into the hall, leaving his employer to her thoughts.

Grace gazes across the room to the large window that faces her favorite view of Ten Mile Range. She thinks of her daughter, and it feels like a vice grip around her heart. The emotions build, and she allows herself a moment to cry.

Her thoughts return to that night, as they often do. The night they went from being a happy family, living in Kentucky, to this.

Her grief slips to anger, as if on cue, and the tears dry.

She looks at the tea waiting for her on the tray and notices that Spencer left a book from the pile she had been meaning to read next to it. Grace smirks at his thoughtfulness.

"I get the hint," she says to herself.

She reads until her eyes get heavy.

Grace awakens to the clock's chime. Confused, she focuses her blurred eyes to see that it's eight o'clock.

She runs a hand through her hair as she reaches for her phone. "Shit!"

A sigh of disappointment escapes her when she sees there are no missed calls.

She sends a text to Hadley.

*Have you made it?*

Surprised that her daughter, with her first phone, doesn't immediately text back, Grace masks her growing fear with annoyance.

After another minute passes, she texts Raymond.

*Please check-in!*

Recalling the time they left, she knows they must have been there for a while.

She opens the GPS tracking app she installed on Hadley's cell phone. The app shows her phone is just shy of the lodge by a few miles. The icon also indicates that it hasn't moved in quite some time.

Assuming they must have lost cell service, she calls the lodge.

"Bear Canyon Lodge, may I help you?" A cheery voice on the phone asks.

"Hello, I'm trying to reach one of your guests, Raymond Pollard. He should've arrived with our daughter hours ago."

The man is quiet for a moment before he says, "I'm sorry, ma'am, I have the reservation, but he hasn't checked in yet."

Grace says, "I'll try back in a few. Thank you."

She looks at the GPS app and sees Hadley's phone still hasn't moved. She refreshes the app, and after a couple of seconds of watching a circle go round and round, the icon turns red and reads, "Unavailable."

# Chapter Two

**The rubber tires** touch down on the tarmac at the Denver airport, letting out a long, wailing cry. A few of the passengers clap in celebration of a successful landing.

Rolling his eyes, Clifford Dee sighs in relief. Flying has never been his favorite thing. He's always happier with his feet firmly planted on the ground.

Clifford would have preferred to use the time on the flight to prepare for the case, but he's still unsure why Grace reached out to him. She had insisted he come alone. Clifford's partner and technology lead, Bailey, wouldn't let him take the job without being allowed to at least track location and vitals.

She agreed to that.

Clifford hadn't seen Grace in a few years. Not since their brief run-in while Clifford was working a case that involved mafia boss E.I. Bandoni in Kentucky. Between the two of them they managed to get her family out of the kingpin's crosshairs.

Clifford's certain Bailey already knows, but decides to be courteous and send a text to let him know he'd landed safely. He turns his phone off of airplane mode and a queued text from Grace comes through.

*Level 6 road. Black SUV. Driver will find you.*

The windows alongside the main terminal's wall allow a spectacular view of the sun setting over the mountains, causing the sky to light up in an array of oranges and pinks. The glow highlights the darker clouds approaching.

Bailey responds with only a thumbs-up emoji to his earlier text. Clifford pockets his phone as he secures the rest of his luggage from baggage claim and heads outside toward level six.

The crisp air cuts through the coat Clifford had believed would be warm enough. He places his bags at his feet to put his bare hands in his pockets. While thinking about digging into his bag for gloves a customized Range Rover pulls up, and the passenger window rolls down.

"Mr. Clifford Dee?" the driver yells across to him.

"Yeah!"

The liftgate opens as the driver gets out and rounds the front while buttoning his coat.

"Mr. Dee, I'm Jimmers, your driver for this evening. Let's put your bags in the back."

Clifford walks alongside the driver toward the back of the car.

After placing his bags inside and closing the back, Clifford walks around the car heading toward the front passenger side. Jimmers stops him at the rear door and smiles politely.

"You'd be more comfortable in the back, Sir."

Inside the warm luxury SUV are cold beverages. Bottles of water, beer and soda gathered in ice. Next to them are paper wrapped sandwiches that make his mouth instantly water. Above those, on a secured mini shelf is glassware, and a bottle of Kentucky whiskey.

Clifford smiles at Grace's subtle nod to their past connection.

Next to the bottle is a basket of various pretzels and chips.

Clifford finds himself sinking into a lush rear-facing leather seat. The seat warmer takes little time to ease his muscles.

"You were right. I am quite comfortable," he quips.

Jimmers chuckles. "Your destination is approximately ninety-five minutes away. Sit back and enjoy the refreshments while we travel. The satellite radio is set for relaxation, but you have complete control on what you'd like to listen to," he says from the front seat.

"Thanks," a famished Clifford says as he grabs a sandwich before indulging in anything else.

"You're welcome. Give the partition a gentle tap if you need me for anything."

As they begin to travel down Peña Boulevard, the glowing red eyes of Blucifer catch his attention through the rear window.

Clifford can't help himself. He takes a dozen photos of the mountains before the sun goes down and sends them to his crew.

Their texts come in, one after the other.

Dan: *Think u caught the best case ever!*
Bailey: *Nice view*
Sara: *Happy for you. Not jealous at all...*

Clifford pours himself two fingers of the whiskey, sits back and enjoys the view. The roads change from busier highways to less traveled routes as the landscape alters. The mountains inch closer, and the range seems to surround them as Jimmers navigates the weather on the paved narrow incline.

Clifford can see individual properties lit up as they nestle between wooded groves; each appearing more impressive than the next.

The feel of the road changes. Clifford turns to see they've pulled onto a long driveway that bends around a copse of trees. The main house reveals itself on the other side.

Clifford dons his coat again as the car comes to a stop.

The partition slides open.

"Mr. Dee, we've arrived."

The liftgate activates, and Clifford's car door is opened by an older man in a suit with leather gloves, wearing a cashmere scarf around his neck.

"Mr. Dee, my name is Spencer. Please follow me inside. The valet will handle your luggage."

Clifford steps out, taking in the view of the spectacular home.

The front door swings open, and his client Grace steps out under the portico.

"Clifford Dee. I am so relieved to see you."

Before Clifford steps inside, he knocks the snow off his shoes.

"I regret packing my winter gear, but we're having a false spring in Virginia," he says with a chuckle.

Grace looks him over.

"Well, I'll admit the amount is quite unusual. We typically get storm after storm in March, not January," she says before looking at Spencer. "Have them put Mr. Dee's belongings in the main guest room."

She escorts Clifford into a rustic chic sitting room with a fire roaring by a large window.

"I must say, this is a huge upgrade from your last place," he says, looking around.

An oversized cream sectional sits in the middle of the room, and Clifford is directed to take a seat.

"How's the hand?" he asks.

Grace instinctively looks at the scar on her left palm, intersecting the distal transverse crease. Only Clifford and Raymond know what she did to get it.

"Healed nicely, thank you. Can I get you anything, Clifford?" she asks as she picks up a cup of tea from a tray.

"Oh, no, I'm fine, and please call me Dee."

She forces a smile as she takes her own seat on the sectional across from him.

"Raymond, my *ex*-husband, was one of the real estate attorneys for the Bandoni crime family. He was paid handsomely to make their illegal properties legal, but he started taking some side-money from two of Bandoni's employees to help them set up gambling nests all over town. Didn't take long for him to develop a gambling addiction."

Clifford nods, knowing the two employees she's referring to as the infamous Tye brothers.

"Anyway, I took what I could from our accounts and protected our money from his vice. I'd developed my own company when we were financially secure and made decent investments."

She stopped to look around at her home that felt more like a prison without her daughter in it.

"My own blood, sweat, and bitter tears created this upgrade. My security is more impressive than the house. I don't know how long Bandoni's tentacles are. If he finds out we survived that night..."

Clifford begins to understand why she had asked him to come alone.

"I've kept tabs on you," she continues," I read what happened in Kentucky after we left. Bringing down Bandoni and having his property seized couldn't have been easy."

"I had a team to help me - which, and forgive me, Grace, but why exactly am I here?"

Grace respected his directness.

With a shaky breath, she says, "My daughter, Hadley, is missing. She left a few days ago on a trip with Raymond, and I can't reach either of them."

Clifford perks up. "The police are involved, yes?"

"Well, if Bandoni's the reason, I thought you'd be best-equipped-"

Clifford shakes his head vehemently.

"Highly unlikely, Grace. You need to contact the police! Raymond could've kidnapped his own daughter, or they could both be hurt from an acci-"

"I know Raymond. He wouldn't have gotten Hadley excited for all the fun activities he booked.

"My team already confirmed everything he'd arranged for them to do was paid for. There were also no accidents reported on the roads he would've taken to get there from here."

"I still don't understand why the police aren't all over this," Clifford says in frustration.

He watches her face change and spots shame.

"I think I did something stupid," she whispers. "This could all be my fault."

"Oh, Grace. What did you do?" Clifford asks.

Grace takes a deep breath and slowly exhales. "I'd suspected that he might be gambling again. The trip was already booked and Hadley..." Grace's voice catches.

"She looks at him like he hung the moon. She was so happy and excited. I couldn't ruin that for her, not again.

"The divorce has taken its toll on our relationship. Fred, my head of security, kept tabs on Raymond, for Hadley's safety, of course. Raymond had been doing well; going to meetings. But, about six weeks ago, he spent an entire weekend inside a casino- *losing*. Fred told me he took a marker worth nearly forty grand in one of those tourist-trap towns up north."

Clifford lets out a low whistle at the amount.

"Obviously, I was livid. I felt like I couldn't really do anything so, I figured... maybe if he was scared straight-"

"Oh no, Grace. You didn't!" Clifford says with worry.

"The divorce didn't faze him. I thought losing custody did the trick until... I was angry, and I thought that if he felt genuine fear - maybe even a hospital stay - he'd *finally* stop.

"I imagined Hadley would be disappointed that she couldn't go, but... I wouldn't be the bad guy for once.

"Fred said he'd handle it. He called in some favor and assured me it'd be taken care of before their trip. But when Raymond showed up that morning... I knew something had changed. I couldn't just keep Hadley here."

She stares into the fire, clutching her teacup.

"And they never made it to the lodge?" Clifford asks.

"No. I wanted to call the police. Fred said he'd handle it, so I gave him twenty-four hours. He knows I've called you and assures me he'll cooperate."

Clifford nods, silent in thought for a few moments. "I see. I'll need the address of the lodge, the information of everyone involved, including Fred."

Grace sits up and says, "I'll make sure that you have all of that. Fred should join us for breakfast in the morning. His office is on the property. He was supposed to have been here to greet you with me, but a personal matter came up that he needed to attend to.

"Oh, Clifford, before I forget, I have a reloadable debit card for you to use for all your expenses."

She heads over to a small table opening a drawer.

"There's currently ten thousand dollars loaded on the card. That should get you started. Use it to pay for meals, rooms, supplies... whatever you need. If you run low, text me and I'll add more."

"This should be plenty. I appreciate it. Did you by any chance take a picture of her before she left? I'd like to see what she was wearing. Also, did Raymond give you their itinerary? Besides the lodge, of course."

Grace smiles and walks back toward Clifford with a manila folder. She says, "I had all that information prepared for you," as she hands him the folder with the debit card clipped to the front.

He flips through it, pulling out stills of security camera footage from the day. He had a clear look at their clothing, and the car Raymond was driving. His license plate, a copy of his license with his home address, his cell phone number, Hadley's cell phone number, and a photocopy of her school ID.

Clifford points to neatly handwritten words on the corner of a page. "What's this?"

"Say that to Hadley once you see her. She'll know you're a safe person."

He looks at her, confused by the choice of words.

Grace shrugs, "No adult trying to take a child would say that. Tell absolutely no one what it's for. Including that team of yours. Not even Fred knows it. Do you need anything else?"

Clifford purses his lips and says, "This should be enough to get me started. Thank you."

That night, Clifford looks over every piece of information in the file. He takes photos of everything and uploads them to the cloud Bailey had set up. Clifford sends a text to him before realizing the late hour. Paired with the two-hour time difference, he knew Bailey would be asleep.

The heaviness of the jetlag sets in, and Clifford decides he's done all he can for now. Sleep takes over when his head hits the pillow.

# Chapter Three

**The next morning,** Clifford wakes only to realize his internal clock is still on Eastern Standard Time. He looks at his phone, disappointed his day is starting just before 4am.

Rotating his shoulders and tilting his head from side to side, Clifford is rewarded with satisfying cracks and pops.

He opens Google Maps and looks over the two routes and trails Raymond would have traveled from Grace's to Bear Canyon Lodge. One is a more direct route and makes more sense for his vehicle. The other is several miles out of the way, and the terrain becomes rougher the farther north it goes.

Bailey's text comes through before he puts the phone down.

*u up?*

Testing his bad knee, he's surprised it feels good as he slowly stands from the bed. Clifford stretches his back a little before returning to the warm and comfy bed.

He answers Bailey.

*Yep. Can I call?*

His phone vibrates in his hand, and he chuckles when Bailey calls first.

"Of course you would," Clifford says to himself before answering.

His original battle buddy on his team; Bailey is trusted personally and professionally. Clifford even made him a partner in his company, BluTrace Investigations, after the last case.

Bailey's brain can make order out of chaos quickly, but he's also a bit of a 'mother hen' for the team.

"Hey!"

"What's up, Dee? I didn't expect you to be up."

Clifford sighs, "Yeah, brain and body are fighting over what time it is."

"Jetlag's a bitch. How's everything goin'?" Bailey asks.

"Good. Cold. Snowy. The client sent a luxury car with heated seats and a minibar in the back."

Bailey can sense Clifford's smile through the phone.

"Sweet! Can't complain about that!"

Clifford chuckles a bit. "Yeah, no complaints about the transport. She set me up for the night in her house, but I'll be staying in hotels from here on out while I look for her missing daughter and ex-husband. It's a long story, but she prefers to keep the cops out of it."

"The fuck!?"

Clifford, involuntarily nodding in agreement of the sentiment, sighs. "That's the long story part. The short is; she tried to teach the ex a lesson. It backfired, and the daughter might be collateral damage."

"So where are we thinkin' about starting?" Bailey asks.

"Her security guy, Fred. He's involved in setting up that lesson. It sounds shady as fuck, but I'll take his temperature in a couple hours. I'm supposed to have breakfast with him."

"Cool, just make sure you wear that watch I gave you. It's been off your wrist almost 6 hours," Bailey says sternly.

"Wait, you want me to sleep with it on?" Clifford asks.

"I want you to *bathe* with it on, Dee. Never take it off. Okay? It measures your vitals and lets me keep tabs on you always. I need to make sure you're safe."

"Say less," Clifford says, rubbing his face as a yawn escapes him. "I'll put it on when I get up, and I won't take it off again."

"Thank you!"

Clifford continues, "Not until you tell me I can. Even if it chafes my arm."

Bailey chuckles.

"Okay, man, I know you've got stuff to do. Just remember, that watch lets me know if I need to send in the cavalry."

"Okay. I sent everything I have so far into the portal. That includes Ray and Hadley's phone numbers. See if you can trace them."

"Sounds good, Dee. I'll run those through today. Oh, and if Grace has the password to her daughter's phone, try to get that as well," Bailey responds.

"Will do," Clifford says.

Clifford places his phone in his lap and picks up the watch from the nightstand. He smiles as he tightens the buckle around his wrist.

His phone vibrates.

*Thank you!*

After a quick shower, Clifford dresses and makes his way downstairs. Spencer greets him and escorts him into a small sitting room.

"Sir, Ms. Dillenger thought it would be best for you and Mr. Polter to get acquainted before she joins you for breakfast. Would you care for some coffee? Tea?" he asks, walking over to an antique sideboard.

"Coffee, please. Black."

Clifford looks around at the navy and cream striped cotton-blend wing-backed chairs. A small table between the chairs holds flaky cookies and stroopwafels.

Spencer hands him his coffee and quietly retreats into the main hallway.

Both walls to the side of the window across from the chairs have floor to ceiling bookshelves filled with fiction and nonfiction works. A horror novel about haunted woods catches Clifford's eye. He pulls it down to read the jacket cover.

"I think I'm done with scary woods," he says to himself as he sets the book back in its place.

He goes to the tray and places a stroopwafel on top of his cup to warm as he sits.

"You must be Mr. Dee."

Clifford looks up to see an older gentleman enter the room wearing a polo shirt tucked into dark khakis with a belt and nice loafers. He looks about five foot ten, but with a stocky, muscular build. His face is deeply pock-marked, but the neatly trimmed mustache softens his facial features. His greying hair is freshly cut.

Clifford stands up as the man steps closer with a confident smile, extending his hand.

"Name's Fred Polter. Grace told me you were coming."

"Ah, Fred. I was sorry to hear I had to wait to meet you," Clifford says with a smile while returning the firm handshake.

Spencer prepares Fred's coffee and hands it to him without a word before leaving again.

"I had an appointment that couldn't be rescheduled. How do you know Ms. Dillenger?" Fred asks.

"It's a bit of a long, complicated story. But the short version is: back in Kentucky, I was told to kill her, and I didn't."

Fred's smile widens.

"I know the Kentucky story very well. She keeps your name out, though."

Clifford waits for Fred to take a sip of his coffee before he dives into his questioning.

"So, tell me about yourself, Fred. How did you come to work in private security for Grace?" he asks, bringing his own cup to his mouth.

"Former Sacramento PD. I retired about 4 years ago and moved out to Denver. I met Grace and Raymond soon after, and they were looking for someone to run security for them over the Bandoni situation."

Fred adjusts his position and picks up a palmier cookie.

"Were you a cop before becoming an investigator?"

Clifford shifts and takes the stroopwafel from his cup.

"Nope. Army Infantry. Special forces. I did some time in Afghanistan before deciding to get out and start my practice. What about you? Military?" he asks before taking a bite.

Fred shakes his head as he licks his fingers.

"Never joined. I thought about it but went to the academy instead."

Clifford licks the sweet caramel left on his thumb.

"Grace mentioned last night something about a guy you hired to scare Raymond. Mind explaining?"

Fred exhales through his nose, and Clifford notices his jaw flex.

"His name's Jack Hayden. I met him about six years ago or so. I was still on the force. A confidential informant on a case I was working on. He let it slip that he was a former government agent. I assume the CIA or FBI never asked, but anyway, we did favors for one another. Nothing too bad, just looking the other way on something minor, or access to some place before a warrant cleared."

Fred sips his coffee and crosses his legs as Clifford tries to keep his facial expressions neutral. Fred had casually alluded to being a dirty cop. He knows the type and surmises Fred would argue a 'greater good' defense.

Clifford continues to mimic Fred's physical actions to build rapport during the informal interrogation. He shifts to bring his leg up in a figure-four lock.

"Do you still have contact with the CI?" he asks before taking his own sip of the delicious brew.

"Unfortunately, no. When I tried making contact after Ray and Hadley went missing, he'd already gone dark."

Clifford shakes his head. Fred's demeanor and posture suggest he's calm, but what he says has alarm bells going off for Clifford.

"He went dark? That's suspicious, don't you think?"

"It's what he does. How he operates," Fred says with a shrug. "Look, I know how my arrangement with him may look, but I don't think he'd go rogue. He might've gone dark just to protect himself. That seems the most logical answer."

"It's not just how it looks. It doesn't sit right."

Fred leans in towards Clifford. "I'm trying to find him. I am. Gracie is a mess, and I want to get her daughter back."

Spencer walks into the room.

"Gentlemen, breakfast is served. Follow me."

Clifford isn't as relieved as Fred is for the interruption. He takes another sip of his coffee before leaving the chair and follows a step behind.

The three men walk into a formal dining room.

"Wow!" escapes Clifford's lips as his eyes lay upon a small feast.

A buffet table to the side displays eggs, bacon, waffles, fruit, and oatmeal. A variety of juices, and more coffee sit at the end.

Grace is already sitting at the head of the table. She smiles warmly as they enter.

"I take it you two had time to get to know one another?"

Fred chuckles as he grabs a plate. "We have. Were you able to get any sleep?"

"Some," she admits.

Clifford prepares his own plate and sits on one side of his host. He pays close attention to her interactions with Fred and Spencer while he eats his eggs.

"I take it you finally quit smoking?" Clifford asks, remembering the hidden pack of cigarettes she kept in a kitchen cupboard years ago.

Fred chuckles and looks at Grace.

"Oh, I haven't quit exactly. Spencer keeps my... vices on-hand, but he's hidden them. He also replaced my nightly whiskey with tea. If he weren't so damn good at his job-"

"Yes ma'am. I know. You'd fire my ass," Spencer says dryly.

Fred laughs as he gazes at Grace. Clifford observes that he often watches her when she's unaware.

"Would you like me to get some of the food for you?" Clifford asks Grace, seeing she's only drinking coffee.

"I haven't had an appetite, but thank you for your concern," she says, running her finger around the mouth of her cup. "I had Spencer reserve a suite with an open-ended checkout date under your name at the lodge. You did say you wanted to start your search there, right?"

Clifford nods as he wipes his mouth.

"That's great, yes, thank you. Fred, I'd love for you to join me when you can. Since you know more about the man you hired."

Fred shifts in his seat uncomfortably. The smile plastered on his face falters.

"I have a lot to do here, but I'll make my way up as soon as I can."

Clifford nods and changes the subject.

"If you don't mind me asking, what was the company you started that helped build all this?" he asks Grace.

She smiles with pride and takes a sip of her coffee.

"I was a partner in a small software development company. We developed software that strengthened the algorithms that made it possible for more secure video communications and teleconferencing. When the pandemic hit, our company made hundreds of millions after partnering with several big tech companies. I retired and sold the majority of my shares. Between that and other ongoing investments, my daughter and I can live quite comfortably."

Clifford raises his cup, impressed with the woman's fortitude.

Grace takes a sip of her coffee and asks, "How about you? How are things in DC?"

"Great," Clifford says quickly before continuing. "My team and I just finished a major case we didn't think would ever end. We have a few other smaller cases that are keeping us busy."

Fred excuses himself from the table.

"I should get going on my duties so I can meet up with our new investigator as soon as possible," he says as he walks away from the table.

"Fred takes his job very seriously. He was gutted when..."

Clifford watches her stare at the coffee she's barely sipped.

She blinks and takes a deep breath.

"If you're ready, we can head over to the garage and pick out your car."

The garage is at least three times the size of Clifford's townhouse. Grace explains that the area is climate controlled to stay at sixty degrees with fifty percent humidity. The air circulation is optimized to prevent any moisture buildup, and it's completely shaded from the sun and UV rays. A stable for automobiles, several motorcycles, golf carts, mini-bikes, and collectibles. The perfect garage.

Clifford whistles as he looks around at a vast collection of cars.

Grace raises her eyebrows. "I guess you approve?"

Clifford shakes his head in disbelief.

"Is this an underground bunker?"

"One of them. I have a panic room on the other side of the grounds."

"Jesus! You weren't kidding about your security!"

He looks around some more.

"You own a dealership, or somethin'?"

"Two, actually. A pet project that *kinda* took off," she says with a shrug.

"I think one of the SUVs would be the most practical," Clifford mentions as he runs his hands down the body of a tiny sports car.

"Agreed," Grace responds.

Clifford looks over at a Ford Bronco while an attendant walks up to answer questions.

Grace makes the introduction. "Dillon, this is Mr. Dee. He'll be taking a vehicle to help look for Hadley."

"You want the Badlands?" Dillon asks Clifford, referring to the model.

Clifford nods and says, "Yeah, that should work. I just need something that can get me from A to B, really."

Dillon goes over the amenities and mentions the hands-free phone features, which triggers a question Clifford wanted to ask Grace.

He turns to Grace and asks, "I forgot to ask you earlier, but you wouldn't happen to have the password to Hadley's phone, would you?"

Grace nods and says, "I do, but I'll need to look it up. I'll get it to you."

Clifford nods, "Thanks."

# Chapter Four

**The overnight snowfall** amounted to only a few inches, which accumulated on the asphalt. The snow was dry and airy, unlike the heavy and wet East Coast snow.

Clifford rounds a bend in the Bronco. Up a steeper incline, he slows down as the left side of the road is a very steep drop-off.

He notices that a portion of the guardrail looks damaged. A scenic overlook provides the perfect area for him to pull over and investigate. He steps out of the vehicle and carefully walks across toward the damaged guardrail.

A whipping wind blows across the road, making the mid-twenty degree air feel closer to zero. A car slowly approaches and stops as Clifford reaches the guardrail. He rolls down the window and yells toward Clifford.

"Everything okay, sir? Do you need me to get help?"

Clifford glances over and says, "No, I'm okay." He turns fully around and asks, "How well-traveled is this road?"

The man in the car thinks for a moment. "Not very traveled, I guess. This is more of a scenic route that takes you to Bear Canyon Lodge. Only locals really use this road. When you get to the top, it merges with the main road again."

Clifford nods, thanks the man and continues toward the guardrail as he drives away. He sees a few scratches and some paint transfer.

The color was light blue.

A few feet down, he spots a small piece of plastic, most likely part of a taillight. He sees a few more dings in the metal rail, but no breaks or serious damage that would indicate a car going down off the edge.

He takes a few pictures with his phone, snagging proof of the paint color, the shards of colored plastic, and even the road marker for reference.

As he walks back to the Bronco, he spots something on the ground out of the corner of his eye.

He heads over and pulls a pen off the road with his gloved hand. 'Wild Willies' was printed on the side of the cheap click pen along with the address. He shoves it into his breast pocket and heads back to the warm vehicle.

Clifford sits for a minute, allowing the seat warmers to soothe his cold body. As he sits, he uploads the photos to Bailey's portal.

He looks at the map on his phone and realizes he isn't too far from the lodge and continues on his way.

As he enters the property, there's a fork in the road. To the left, he spots a small cabin-like building with an old Jeep sitting in its parking lot. The sign with an arrow pointing reads, "Park Security Office."

He continues to the main building, but makes a note to venture over and chat with whoever's in the cabin. He continues on the narrow path leading up to the lodge and pulls up to the valet.

"Welcome, sir. Checking in?" the front desk receptionist asks.

"Yes, Clifford Dee," as he hands her the credit card from Grace.

A man rolls a cart with Clifford's luggage behind him and waits.

Clifford glances over his shoulder and nods.

The receptionist hands Clifford his electronic key and credit card and says, "Room 303."

Clifford smiles and says, "Add fifty for the attendant," to which the receptionist smiles and nods. Clifford turns to follow his luggage when a question hits him.

"The Park Security Office?" He begins, pointing in the direction of that cabin. "Does that include the Lodge?"

Debbie nods. "Yes, in the event a guest needs assistance in the park, they're close by."

"Great," Clifford says with a smile.

Clifford texts Bailey once he's alone in his room.

*At Lodge. Tagged location of possible accident. Paint transfer looks like R's car color.*

*Grace is getting pw for H's phone.*

*Look into Jack Hayden pls.*

By the time he's going over notes and unpacks, it's mid-afternoon. Clifford decides to visit the security office and heads back down to the lobby.

The receptionist motions to Clifford after he exits the elevator.

"Sir, do you need your car pulled around for you?"

"No, thank you. I'm just going to go for a walk."

"The sun will be down soon, and the temperature drops quickly."

Clifford nods, appreciative of the tidbit.

"I'll be back before dark. Thank you."

He turns to leave but stops for a moment to ask another question.

"What time is sunrise?"

The fresh air is brisk. As he inhales, it stings the inside of his nostrils. Clifford takes another deep, cleansing breath, and lets out a lungful of steamy air. He pulls his gloves out of his pockets and adjusts his scarf over his ears.

He takes a few steps and stops to admire the beautiful snow-dusted blue spruce, Ponderosa pines, and other conifers that claim this area as their home. This is his first trip to Colorado, and he's never seen a more picturesque winter landscape.

Clifford stops to check his buzzing phone.

It's a text from Grace.

*Hadley's password.*

Clifford thanks her and then shoots the info to Bailey before walking up the steps to the Security Lodge.

He lightly knocks on the door.

"It's open," a voice from the other side barks.

Clifford pushes open the door to a welcoming blast of warm air.

"What can I do you for?" the Hispanic gentleman behind the desk playfully asks.

The name tag over his badge reads, "Ramos."

Clifford smiles and walks closer to the desk.

"Hey there, Ranger Ramos! My name's Clifford Dee. I'm an investigator, hired to look for Raymond and Hadley Pollard. They were supposed to check in here last week, but never did."

"I'm not sure how much I can help, I'm not that kind of Ranger. I work with Lodge security and keep to the grounds. You can call me Luis. I'm not a cop."

Clifford says, "Luis, that's even better. My client needs discretion and isn't willing to have law enforcement involved yet. Hadley Pollard is the main priority. She's my client's teenage daughter. She was traveling with her father. If there's anything you can do to help, I'd really appreciate it."

Luis says, "I can try to help. What do you need?"

Clifford hands him the photos Grace put in the file.

"Father and daughter were traveling in a light blue sedan. The GPS on Hadley's phone stalled for some time before losing signal on the main road up here," Clifford gestures toward that area.

"Given the proximity to cell towers and signal interference from the mountains, it's accurate to about a half-mile. Give or take," Clifford says, pausing for a moment.

"On the way here, I noticed a dented guardrail. I stopped to get a closer look, and there was light blue paint transfer in the dents." Clifford opens his phone and shows Luis the picture of the guardrail.

Nodding, Luis asks, "You think that was from their car?"

Clifford says, "I do. Same color. I looked down the drop-off, and it looks like there's some snow disturbance, but nothing near the size of a car, and there were no breaks in the guardrail that would indicate a car went over the rail. I think somehow he bumped the rail but didn't go over. Were there any reports of an accident on the road last week?"

Luis shakes his head and says, "I don't think so, but you piqued my interest. Wanna go for a drive?"

Clifford smiles, "I'd love to."

Luis grabs his hat from the back of his chair.

"We gotta be quick. The sun will be down soon."

They slow to a stop beside the dinged guardrail, and Luis throws on his overhead yellow and white lights.

They both step out, and Clifford points out the blue paint as they get closer.

"Here, you see the light-blue paint transfer? It goes on for about twenty feet, like he skid across it."

Luis examines the paint, and he glances over the side. "Yeah, I see what you mean by the snow disturbance too. But that could easily be a small boulder falling. It's frequent."

Clifford nods, understanding that it's likely.

Luis continues to look down the drop-off.

After a few long seconds of silence, Clifford asks, "How far down do you think that goes?"

Luis' eyes widened. "A-ways. That gully at the bottom runs out to the creek, but there's no easy way to travel down there. You'd need to get a crane or something."

"And how hard would that be?"

"Let's go find out."


Back at his office, Luis says, "Wait here," as he heads into a back room.

Clifford looks around at the pictures hung on the wall. After a few minutes, Luis returns with a plat map of the park property.

Clifford pulls out his phone and asks, "Do you mind if I take pictures of this?"

Luis smiles, "Not at all."

Clifford texts the pictures to Bailey with notes describing what they are.

They continue to look over the map to find the incident area is on the resort property, which means Luis can request assistance without involving the police.

"We'll have to wait until tomorrow," Luis says, looking at his watch.

Clifford shakes his head. "Shoot, okay. When should we meet up in the morning?"

"Let's say seven. I need to close up the park and do my checks. If you need anything else, contact the resort security at the hotel. They have my direct number if you need me."

Clifford nods and says, "Thanks for your help."

"Sure, see you in the morning."

"See you then," Clifford says as he heads out the door.

As he reaches for the handle, Clifford turns back and sincerely says, "Thank you."

Luis looks up and nods. "We'll find that girl."

It takes a little over an hour for him to complete his evening tasks before Luis is on his way home.

He shuffles into the house and is greeted by his youngest daughter.

"Daddy!" she yells as she runs up and hugs him around the waist.

He reaches down and rubs her hair. She looks up at him with a smile and runs off into the other room.

His wife, Daniella, walks into the foyer and says, "Mi amor, dinner will be ready in half an hour."

Luis lets out a comforting sigh and smiles. "Thank you, mi vida."

Daniella looks at him, analyzing his demeanor, and asks, "What's on your mind?"

Luis shakes his head and tells her all about his conversation with Clifford Dee.

"I need to get equipment up to the lodge from the county road crew, but I'm afraid it will take weeks once I put the request in."

Daniella shakes her head. "No, no, no," she says. "Stay right here; I'll call Valerie Benson."

Luis, confused, asks, "Wait, who's Valerie Benson?"

Pulling her cell out of her pocket, she scrolls through her contacts. "She's helping me run the Rocky Mountain Mamas' social group. She works in the Mayor's office and oversees the road department. I'll see if she can get a crew there in the morning."

Luis says, "You don't need to -"

Daniella holds up her finger and walks away as Valerie answers.

After a quick chat about the situation, she ends the call and smiles at her husband.

"Good news?" Luis asks.

"Tell me you love me first."

Luis narrows his eyes.

"Mi amor, I cannot tell you enough how much I love you."

"Then tell me."

"Te amo mi amor. Siempre."

Daniella smiles and wraps her arms around her husband.

"Call Val's office first thing tomorrow morning. Tell them where, and the crew will be there before noon. I texted you her office number."

Luis drops his jaw. "Wow! That's amazing."

"The mom network is strong. Never forget that. Now, go wash up for dinner."

# Chapter Five

**Bailey** takes a break from looking over all the files Clifford uploaded during the investigation.

He rubs his eyes and pushes away from the desk. He wheels over toward the kitchen and pours himself a small cup of tea that was already steeped in a pot. A little bit of THC-infused honey is his sweetener of choice. He gives it a quick stir and sets it down to cool when there's a knock at the door.

Bailey looks at a screen to see his teammate Daniel on the other side of the door.

He presses a button on his phone that unlocks the door before yelling, "Come on in, Dan!"

Dan pushes the door open, and Bailey turns back to fetch his tea.

"Tea?" Bailey offers.

"Nah, I'm good. I was just wondering how Dee was doing," Dan says as he shuts the door.

Bailey takes a swift, tight-lipped sip of his tea and lets out a cooling breath and says, "That's still too hot," under his breath, setting the tea back down on the table.

"Dee's good. I'm going through a lot of the data he's sending over. Come, take a look."

Bailey wheels over toward his office and turns on his wall display to easily show Dan.

Bailey's home office is a telecommunications command center. He has displays all over the walls he can control remotely with his phone and virtual keyboard / mouse application he developed.

He prefers the term 'Technologist' to describe his passion for his skill set. He studies technology, versus adapting to it.

Dan watches closely as Bailey shows him the way to read the maps, identify elevation, and other cartographic techniques.

Bailey finishes his display and says, "I sent this all to Dee, and he can open it with the app I created on his phone."

Dan asks, "Do you need the app to open it?"

"Yeah, you need the app, create a password, add your fingerprint. It's a whole process. Didn't you get the memo about it?" Bailey replies.

Dan smirks and says, "I didn't quite understand what that meant. Can you show me?"

Bailey smiles and says, "Dude, that's why you haven't been uploading anything? I thought you knew about it this whole time. Say something next time. Okay, so I already pushed the app to your phone. The company cell phones are linked to a server on my network that acts as a huge application store for all my software."

Dan pulls out his phone and looks through it. Bailey shows him around the apps, explaining to him how it works, and then asks, "So, how's that custody case coming?"

Dan nods and says, "Oh, it's pretty much done. I just need the last payment, and I hand everything over to the client."

"Oh! Check this out," Dan continues as he comes across a photo he took. "I tracked the subject to a sketchy part of D.C. and got pics of him making an exchange with a known dealer. He's still using, just as she suspected," he says, showing Bailey with a proud smirk on his face.

Bailey nods and gives a little golf clap. This was Dan's very first solo assignment, and he did everything himself from start to finish.

"How's Sara? Have you heard from her? Getting much-needed rest and relaxation, I hope."

The smile fades from Dan's face.

"Yeah, the Senator's case was rough on her. All of us, really, but..."

Bailey's expression turns more somber.

"I still haven't got any pings on Paul Michaels."

Their first major case in the DC area, "The case without end" as they refer to it, started as an investigation into an unfaithful senator and ended with them uncovering a high-ranking government official trying to conceal his attempts to smuggle guns into Africa.

They all barely escaped death, thanks to one rogue aggressor with the code name Dorothy.

"Yeah, thanks for the app demo. That's great. I need to prep for my meeting tomorrow, and I'm going to hit the gym. Is there anything you need from me?" Dan asks.

"Nah, I'm good. I'm glad your first solo case is almost done. You did a great job."

Dan blushes when he smiles again.

"I'll call you tomorrow after my meeting."

Bailey shouts back, "Don't take kisses as payment!"

Dan laughs, "I dunno, the client is pretty cute, but don't worry, I won't."

Bailey smiles to himself as Dan heads out. He fetches his tea and wheels back over to his computer to continue his work.

Looking over the picture showing Hadley's password, Bailey has an idea.

He takes a quick sip of his tea before wheeling over to a cabinet. He pulls out a brand new cell phone, and enters her phone number and email address into the login prompt and uses the password provided by Grace.

***

Clifford Dee is sitting in his hotel room reviewing the file that Grace put together for him when he gets a call from Bailey.

"Hey B, what's up?"

"Dee, check it out. I used Hadley's cell phone account information to log into a new phone, and I have access to everything she uploaded to her cloud storage."

"Sweet! That's good thinking. Anything useful?"

"Uh, yeah. I'm uploading the files to our app now. Take a look at the first video. This is the last thing loaded onto her phone. The phone's GPS pinged off the same cell tower about two miles away from the dented guardrail."

Clifford's phone dings, and he clicks the 'new files' notification to open what Bailey uploaded.

It's a zip file with a bunch of folders and files inside.

He sees the first is a video, so he clicks to watch it.

He recognizes Hadley hiding in the back of a car. Her face is half in frame as she whispers to the camera.

*"Dad was just run off the road by some jerks. He got out, and now they are all yelli-".*

Off-camera, a gunshot rings out, echoing through the mountains. Hadley looks up toward the sound, horrified, and her eyes widen in terror. *"Oh my G-, Oh m- Oh my God, Daddy!"* she screams out in a faint and shaky voice, lips trembling.

The video ends.

Clifford puts the phone speaker to his ear to replay it, and says, "Holy shit! Was that a gunshot?"

"Sure was, and it looks like she tried to send it to her mom, but it failed. She's also on social media, so I'm going to review her account. Maybe I can find you some people to talk to."

"Good thinking. I'm gonna sit tight on this, because I don't want Grace knowing about it until we have more information. I'll start going over the rest of these files. Oh, and I've been working with a park ranger up here named Luis Ramos. I'll share this info with him tomorrow," Clifford says.

"I thought Grace said no cops?"

Clifford clarifies, "Not that kind of ranger, but he's willing to help. Oh, did you get anywhere with the name Jack Hayden?"

"Nah. A couple obits from decades ago, but nothing that screams former CI who may or may not've been a spook."

"Okay man, sounds good. I'll let you know what else I find," Bailey says as he ends the call.

Clifford spends the next few hours going over the pertinent pictures and videos that Bailey found on the cloud account associated with her phone.

He earmarks the video and some other photos Hadley took that day before he calls it a night.

The next morning, Clifford wakes up to a text message from Bailey.

*"HMU when you get this. I got something."*

Clifford rubs his eyes and swings his feet off his bed. He stands and stretches before hitting the call button on his phone.

"Hey Bailey, what'cha got for me?" Clifford asks with a yawn.

"So, I had an idea. Since her phone pinged off the cell tower, we got a timestamp of that. I was able to find there were three other phones that pinged the same tower around the same time.

Raymond's was one. The other two were burner phones that also pinged near a casino off of Route 119 just a few hours before."

"Out-damn-standing! What about Raymond and Hadley's phones? Where did they last ping?"

Bailey takes a breath. "They didn't ping anywhere after that tower. So either they were turned off, or broken."

Clifford was quiet for a moment.

"It doesn't mean they, uh-"

"I know," Clifford says with a sigh.

"Yeah, but we have a thread, Dee. Let's get to pullin' on it," Bailey says.

"We do and we will. Let me talk this over with Luis and get back to you in a few hours."

# Chapter Six

**The air** is crisper than the day before as the crest of the early morning sun casts its rays to sparkle through snow-laden trees.

Clifford arrives at Luis' cabin office with two hotel coffees in his hands. The steam rolls off the tops of the cups, leaving a lingering warm, nutty aroma in the air.

He shuffles the cups into one hand and opens the door.

Luis, standing by his desk, looks over as the door opens.

"Dee, hey," Luis quickly says.

Clifford stops as he realizes they're not alone. Two other people are looking over the plat map on Luis' desk.

Luis continues, "This is Clifford Dee. He's the investigator the family hired. Dee, this is Janice and Mitchell. They work at the road department and are here to search the ravine."

Clifford displays a thin-lipped-grin and raises the coffee as a hello.

"I brought some coffee, but only two."

Luis glances over at a big to-go carafe from a local donut shop with a plethora of cups, creamers, sugars, and donuts.

"Janice's treat," Mitchell says.

Janice raises her coffee with a welcoming smile.

Clifford nods and sets the cups down on the desk next to her offerings.

"Sorry, I wasn't expecting them so early. I should have texted you."

Janice says, "When we heard a child's involved, we came right away."

Clifford asks, "No worries. When are you guys getting started?"

"Well, the sun will be optimal in about two hours. We already have all the gear in transit. We're heading out now to meet them to set up. As soon as we get something, we'll loop you in," Luis says.

Clifford nods, impressed by how quickly they're moving.

"Okay, great. I'll stay out of the way. I have a few strings I can pull on in the meantime."

"Cool. Like what?" Luis asks.

"I got word that there were two cell phones that pinged the same tower at the same time as Hadley's phone. I'm going to look into that."

"Excellent. Let me know if you need any help," Luis says as he glances back toward his desk.

"Call or text as soon as you get anything. I'll let you know if I dig up anything."

Luis nods and goes back to looking over the map, discussing the area they are going to search. Clifford grabs a donut, places it on top of the coffee he brought with him before heading back toward the lodge.

Three bites later, Clifford's donut is gone. He takes a big sip of his now cooled coffee before reaching the front door of the resort, then asks the front desk for his car to be brought around.

"I just need to scan your keycard, sir, and we will bring your vehicle around shortly."

After the scan, Clifford sits in a chair in the lobby near a window. He sips his coffee, taking in the winter-scape, while waiting for the car.

The valet pulls up and enters the lobby. He walks over to Clifford.

"Your keys are on the dash. I took the liberty of turning on your seat warmers."

Clifford palms the young valet a twenty-dollar bill and heads out to the Bronco.

While carefully passing the worksite, Clifford spots Luis talking with a small group on the side of the road, looking over the side.

As the road opens back up to both lanes, he picks up speed, heading toward where Bailey said the burner phones pinged a tower.

***

Clifford reaches a small town, talking with Bailey on speaker in the car.

"Okay, Dee, you're about two miles from the tower that was the last to ping those burner phones. The casinos I saw are a few miles farther up the road. I ran a report on Raymond's phone. It connected to the same tower a few weeks ago and sat connected for hours."

"Well, at least we know Fred's intel that Raymond was gambling again was right."

Clifford looks over and spies a novelty shop and decides to check it out.

"Hey B, there's a little shop here that looks like it would sell burner phones. I'm going to get a closer look."

"*Looks* like it sells burner phones? How's a building do that, Dee? Genuinely curious."

Clifford chuckles. "I can't explain it. It just fucking does, man."

Bailey laughs. "Alright, man. Be careful."

Clifford pulls off the road and into the small parking lot of the store.

"Hey there, friend, what can I do for ya?" A short, older man with a slender build sits behind a counter.

Clifford looks around the shop. Beautiful ornate glass and ceramic bongs sit behind glass cases. In a smaller display case were various pocket knives, some coated in titanium nitride to give them a rainbow shine. Clifford continues to look around until he spots a rack with reloadable phones next to phone cards.

"How much are your burner phones?"

The clerk looks over and says, "Depends on what you're lookin' for. Smartphones cost more. The prices should be on 'em."

"Ah, yeah, I see. You sell a lot of these?"

"They sell pretty regularly," he replies.

"I guess with the casino up the way…"

Clifford notices the clerk shift his stance.

He looks confused as he stammers a bit.

"I don't see what that has anything to do with the phones," he blurts out.

"I didn't mean anything by that; just presuming some visitors of the casinos might not want their personal phones located inside."

"Oh, no sir, they have signal blockers in the casinos. You can't use your phones up there. Even the beepers don't work so good. Cuz, cheatin' 'n all."

Clifford rubs his stubbly chin.

"Hmm, yeah, I guess that makes sense."

The clerk smiles conspiratorially as he leans toward Clifford.

"Most of the people who get the phones are guys staying in the hotels. It's so they can call their mistresses without their wives tracking their calls."

He chuckles for a moment and pauses, giving Clifford a serious look. "Some of the casino workers will buy 'em too, but hell if I know why. They can't use them at work. But they come back in for new phones every so often."

"Good to know," he says as he continues to look around the shop.

Clifford looks over all the devices, including vintage beepers, headphones, and portable batteries.

He stops at the camera display and grabs a top of the line camcorder, and takes it up toward the counter and sets it down. He points at a knife in the case and says, "I'll take that as well."

The clerk smiles and asks, "No phone?"

Clifford smiles back and says, "Nope. I was just curious. Keeping track of one phone's bad enough, right?"

"Don't have that problem. I ain't got a cell. Those things give you a brain tumor."

Clifford, noticing the pack of cigarettes in his breast pocket.

"Come on now. You're worried about cancer?" he asks as he points at the man's shirt.

"Yeah, them brain tumors develop quick - It's documented. Smokes take like twenty years."

Clifford gives a tight-lipped smile. He knows when to back out.

"I guess you've got a point."

Using the prepaid card Grace gave him, he makes the purchase and continues up the road when he spots a sign for a gun store across the divided highway.

He finds his way back to the gun shop after a U-turn.

The gun shop clerk is a lot less friendly than the guy from the previous shop.

Clifford spots a SIG Sauer M17. He'd carried one just like it in Afghanistan.

"How much for the SIG?"

"$750 plus tax."

Clifford nods as he looks around.

Realizing the cheap novelty knife is the only weapon he has, he turns back to the clerk.

"I'll take it."

"ID?"

Clifford fishes his license out of his wallet and sets it on the glass case. He also sets down his Virginia Concealed Carry permit and his DJCS license from Virginia.

The clerk looks down at the documentation and back up at Clifford.

"Mr. Dee, you can put all that away. You can't buy that handgun."

Confused, Clifford asks, "Why not?"

"State law. You're not a Colorado State resident. I can't sell you a handgun."

Clifford scoffs and starts putting his information away.

"Nothing? No guns at all?"

"Only hunting rifles and shotguns."

Clifford shakes his head and turns to look at the long guns.

"I'll take the Winchester up there and -" Clifford pauses while looking at the shotguns.

"And the Remington 870 pump."

The man gathers ammo for each gun, and Clifford selects the quantity.

"How long are you in town for?"

"I don't know just yet. A week. Maybe two. I'm meeting a few friends up at a cabin my buddy owns. We're going buck hunting," Clifford lies.

"Well, I guess you'll be mostly scouting for the next three days. Waiting period. You can leave today with the ammo, but you'll have to come back on Thursday to pick up your guns. ID?"

Clifford hands the man his license.

The man rings up the total and bags the ammo.

"The waiting period starts after the payment's completed."

Clifford hands the man the credit card and looks at the time on his watch.

Something catches his attention. He looks up to spot an unpackaged drone displayed on top of two more boxes.

"Waiting periods for drones too?" Clifford asks.

"Just the guns," the clerk says, handing Clifford his ID and credit card back.

Clifford tosses the ammo into the back of the Bronco. After seeing Hadley's video, Clifford understands the stakes have increased considerably. He'd feel so much better once he has a decent weapon. He also wants to take another run at Grace to get her to call the cops before he does.

He takes a deep breath as the Bronco warms up. Realistically, he knows he'll probably canvass around the casinos over the next few days while Luis and his team of engineers scour the side of the mountain for clues.

A text notification from Fred comes through.

*On my way up to the lodge, see you soon.*

Clifford responds:

*I'm out and about. Check in at the Ranger station with Luis. He's not a cop.*

Clifford calls Luis.

"Hey Dee, we haven't found much yet. We're going to go a little further down the ravine soon!" Luis yells, trying to speak over the sounds of the machinery.

"Uh, great! I guess no news is good news."

"I think so too!"

"I wanted to let you know I'm probably going to be out of town for the next day or two."

"Okay. I'll keep you up to date!"

"Thanks! One more thing. A guy named Fred should be coming by. He works for my client. You can update him."

"Who?"

"Fred. Fred works for my client!" Clifford says, shouting back.

"Hold on a second!"

After a few seconds, Luis comes back to the phone.

"Sorry, I was right next to a crane."

Clifford chuckles.

"Yeah, buddy, I could hear it. I wanted to let you know that a guy named *Fred* might stop by. He works for my client, so you can update him on everything. I gave him your name."

"Oh, okay. Fred's good for updates, you're out of town. Update you when I get something. Got it!"

Clifford takes a deep cleansing breath.

"You're the best. Thank you."

"No worries, take your time."

Clifford climbs into his car and heads back towards the casino. He rounds a sharp bend in the road to an immediate change in scenery. The quaint picturesque mountain-scape yields to a more aggressive atmosphere of flashing lights, signs, tall buildings, and hotels with casinos.

He turns off the major thoroughfare and onto a side access street. The strip is several miles long, so he finds a place to park for the evening and walks around.

# Chapter Seven

**Recalling the pen** he found, Clifford walks up to the historic Wild West burlesque club called "Wild Willies." The outside has an Old-West style aesthetic, with a cabaret character displayed behind the name with red, black, and yellow tones.

Clifford heads inside the club by pushing through the swinging saloon-style doors and rounds a corner to a larger door that blocks the view of the inside from the passersby.

The stage, illuminated inside the dark club, is where a burlesque dancer is finishing her routine. The modest crowd whistles and cheers.

Toward the side, he spots a wooden bar with brass features. He heads over to the bartender for a chat.

A fit and busty brunette with delicate features stands behind the bar, wearing a sleeveless saloon-style dress that shows off her colorfully tattooed arms. Her hair drapes down the sides in loose curls onto her bare shoulders. A small hat pinned on top of her head where her half-updo gathered. The bottom of the dress is longer in the back, and frills out, covering the tops of her knee-high leather boots. The front is short enough to expose her fishnet stocking-covered thighs. Her small nametag on her vest reads, 'My name is: Moxie.'

Clifford approaches and says, "Good evening, Moxie."

She glances over just as the light shimmers across his face and highlights the stubble on Clifford's cheek. The men who usually patronize the club all seem the same. She's disappointed in their character for just walking into the place before they ever open their mouths. *This guy,* she thought, *is very easy on the eyes. Too bad.*

She smiles and begins her usual routine. "Hello handsome, whatcha drinkin'?"

"Whatever you have on tap is fine," Clifford says, looking at his wallet.

He lays down a fifty-dollar bill. She glances at it and says, "Comin' right up. Did you just get in?" She asks as she pours his beer.

"Yeah, well, sorta."

"Oh? Sorta? What's that mean?" She asks, trained to seem interested, for tips.

Clifford says, "I flew into Denver a few days ago. I'm just up this way for a day or two."

Moxie finishes pouring the beer and slides it over toward him.

"A fun day trip for some gambling and a show?" she asks.

Clifford takes the beer as she picks the fifty he laid on the bar. He draws a hefty swig and sets it down.

"Not a day trip. I'm actually looking for someone."

Clifford pulls out his phone and shows her a photo of Raymond. She takes a quick look and shrugs, laying down the change for the beer.

"Sorry, he looks like every other guy I've seen today."

"It could've been anytime in the past few weeks," Clifford begins as he scrolls to a different photo on his phone. "He should be travelling with her," he volunteers as he shows her the photo of Hadley.

Moxie shakes her head. "I'm sorry, I haven't seen either of them."

Clifford pockets his phone, disappointed, and takes another swig of his beer.

Moxie wipes down the tap and notices Clifford staring at the wooden bar rather than the entertainment. She can't help but look at his hands for some evidence that he wears a ring. She watches as he drinks down the rest of the draught, licking the foam from his upper lip.

Clifford lays another fifty-dollar bill on top of his untouched pile of change on the bar and asks again, "Are you sure you haven't seen this guy?"

Moxie's eyes widen. "If I keep saying no, will you keep laying down bills?"

Clifford laughs out loud and says, "Your patience may outrun my funds."

"I get it. Cop's salary?"

Clifford shakes his head. "Not a cop. I'm a P.I. I run an agency near D.C."

Clifford hands her his business card.

Moxie, impressed, takes the cash off the bar and shoves it into the tip jar and puts his card into her pocket. "You said his name's Raymond?"

Clifford nods.

"I may know something. Not here, though. Got enough funds to buy me dinner?"

Clifford smiles. "You think your info's worth dinner?" He asks with a tilt of his head.

"Yeah, if the dinner's at Buffalo Bob's Diner," Moxie says with a smirk.

Clifford chuckles. "I passed it a few miles back. Yeah, I think I can swing that. Dessert, too," he says with a wink.

"Ooh, careful now, or you'll end up buying me breakfast. Meet me there at eight thirty?"

Clifford nods and watches as she glides to the other end of the bar to take a new order. He takes a moment to fully appreciate her entire look.

He can feel his cheeks warm when she catches him as they make eye contact. She smiles and mouths, "Eight thirty," before turning away.

Clifford looks into a few casinos and other places in the area with no luck. He knew from experience to ask service staff rather than management or bouncers first. Private security in places like casinos will usually stonewall an investigation before it gets off the ground. It's best not to push and risk pissing anyone off.

With little else to do, Clifford makes the walk back to his car to drive back to the sad little diner he passed on his way into town. He looks at his watch, noticing he has less than twenty minutes to get there. As he quickens his pace, he can't help but smile. Of all the people he approached today, he's glad Moxie's the one he's meeting for more information.

Using Bluetooth, he connects with Bailey to update him as promised. With little to report, Clifford tells Bailey that he may stay in the area overnight and try the casinos again in the morning.

Clifford pulls into the parking lot of Buffalo Bob's and idles until he spots Moxie getting out of a small, rusted two-door beater of a car. He walks to the front of the diner and waits for her to approach. The tiny hat is no longer pinned to her head. She'd tied her long hair up loosely in a bun with the colorful band he remembered seeing around her wrist earlier. Clifford's thankful to see her sexy leather boots peeking out of the bottom of the long buttoned-up trench coat she uses to hide her uniform.

"After you," he says, holding the door open.

"Oof, and a gentleman. Strike three," she says as she enters the diner and waves at the waitress behind the counter. Clifford continues to follow her as she makes her way into a booth.

"Mind telling me how I struck out when I didn't even know I was at bat?" he asks as he slides into the seat facing her.

Moxie laughs and covers her mouth. "I'm sorry," she says, unbuttoning only the top two buttons of her coat. Her cheeks flush pink in embarrassment. Still smiling, she fans herself with her hand. "I was just making a mental list of all the ways you're not my type."

Clifford chuckles. "That's a bold conversation to have with yourself - wait, being a gentleman's a strike?"

"Yeah. And, apparently, so's having a stable job and being hot as hell, yet here you are. You're probably single and have a healthy relationship with your mother, too," she hilariously accuses. "So, dinner before information or vice versa, I don't care either way."

Clifford isn't sure if she's intentionally hitting on him or naturally funny and adorable.

"I'm very single, my mother and I have healthy boundaries, *and* I'm good to put our order in first. Is there anything here that's really good?" he asks, looking down at the menu.

Rox stares at him for a second. "Um, I typically get scrambled eggs, pancakes, O.J. and a coffee."

Clifford's smile widens. He closes his menu and sits back.

Moxie looks up and says, "What?"

The waitress walks up.

"Hey Rox, not eating alone tonight. Nice. Usual?"

"Yeah, thanks, Frannie."

Clifford waits until Frannie looks at him. "I'll have her usual, too," he says, tucking the menu back in its holder.

Frannie rolls her eyes. "Cute," she says before turning towards the kitchen and shouting, "Two orders of scrambled with cakes!"

Confused, Clifford asks, "Did she call you, Rocks?"

"Rox. R-O-X. Short for Roxanne. Which I hate. So I go by Rox."

Clifford nods. "Got it. Rox, Roxie, Moxie."

Rox smiles, "Yeah, real creative, right?"

"Well, I go by Dee."

"Like, the letter D?"

"D-E-E. Dee. It's my last name."

"Oh, right," she says as she works her hand under her coat and into the pocket of her uniform. She pulls the business card out. "I got so busy I forgot you gave me this," she admits.

Clifford watches Rox's brown eyes as they scan over the card he handed her at Willies. She moves the card between her fingers before laying it on the table, next to the unwrapped utensils. "Totally looking into you tonight when I tuck in with my laptop. So, what's really with the guy you're looking for? And how does that girl fit into it?"

Clifford leans back in the booth. Frannie returning with their coffees and a bowl of cold single creamers gives him the opportunity to weigh how much information he's willing to share with Rox.

"The guy, Raymond, and the girl, Hadley, left for a father-daughter about a week ago. They never reached their initial destination."

"No shit," Rox exclaims as she leans in, more focused.

"My client, Hadley's mother, hired me to find her. Well, preferably both of them, but Hadley's the priority."

"I'm guessing Raymond's status is divorced, and that he's done a stint or two in rehab for... ooh, I wanna say...gambling?"

Clifford smirks, "And I guess you've heard a few loser's stories in your line of work, huh?"

"That and I remember Raymond."

Clifford instantly sits up straight. "No shit, really?" The excitement of Rox possibly giving him a lead in the case takes over.

"Yeah," she says before stopping to smile at how cute he suddenly got. "Um, but first, why aren't the cops all over this? Your client's the mother, and she hasn't tried calling in the National Guard? What am I missing here?"

Clifford sighs. "You're not missing a damn thing. That was my first question, too. All I can say is, she has her reasons, but the second I have cause to involve better-equipped authorities, I'm doing it."

Before telling Clifford what she remembers, Rox sips her coffee, trying to imagine a scenario where she wouldn't want to get as much help as possible.

"A few weeks ago, your guy came in looking stressed. He ordered bourbon - neat.

Not long after, two guys burst in and made a beeline to the tall table directly behind him. They said his name over, and over, again. Even threw balled-up napkins and straws at him. Immature shit. It was like, their job to follow him around and taunt the crap out of him, ya know?"

"What did Raymond do?"

"Nothing. He did his best to ignore them. The guys were eighty-sixed for the night."

"Could you describe the guys?"

Rox grimaced as she shook her head. "I can tell you; they rarely put soap and water together. But you saw the lighting at Willie's. It isn't always the best, especially with the stage lights moving around. I can keep people straight while in there, but I rarely get close enough to see helpful details."

Frannie returns with their juice and meal. "Enjoy your breakfast for dinner, guys," she says as she slides the plates across the table.

Rox dives into her eggs and notices Clifford's slow to remove his fork from its napkin-wrap. His gaze suggests his mind's somewhere else. "Were they gross enough that you think you'd recognize them again if they came into Willie's?" He finally asks.

Rox shrugs. "Maybe."

Clifford pulls out his phone and a pen. He reaches for his business card she left on the table and jots down his cell phone number on the back. "The number printed on the front is for my office back in D.C. This is my cell," he explains as he opens up a tab on his phone for a new contact and lays it in front of her.

"Do you mind? You're a potential witness, so if we find anything big, I may have to give your info to the cops," he explains.

Rox wipes her mouth with a napkin to hide her smile. "Well, yeah, if you need my number, sure. And you may have more questions, too, right?" She playfully asks before typing her number into his phone.

Clifford laughs and feels his cheeks warm. "I may think of a few things I'll need clarification on later," he says, hoping his weak flirting isn't inappropriate. He's been out of practice for much longer than he cares to admit, but there's something about Rox that makes him feel like if he didn't at least try, he'd regret it.

"I really appreciate you talking with me," he says.

Rox sets the syrup pitcher back onto the table. "I'm sorry I couldn't help more. I hope the dinner's worth what I gave you."

Clifford takes a moment to appreciate the beautiful woman in front of him devouring a stack of overly syrupy pancakes after nine in the evening with reckless abandon. "It was more than worth it."

Rox says through a smile, "Well, I usually eat dinner alone, so thanks for the company."

Frannie lays the slip down on the table, and Clifford reaches for his wallet. "Well, I'm probably gonna be around here tomorrow. Maybe I can take you to dinner again?" He asks as he pulls out a fifty and a twenty, laying them on the table.

Rox sips the last of her juice and looks down at the stack of paper. "Dee, that's seventy dollars."

Clifford smiles and says, "I'm a big believer in tipping well."

"Oh, and here I thought I was special," Rox says, trying to feign disappointment, but her smile didn't leave her face.

"You are. I asked you to dinner," Clifford replies as he stands up.

"That's just because I had information and leveraged you."

"Today, sure. But I asked if I could take you out tomorrow."

Rox scoots to the end of the booth and stands up, facing Clifford. "You're right," she says as she looks up and smiles. "I never answered you, did I?"

Inches apart, Clifford shakes his head slowly without breaking eye contact with her. Rox's eyes drift to his mouth and back to Clifford's eyes. "I'd love to," she whispers.

Rox waves and bids a goodnight to Frannie as she passes the counter and makes her way through the front door with Clifford following close behind.

He walks Rox to her car. She buckles her belt and locks the door before rolling the window down.

"So, there's a good chance I'll see you tomorrow?"

"I'll find a way to make it happen," he says with a wink.

Rox sighs and goes to start her car.

<Click, Click, Click>

Clifford notices and turns around.

"Shit! Not now." Rox exclaims.

<Click, Click, Click>

The car doesn't start.

Clifford walks back to her car and says, "This is not how I make it happen," with his hands in the air, professing his innocence.

She laughs despite the frustration she's feeling.

"Need a jump?" He asks.

"I guess I do. Wanna jump me?"

Clifford stammers but says nothing. A smile grows on his face, and he says, "Wait right there."

Clifford pulls his car next to Rox's and gets out. He rummages around the various compartments inside the vehicle, and eventually asks her, "Do you have jumper cables?"

Rox laughs and shakes her head no.

"I was hoping you had some," she admitted.

"How about I drive you home?" he asks.

She throws her hands up in the air. "Shit, why not."

Rox secures her car before walking with Clifford to his SUV. He opens her door and holds a hand out for her to take as she gets in. She smiles and shakes her head.

"You really don't need to lay the chivalry thing on so thick," she says after he climbs into the driver's seat.

She watches as he walks around the front, taking the time to observe him. She notices he looks around the parking lot before opening his own door and climbing in.

Rox points down the road and says, "So, I live about three miles down that way. It's not too far."

# Chapter Eight

**Clifford** turns the car on and presses the buttons on the center console to warm both of their seats. Rox blows into her hands to warm them up and, as if on cue, Clifford moves the vents so that more heat goes in her direction.

"Thank you," she says.

Clifford winks.

"This is really nice! Rental?"

"It's one of my client's cars," Clifford says.

"*One* of her cars? Wow."

"She has a small fleet of cars in one of the largest climate-controlled garages I've ever seen," Clifford divulges.

Rox shakes her head. "A bunch of cars and a private dick instead of cops when her kid goes missing. More money than sense, if you ask me."

"That and misplaced fear can keep a good person from doing the right thing," Clifford says as he continues to follow her direction.

They reach a small apartment complex filled with single and double-bedroom units.

As he turns toward her building, he hears Rox say, "Fuck," under her breath followed by a slight groan.

Clifford asks, "What?"

"Keep driving. Don't even slow down," she says as she slumps down in the seat.

Clifford looks over and sees a guy leaning against an apartment door, vaping.

"Is that yours?"

"Apartment, yes. The idiot standing in front of it, no. That's 'Redacted', my ex. We broke up months ago, but he comes by every once in a while."

"Redacted? That's a strange name."

"That's what I call him. His name isn't important."

"Clever. I like it."

Clifford keeps driving and finally asks, "So, you said he comes by sometimes? What happens when he comes by?"

Rox says, "It's an unhealthy, parasitic relationship. He shows up when he needs money, and he stays the night if..."

Her voice trails off, and Clifford waits to see if she finishes her thought.

"He stays if, what?" He asks when he realizes she has no plans to continue.

She sighs, "He stays if I'm in need."

Clifford clenches his jaw. "Oh. I see."

Rox says, "It's not like that. He's just- all the universe has to offer. Let's go."

"Do you want me to loop around the block?" he asks.

"No, let's just drive. He's... persistent. I don't want to go home right now."

Clifford regrets feeling like he pried into her personal affairs. She doesn't owe him an explanation, and feels how uncomfortable she's become. He knows he has no right feeling jealousy. She's a grown woman with a life, and until today, he didn't know she existed. But damn if he didn't feel like making Redacted disappear from her life so she could go home.

Clifford swipes the screen on the dashboard to show a more comprehensive map of the area they were in.

"Tell ya what. I have to get a hotel for the night anyway. How about I get two rooms for us at the nearest place?" He asks.

Rox sits up. "Really? Are you sure?"

Clifford smiles and says, "Of course. Tomorrow we'll pick up some jumper cables and get your car."

Rox watches in the side-view mirror as her apartment slips farther into the distant night sky and says, "That would be amazing. Thank you!"

About half an hour later, Clifford and Rox walk down the hallway, each carrying a bag of toiletries they requested at the hotel's front desk.

"See ya later," Clifford says after she gains access to her room.

"Later," she says back with a smile.

Clifford walks into his room, tosses his keys, wallet, and phone next to the TV on the dresser across from the bed. He takes off his shoes and walks into the bathroom with his toiletries. He takes his time to splash cold water on his face and brush his teeth.

He sits on the bed and sends a text to Bailey with the information Rox gave him. Another fifteen minutes go by, and he turns the TV on to distract him from knocking on the adjoining door to Rox's room. The dangerous nature of his occupation makes it difficult to commit to romantic relationships, and he isn't a fan of one-night stands.

He picks up his phone to text Sara. Of all the people on his team, Sara's the one he could talk to about this.

Clifford opens his text but freezes with his thumbs hovering over his screen's keyboard. He has no clue what to say. He finally decides that texting will only cause more back-and-forth. She'll need to tease him, like always, before giving advice, and he'd rather get that out of the way faster by talking on the phone instead.

Dee: *Hey there! How's KY? Can you talk for a minute?*

Within seconds, his phone vibrates in his hand, and Sara's number flashes on his screen.

"Hey Sara, I'm not interrupting anything, am I?" Clifford asks softly as he picks up.

He hears Sara's chuckle and slumps into a chair by the window. His view is of the parking lot, but the full moon behind the mountains is a sight he doesn't think he'll ever get used to during his time out here.

"Not really. How's the case? Everything going okay?" she asks.

Clifford smiles. It was just like Sara to get to the point. "The case is slow-moving and frustrating. It feels like people would rather overcomplicate their lives than face reality."

Sara quietly listens as Clifford vents for a minute. "How can I help you, boss?" she asks.

Clifford sighs, "It's not about the case. I need... advice."

"Oh?"

Clifford can feel Sara smiling through the phone. He imagines her sitting up straighter, looking as though she's waiting to hear the hottest celebrity gossip.

"Please?" he pleads, hoping to get through what he needs to talk about as quickly as possible.

"Lay it on me, Dee."

He catches Sara up on how he ended up at the burlesque club and all about the bartender he met there. He fills her in on the conversation at the diner and what took place afterwards.

"I've felt attraction to women before, but this one makes me want to stop the world so I can just focus on getting to know her."

Sara giggles. "Aw, Dee! You're a smitten kitten!"

Clifford shakes his head. He knew this was coming. "Go on. Get it out of your system."

"You wanna kiss her so bad! If she gives you an opening, get out of your head and just go for it."

"And then what? She lives here... in Colorado. "

"So? You just met her. You have no idea if you'll like her in a week. Hell, maybe she's really a man or a trained assassin posing as a bartender!"

Clifford snorted at her last example.

"Hey, none of us knows who the trained assassins are these days," Clifford says with a chuckle.

"Dee, for a smart man, sometimes, you can be really dumb. You're overthinking this. She's a grown woman. She might just want to get dicked-down. Not all of us are looking to settle down. Not anymore, anyway."

Clifford winces. There was a time when Sara was on her way to her own happily ever-after. Before Clifford can say anything, Sara continues.

"You value women as human beings. That makes you special, my friend. If she's giving you clear signals, just lean into it."

"Leave future problems in the future?"

"Leave your imaginary problems on the floor. They don't exist. They may never exist. Live a little, Dee. You deserve to reach for the things you want."

"Thanks. How are you? Really?" Clifford asks.

Sara sighs. "I'm good. The work I put into therapy is helping me have conversations that need to be had with Tracy's mom."

Clifford wishes he could have gone back to Kentucky to support his friend. It was there during his first big case, where Sara's girlfriend, Tracy, along with some of Clifford's closest friends and neighbors, paid the ultimate sacrifice, just for helping him.

To cope, Sara threw herself into seeing Clifford's case through. She discovered she was good at it. She used that as an excuse to run away from her grief.

At the end of their previous case, she finally realized that her mental health was in trouble. She began drinking to keep from grieving. She needed healthier coping skills.

"I'm glad to hear it. If you need more than the two weeks, Dan and Bailey can handle things."

Sara laughs. "Let's be honest, they'd miss me too much. Any messages for the guys at the Dollhouse? I'm gonna take Tracy's sister tomorrow night."

Clifford laughs and says, "Tell everyone that I say hello. I should get going."

As they say their goodbyes, Clifford can't help but think about how Marlon's Dollhouse started as a small strip club that became the venue for some pivotal moments and decisions for the group. The owner became family when he and Bailey's cousin, JJ, started a relationship.

He sets his phone down on the nightstand and lets out a huge nervous sigh.

Clifford, a man who's fought wars, been a POW, hunted down and taken out the ruthless Tye Brothers, needs a moment to muster enough courage to knock on a woman's door.

He unlocks his side of the adjoining door, but hesitates to pull it open and knock on Rox's side. Instead, he takes a step back to look at himself in the mirror when he hears a soft knocking sound.

He slowly opens his door and is stunned by the view.

Rox, wearing one of the hotel's small towels, has showered and stands in front of him. Her hair, still wet, clings to her bare shoulders. His eyes somehow focus on a small droplet of water that runs down her goose-bumped skin.

"Dee, did they happen to put a comb in your bag? I don't have one."

Clifford can only stare, slack-jawed. His reaction emboldens her. She stands inches away from him with only a thin layer of terry cloth between them. His heart is thumping in his chest, and he can feel fluttering in the pit of his stomach. Every bit of his vocabulary escapes his mind at that moment, so he just blinks as words evade him.

She thinks about saying something clever, but chooses to be bold instead, dropping the towel on the floor. The worst he can do is reject her and go back into his room. But before she can convince herself she made a mistake, he wraps an arm around her, pulling her into him.

"Holy fuck," escapes Clifford's lips as hers trail his neck. He places his hand on the small of her back. She leans into him, raising her leg, curling it around him.

He lifts her up, and she wraps her other leg around his waist before he gently presses her back into a wall, their kissing becoming more passionate.

He keeps her pinned to the wall while her hands work on the buttons of his flannel shirt, exposing chest hair that neatly dances across his chiseled chest.

He lightly tosses her onto the bed. She giggles as she bounces, rolling onto her side and sitting up on her knees. She reaches for him, grabbing at his belt buckle, and pulls him closer. Clifford's shirt falls off his shoulders.

Rox kisses his neck as she traces a finger down an old scar on his shoulder from his time in the military as Clifford works frantically to unbutton his pants.

Her lips follow the trail of her finger. She gently bites his shoulder before doing the same routine with each scar she encounters on his body. Clifford closes his eyes as he recalls the story behind each of his many imperfections while she explores. Her kisses can't take away all that he's been through, but he'd never been so happy to have them until now.

His fingers move, entangling in her wet hair. He inhales the light fragrance. "Do you want me to shower first?" he asks in a harsh whisper against her ear.

She wraps her arms around his neck and pulls him down onto the bed. "I don't think I can wait any longer for you, Mr. Dee."

Clifford rolls onto his back, and she straddles him. She leans down to kiss him.

"You're so beautiful," he says, moving her hair away from her face. After a passionate kiss, she smiles and leans back, smoothing her hair with both hands so he can watch her face as her eyes roll backwards as she moves.

Over two hours later, Rox drifts off to sleep while rubbing the hair on Clifford's chest. She's snug under his arm, plastered to his side as close as he can hold her. They'd made their way back into his room to raid the mini fridge before succumbing to round two. He kisses her head and closes his own eyes, drifting off to sleep.

# Chapter Nine

**The phone** buzzing awakens Clifford from a sound sleep.

With barely one eye open, he blindly searches for his phone on the nightstand. After eventually finding it, he glances to see it's Bailey, who has called four times already.

He grimaces as he puts the phone to his ear. He knows he's about to get yelled at.

"Hey Bailey, what's up? It's really early," Clifford whispers.

"Okay, you're good."

"Yeah. I'm good. Can I go back to sleep?"

Bailey's tone changes now knowing his friend's okay.

"Your heart rate went nuts. Wait, why are you whispering?"

Clifford quietly answers, "Seriously, I'll call you later."

He ends the call and sets the phone back on the nightstand.

A moment later, he hears a single, long-buzz, and glances over to see a light blinking, indicating a text message.

He picks up his phone and glances at the message:

*"Was worried over ur vitals."*

*"forgot that you're monitoring that."*

*"bet!"*

*"I'll call later. Promise."*

Bailey responds with a thumbs-up emoji.

Clifford sets the phone back on the nightstand.

Rox rolls over and throws her arm over Clifford's bare chest and mutters, "I didn't get you in trouble, did I?"

Clifford adjusts his weight to wrap his arms around her again. His fingers trail down from her shoulder, along her side, and rest on the lowest part of her back.

"No, it's just my business partner. He's back in Virginia, but keeps a close eye on us when we're out in the field."

Draping her leg over his, she nuzzles his neck. Her sleepy sighs make his body react. Her hand lies on his chest, scrunching his chest hair. He curls his fingers around hers, interlocking them, and he kisses her forehead.

He hears her soft chuckle. "Mr. Dee? Are you hinting at round three?"

"I thought you were," he says.

They gaze into each other's eyes and smile.

Over three hours later, Rox is back in her room to redress and gather her things. Clifford grabs his phone off the nightstand and notices another text from Bailey sent not long after Dee's promise to call.

*HR spiked again after we talked.*

Clifford didn't feel like explaining, but he knew who'd love to.

*Tell Sara all about it.*

After taking a quick shower, he gets dressed, and they leave well before checkout time. He drops Rox at home to change and leaves to purchase the jumper cables. When he returns, she's waiting outside in a pair of jeans and an oversized sweatshirt with her hair gathered in a high ponytail. Clifford sees a huge smile grow across her face when she recognizes the Bronco pulling up, and it makes him melt inside. Catching his own wide grin in the rear-view when he stops in front of her place makes him glad his team isn't there to see him.

Happy to have her in the passenger seat again, they take off for the diner to jump Rox's car.

Just before they arrive, Clifford receives a call from Luis.

He taps the phone icon on the car's dashboard to answer via Bluetooth.

"Hey Luis, What'cha got for me?" He asks.

"Hey Dee. I just wanted to let you know, Fred stopped by and he's been updated. You might want to head back this way soon. We found something last night."

"Okay, I'm about 3 hours out." Clifford says.

The smile on Rox's face fades as she realizes he's being called away.

Clifford ends the call and Rox asks, "A possible break in the case? That's good."

"Yeah, Luis is from the lodge they never made it to. He's looking into evidence of a crash that may have involved Raymond's car on the property."

Rox nods, "I see."

It's quiet for a long, uncomfortable time, and Clifford has conflicting emotions. A girl and her father are missing, and he desperately hopes to find them alive. He's excited about the call from Luis. This case needs a big break in it, but he also doesn't want to say goodbye to Rox yet.

It's made even more bittersweet when he realizes she's not ready for goodbye either.

Clifford pulls onto the road of the diner.

"Do you work the same shift today?"

Rox nods. "Duty calls for both of us, huh?"

Clifford reaches for her hand and feels his stomach flip when she laces her fingers with his.

He pulls into the parking lot of the diner, parks the car and turns to fully face her. She's an unexpected complication, and for once, he wants to complicate things.

"I'm coming back. I just want you to know that, okay. I have a job to do, and I need to see it through."

Rox places a hand on his cheek. "I get it. Really," she says.

"I had a great time and would love to take you out again. Someplace better than a 24/7 diner."

Rox smiles and runs her hand down Clifford's neck and lays her hand on his warm chest. "I'd like that."

Clifford smiles and says, "Let's go jump your car."

"I'd rather you jump me again, but okay."

Clifford flashes a sheepish grin. "There she is."

After a few minutes and several attempts to start the engine, Rox's car is brought back from the dead.

She steps out of the car as Clifford's removing the cables from the battery. He slams the hood down and takes the cables over to Rox. "All set. I think you should keep these," he says.

She throws her arms around him and whispers into his ear, "Thank you."

Clifford wraps an arm around her waist while his other hand moves to her face. His fingers trail until they wrap around the back of her neck. He kisses her with as much passion as he can without committing a misdemeanor.

"My pleasure," he says as he places his forehead on hers.

"Well, if anything, we'll always have Buffalo Bob's," she says with a big smile.

"I'll never eat eggs and pancakes again without thinking of you."

"I know. I know."

After sharing a laugh, he lets her go, and she climbs into her car. He watches as she drives out of the parking lot and heads toward her apartment.

Clifford pulls up to the lodge just as the sun hits its highest point in the sky. He skips the valet and parks directly in front of the security lodge, next to a car that looks familiar.

He quickly heads inside and spots Luis on the phone, and Fred in a chair next to his desk.

Fred, with a stern, expressionless face, gives an upward nod to Clifford as they make eye contact.

"He's here. I'll fill him in and get back to you."

Luis ends his call, faces Clifford and says, "Dee, we found Raymond."

# Chapter Ten

**It's late afternoon** when Clifford and Fred pull into the driveway of Grace's estate.

He circles around the front of the home and stops the car, with Fred in a car just behind him. Clifford sits in the driver's seat for a moment longer, preparing himself for the news he's not ready to deliver.

Fred taps on the window and opens Clifford's door. "Ready?"

"Not really," Clifford replies with a glance up toward Fred.

At the front, Grace is waiting and watching their body language. She looks terrified and close to tears.

"Grace," Fred begins. "Raymond's body was found in a ravine. I'm so sorry."

She closes her eyes. "Hadley?" She asks as she opens them again.

Clifford put his hand on her shoulder. "She's still missing. We believe she's alive."

A huge sudden exhale leaves Grace, and she gathers air into her lungs instantly. A little bit of hope has returned to her, and she holds onto it. Fred slowly walks up next to Grace, allowing her to lean into him for strength.

Fred holds her and says, "We had no choice; we had to get the police involved. They've been notified, but we've asked for discretion."

Grace pushes away from Fred as she stands to her full height.

"Should I even ask for the details?" She asks as she turns back into the house.

Clifford and Fred follow her into the warm home.

After delivering the news, Clifford explains he wants to get back out to the casinos and search for clues regarding the whereabouts of Hadley. He suspects at least one casino may be involved. There's already a search team combing the mountainside where Raymond was found, and Fred mentions he will stay with that crew at the resort while Clifford investigates the leads. Grace likes the idea of having Fred as the trusted point of contact with the search team.

After meeting with Grace, Clifford and Fred part ways. Fred heads toward the resort. Clifford continues on to meet Rox back at the club. While driving, Luis sends Clifford a text. He clicks the read-aloud button on the dash:

*"Initial report advised no GSW. Few broken bones, including neck. They're running tests. More results are coming in a few days."*

Clifford hits the Bluetooth button and says, "Call Bailey."
After a few rings, he picks up.
"Hey Dee, what's up?"
"B, the coroner didn't find any gunshot wounds. Are you sure it was a gunshot we heard in the video?"
Bailey replies, "Oh yeah, for sure."
"Yeah, it really sounded like one. They're doing an extensive exam right now and said it would be a few more days. I hope they find something to go on."
Bailey sighs, "Yeah. Sometimes things get overlooked on the first pass. Let me know when the full report is out."
"Will do."
Clifford hangs up with Bailey and calls Luis.
"Hey Dee, did you get my text?"
"Yeah, buddy. I'm headed back up north. Fred's headed your way. He is going to be the POC for the search, and I am going to continue investigating up at the casinos."
"I'll let the police know. They took over the investigation."
Clifford is relieved the police are now involved.
"Awesome. Fred should be there soon."
"Sounds good. Be careful, my friend."

***

It was really slow at Wild Willies, and Rox is tired of flirting for tips with the same three current customers at the club. Especially since Clifford isn't far from her mind. She has a love-hate relationship with her job. The lunch rush is nice, but it's ten times slower than the dinner rush. She makes about a fourth of what the night crew makes, but she also doesn't have to deal with nearly the same amount of drunk assholes looking to cop a feel.

The only server on duty is taking a smoke break, so Rox comes out from behind the bar to deliver an order. The gentleman is sitting alone two tables back from the stage. He's older, possibly stopping in to catch a show before heading home from work.

He smiles at Rox and hands her a twenty for the food and beer and says, "Keep the change." It seems like a gracious gesture, but the total was nineteen dollars. She waves the twenty in the air and says, "Thanks."

Clifford Dee slips right back into her mind. She couldn't help but think of the generosity he had shown Frannie, the waitress at the diner.

Truthfully, she couldn't help but think of all the ways he had shown his generosity last night.

The other two gentlemen sitting a few tables away snap and wave to get her attention. She looks over and mouths, "One sec."

She heads up to the register at the bar, cashes in the twenty and tosses the one-dollar bill into the tip jar.

She swipes the order pad and returns to the other table.

"Hey guys," she says with a smile. Something about them felt familiar, but she couldn't really be sure.

One man has greasy long hair, and she wonders when his last shower was.

That's when the memory of who they are hit her, just before their smell did; the two men who harassed Raymond.

Getting a closer look at them, Rox spots a strange tattoo on the inside of his wrist that looks like an infinity symbol shaped like two diamonds with devil horns coming out from it.

He smiles and says, "Hey, sweetie. I'm really digging those fishnet stockings and boots combo. Nice touch." He reaches out to rub her leg, but she steps back and to the side to avoid it.

Creeps are a work hazard she has become used to dealing with.

Rox smiles and says, "Thanks. What can I get you?"

"Another round for me and my buddy here. I'd also like an order of the pretzel bites and some chips and salsa, please."

His friend raises two fingers and says, "Make mine a double." Then, he switches his gesture to the "shocker symbol" and makes a kissy face.

He had the same tattoo as his friend.

She glances away for just a moment because of the gesture, and he makes another move.

The greaseball succeeds in placing his hand on her leg, curling it around her thigh. She shimmies to the side, so it falls off.

The other man quickly reaches out and grabs. Rox immediately turns around and says, "Hey! Be respectful! It's not that type of bar."

The man raises both hands in the air and says, "Sorry, couldn't help it, you've got a great ass!"

The greasy guy says, "Chill, Rocco! Jerry already banned me from one of his establishments. Be nice to the ladies."

Rocco flashes a sheepish grin and a wink. Rox glares back. She looks over to the other man and says, "I'll have your order ready in a few minutes. Be nice to your server when she brings it, okay?"

Rocco looks at his greasy friend and says, "Well shit, Louie, I think we made her mad."

Louie responds, "We? That was all you buddy."

Reaching the bar, Rox sends Clifford a text:

*"Those two jerks who harassed Raymond are here. Hurry back."*

After a few minutes, the place livens up. A few more men come in to catch the early show. It's a typical occurrence for guys to get pumped up with a good show before heading into the casinos to lose all their money.

Two other men enter the club and head over towards the table with Rocco and Louie.

Rox quickly glances at the text Clifford just sent:

*"omw to you now."*

She looks up from her phone and notices the server heading over to a different table with a large party. She helps her out again and takes the food and drinks over to the men who groped her a few minutes before.

She picks up the tray and lets out a tremendous, disgruntled sigh.

Making her way over toward them, she sets the tray down on a neighboring table. She sets the beer down and then the snacks.

Louie smiles and says, "Welcome back."

She ignores him.

She glances at the other two men, who are dressed much nicer. They were almost out of place in their designer suits and kempt appearance.

"Anything for your friends?"

The other two men silently wave her off, and she nods and grabs the tray and heads back to the bar.

She sets the tray down and starts looking for the order pad. She looks over, seeing she dropped it behind a pillar near their table.

Rox rolls her eyes and quickly navigates over toward the table to grab the pad, trying not to be noticed by the perverts.

She overhears Rocco talking.

"That fucking idiot Raymond tried to pull a gun on me."

The men show with their hands that he should whisper.

Rox tries to listen but can only make out a few words through the music.

During the conversation, Rocco makes a slide-whistle sound, and motions downward with his hand, to emphasize how cartoonish Raymond's death was.

Louie laughs and loudly says, "One less idiot in the world is a start, Amirite! Had to drive that pussy's car into one of the reservoirs to get rid of it."

Rox hears one of the suited gentlemen ask, "And our money?" She couldn't place his accent, but it surely isn't American.

She shuffles closer to listen.

Rocco stammers and says, "Well, so he didn't have it, but get this; his daughter was in the back seat of the car. I saw she had her phone, so we grabbed her. Still got her. We figure she might be worth something to you, considering who her mother is."

Louie turns his head and spots Rox near the pillar. He places his hand on Rocco, turns his head back and says, "Oh, hey baby, did you need something?"

Rox stammers and says, "What? I can't hear you over the music."

Louie smiles and says, "Come here."

She slowly walks over and says, "I'm sorry, I couldn't hear what you said." She hoped they wouldn't think she could overhear them if she kept playing dumb.

Louie says, "I was just wondering what you were doing standing there."

She smiles and waves her order pad and says, "I dropped my pad. I was looking for it. I got it."

He nods and says, "Well, since you're here. I'll have another beer." He points at the other gentlemen, who raise their hands, declining again.

Rox smiles, grabs the empty mugs, and heads back toward the bar.

She picks up her phone and texts Clifford:

*"I heard them say he fell down a mountain and they have his daughter."*

Her phone immediately rings. It's Clifford.

She declines as she spots Rocco glaring at her from across the club.

To avoid suspicion, she acts as if she were cleaning a glass. She then pours the beer and takes it over to the table and sets it down.

"Okay, guys, here's your beer. I'll be sure to have the server come back to take care of you."

She returns to the bar with her heart beating out of her chest, and glances at her phone.

Three missed calls from Clifford.

Looking around, her gaze lands back on their table. Rocco is looking back in her direction.

She palms her phone and shoves it into her boot so it's out of sight.

She waves over toward a server, who walks up to the bar.

Rox says, "Hey, I need to take a bio-break. Would you watch the bar for me?"

"Sure!" she says with a smile.

Rox turns and heads out the side and angles toward the ladies' room.

She taps a bouncer on the shoulder, and he follows her to the back near the bathroom.

"Hey Matt, the table on the left. Two greaseballs and two fancy guys. Keep an eye on them, please. They're creeping me out."

Matt rolls his shoulders and says, "You got it, Rox."

Rox ducks into a stall and immediately calls Clifford.

"Hey! Got your text!" Clifford says as he answers the phone.

"Dee, I have a bouncer watching their table. They have Hadley and said they should exchange her for money."

Clifford sighs and says, "Stay put, don't raise suspicion and I'll call the cops. I can get to you in about an hour."

"Okay."

"Be careful, Rox!" Clifford says.

"I will."

Rox hangs up the phone and comes out of the stall.

She turns the water on in the sink and runs her hands under it for a moment.

After drying, she looks in the mirror to make sure her makeup is still perfect. She closes her eyes for a moment and takes a huge breath of air into her lungs and slowly lets it out. She tucks the phone back into her boot and heads back toward the bar.

She notices Matt standing near the table she mentioned, watching the rest of the crowd. He's excellent at slight intimidation, and the men seem a little anxious with him standing so close. Matt walks a few feet further away but stops and starts looking around again. He spots Rox as she leaves the bathroom and gives her a little nod.

Rox reaches the bar and notices the club is almost twice as full as it was when she went into the bathroom. The nighttime crowd is finally showing up.

She glances at her watch and sees it's just before six. The night bartender should arrive to help, and they're supposed to be getting a few more servers on shift soon.

As she scans the club from behind the bar, she sees Rocco is no longer interested in glaring at her and the entire table is more focused on the proximity of Matt.

She pours four beers and sets them on a tray. She waves over a server and sends her over to their table with the beer.

The server arrives at the table and says, "Here, fellas, it's on the house."

Matt overhears and looks over toward Rox. She nods to signal him to go with it. He nods back.

After a moment, Matt changes his vantage point and moves to a new spot in the club. He stays for a few minutes and then changes again. After several position changes, Matt eventually ends up near the bar and walks up to Rox.

"Hey, what's with the free beer?"

"We need to keep them in the club."

"Okay, it's kinda the opposite of what I do, but I'll make sure they don't leave."

Rox smiles at Matt.

Matt positions himself midway between their table and the front door.

He notices one of the suited gentlemen reach into his jacket and pull out a phone.

He shows his phone to his equally dressed counterpart, and they stand.

Matt heads over toward the table and says, "Gentlemen, your table won a raffle and you're all getting a free private show with bar service in the back room, please follow me."

"We are on our way out. Give it to another table," one man with a thick accent says.

Matt protests, then the same man reaches into his jacket once more and pulls out a revolver. He fires it directly into Matt's chest.

The gunshot sends panic across the club. Rox looks up from behind the bar and sees Matt falling backwards as the other three men draw their weapons.

Rocco turns and starts shooting across the club above people's heads to get them to scurry.

Louie bolts toward the entrance, swings open the door and stops as if he's surprised by something. He points his gun out the door, fires two shots, and three rounds immediately hit him directly in the chest.

Rox sees him fall backward back into the club and the door swings shut.

Rocco points his gun at her. She looks at him in time to spot his aim, diving behind the bar just as he pulls the trigger.

The bullets strike the mirror behind her, shattering the glass across the bar and floor. She shuffles carefully across the broken bits, trying not to cut herself. She hears several more shots ring out.

The front door swings open, and the cops pour into the club. The two suited gentlemen fire at them.

They flip a table and crouch down. Rocco dives out of the way and starts running across the bar, heading toward the back emergency exits.

The cops fire at Rocco, hitting him once in the leg and again in the back. He falls onto a table and rolls off onto the floor.

The cops pour in and start laying suppressing fire so they can get the injured police to safety.

The suited man on the floor pulls another gun from his boot and starts shooting at the police helping their injured.

A cop fires a single shot and hits him in the head.

The other suited man backs up and angles toward the back of the club. Two cops flank his position, and they fire, hitting him multiple times.

Rox looks up from behind the bar to see cops, chaos, and bloodshed everywhere.

# Chapter Eleven

**About an hour later,** Clifford arrives at the bar to see that the cops have cordoned off most of the parking lot.

An officer stops him. "The strip's closed," he says bluntly.

"I'm Clifford Dee, the P.I. that called about the intel on Hadley Pollard."

The cop relays the information through a walkie-talkie. A second later he's being told to allow Clifford through.

"Okay, Mr. Dee, park over there and head on in."

Clifford asks, "Is everyone okay?"

"A couple of fatalities, but a helluva lot more injured."

"What about the bartender? Roxanne?" Clifford asks.

"I don't know any specifics, but if she survived, there's a good chance she'll be over by the ambulances."

Clifford runs over toward the flashing lights. Faces blur as he passes them by. He can feel his heart racing as he spots the front of an ambulance. He sprints the length of it to stop suddenly once he sees her sitting in the back. Her arms are in bandages from crawling over broken glass.

"Rox!?" Clifford shouts.

She looks up, wrapped in a blanket. "Dee!"

"Please tell me you're okay?" he asks as he approaches. Dried blood smeared her forehead, and her mascara smudged under her eyes. She'd clearly been crying.

"I'm scared. I've never seen a gun aimed at me before," she says in a hoarse whisper.

"You never really get used to that. Are the cuts deep?"

The paramedic answers. "It looks worse than it is. Only one needed suturing. The rest are superficial, but your girl's a bleeder," he says as he pats Rox gently on the shoulder and hands her an extra pack of gauze.

Rox looks up at Clifford as she stands. "Bet you didn't think you'd learn that about me before the second date, huh?"

Clifford smiles in relief and shakes his head. "How did all of this happen?"

"Well, after we talked, I told Matt, the boun-" she chokes on a sob. Her eyes go wide. "Oh God, Matt!" Rox openly sobs.

Clifford steps in closer and guides her head to his chest to let her cry. "I'm so sorry. You don't have to tell me right now. It can wait."

Rox wants to allow herself the time to cry, to feel sad, but she's also angry.

She pushes away and sniffs.

"No, I'm okay. So, I say to Matt, don't let those guys leave. He told me he wouldn't. He didn't even ask any questions. That's the type of guy Matt is."

Rox takes a deep, shaky breath and wipes her nose. "We did everything to keep them in the club," she swallows hard and continues, "They shot Matt."

"I'm so sorry, Rox."

"He was rushed to the hospital. I don't know if..." Rox shook her head, unable to finish her sentence.

Clifford rubs her back. "I'll see what I can find out. In the meantime, why don't you go wait in my car?"

She points over toward a cop and says, "I can't. I have to go to the station to give an official statement," she says, realizing her purse is still in Willie's, an active crime scene.

The cop who'd been waiting for her at the ambulance walks up to them as if on cue.

"I need my stuff," she says regarding the bag she had with her.

"I can get it and bring it to you at the station," Clifford suggests.

She gives him the combination to her locker and walks off with the young officer assigned to her.

Clifford heads into the club and spots an officer. "Hey, I'm Clifford Dee. I called this in. Who's in charge here?"

The officer says, "We called the CBI in. They took over the case."

Clifford nods. "Great!" he says with a hint of frustration.

He's escorted over and introduced.

"This is Clifford Dee. He's the guy who called us."

The agent turns around and says, "Dee, huh? I'm Agent Fulk. You could have warned us they were armed."

Clifford says, "I had no idea. Rox, the bartender, told me they were talking about a missing person, well, now kidnapping case I'm on. When I called it in, I said to approach with caution. I mentioned 'no lights' if I remember correctly. I didn't want them running."

Fulk looks around and says, "Kidnapping case? We'll circle back to that later. But," he pauses with a huff, "they must have been tipped-off somehow. My guess, they had people waiting outside."

A cop from across the room shouts, "Hey, this guy is still alive over here."

Medics run toward the call. Fulk and Clifford hurry over.

It's Rocco. He's coughing up a lot of blood. They roll him onto his back.

Clifford asks, "Where's the girl?"

Rocco smiles and attempts to spit blood at Clifford, but it just pools out of his mouth and runs down his cheek as he chokes.

Fulk yells to the medic, "Don't let this asshole die!"

A BLS apparatus is placed on Rocco's face to pump lungs with air.

He coughs up more blood, splattering it across the clear face mask. They remove it and shove a tube down his throat to help him breathe.

Moments later he starts convulsing, and they call for a crash cart.

They tear open his shirt and start shocking his heart.

After a few attempts, the medic looks over at Fulk and says, "I'm sorry."

Fulk closes his eyes. "Fuck!"

"Try again!" Clifford demands.

"I can't. He's gone!" The medic yells.

Clifford says, "I need to find the girl."

Irritated, Fulk says, "We can't get anything out of a dead man. I should probably talk to the bartender. She seemed to know a lot."

"Her name's Roxanne. I know her. She just left to give a statement at the station."

Fulk says, "Well, let's go chat with Roxanne."

"Right after I get her things. She needs her stuff."

Down at the local station, Rox is sitting in a room with a cup of tea. Fulk and Clifford step into the room.

"I'm Agent Fulk, and this is Mr. Dee. I believe you know each other already."

She smiles and says, "Yeah, we know each other."

Clifford hands her bag to her and winks when she looks up at him and smiles.

She immediately digs into it and pulls out a bag of wipes.

Fulk pauses for a moment and says, "Okay, well, we need to know everything that happened."

Rox recaps the entire story while cleaning the smeared make-up and dried blood from her face.

Fulk rubs his own face with his hand and says, "At no point did you hear where the girl was located?"

"No, sir."

Fulk taps on the glass of the two-way mirror. A few seconds later, an officer peeks into the room.

"Run a search for any properties these guys would have owned. Start searching the most secluded."

The officer nods and shuts the door.

"Dee, do you have questions for Roxanne?"

Clifford shakes his head and says, "No. I think she should head home and get some rest."

Rox smiles with relief at Clifford.

Fulk says, "Okay, but Roxanne, you need to stay in communication with us if you remember anything else, okay? Any minor detail can be important."

She nods and stands up.

Clifford says, "Agent Fulk, I'm going to take Rox to her car and try to stay out of your hair, but I'd appreciate you keeping me in the loop with the case."

Fulk nods, "Sure, as long as you reciprocate."

"I'll send you everything I have."

He picks up his phone and shoots Bailey a text informing him to send everything to Fulk.

He looks back up from his phone and says, "My associate should be sending you all our files shortly."

Fulk nods and says, "Great, thank you, and I'll return the favor. Oh, why didn't your client reach out to the police when her child went missing?"

"It's a long story that she'll need to explain. She has her own private security on the case as well. A guy named Fred Polter. He's a former cop from Sacramento, so I am sure you'll be able to get a lot of his info. He's out at the lodge helping with the investigation."

Fulk nods and says, "Can't wait to look over your report. Thanks."

Clifford smiles, puts his arm around Rox, and escorts her out of the station to his car.

# Chapter Twelve

**Fred steps into** the Ranger's lodge from the cold. As he removes and hangs his coat, he looks over toward Luis and says, "The guys said they're closing up for the evening. The wind picked up, visibilities about zero, and the temperature dropped significantly."

Luis nods and starts looking over the terrain maps when his phone rings.

"It's Dee," he says, looking over to Fred.

"Hey Dee, you're on speaker. Fred's here, too."

Clifford says, "Great! I have news. Kinda good and bad."

Fred sighs a slight relief and says, "What's the news, Dee?"

"Hadley is still alive. There were guys up here in a club talking about having her somewhere. They tried to sell her. But the bad news is, those guys are dead. The sellers and the possible buyers."

Fred slams his fist down on the wooden desk. "Fuck! You've gotta find her, Dee."

"That's not all the bad news, Fred. It was a public shootout at the club. So, the Colorado Bureau of Investigation is now involved. I couldn't avoid it."

"Send me your location and I'll come up there and help. I'll work with the bureau. I know how they think."

"I'll text you the info."

Fred looks over at Luis and shakes his head.

Luis shows a reassuring tight grin and says, "At least we have hope she's alive."

Fred runs his hand through his thinning strawberry-blonde hair. "Yeah, at least."

His phone buzzes, and he glances at it. It was another call.

Luis asks, "Is that Dee again?"

Fred shakes his head. "No, not Dee, but I need to take this."

He hits the answer button, puts the phone to his ear and says, "One second, I need to step outside."

He grabs his coat and walks out the front door, into the dimly lit evening. "Hey sorry, I'm good to talk now," he says as the door closes.

Luis spots Fred through the window walking around toward the side of the cabin where he can be alone.

Curious, he heads toward the side of the cabin where Fred headed. He couldn't make out anything Fred was saying until he became agitated, raising his voice.

"That wasn't the job! No one was supposed to take her!"

Luis' eyes widened, and he tried to listen more intently, but Fred became quiet again. He ends his call and starts back toward the entrance of the cabin.

Luis sits and pulls his revolver from the drawer, laying it on top of his desk.

Fred steps back into the cabin. After hanging up his coat, he turns and notices the gun.

"What's that for?"

Luis places his hand on top of the gun. "Explain how you're *really* involved."

Letting out an enormous sigh, Fred sits in the chair across from Luis.

He runs his hands over his face and then smoothes out his mustache with two fingers.

"I guess you overheard my conversation?" Fred asks.

Luis simply shrugs.

Fred sighs and then describes Raymond's actions, gambling, the dangerous environment he created, the opportunities he had, and the favor asked.

"It was supposed to take place before the day he picked her up. When Grace realized it hadn't happened in time, she begged me to call it off."

"You didn't call it off, did you?" Luis asks.

Fred shakes his head. "I reached out, told them Hadley was going to be with him and not to lay a finger on her. I even thought maybe having his daughter witness his beat-down would be embarrassing enough to get him to finally stop, but something else happened."

Luis huffs and says, "You can say that again."

"I don't have the slightest idea where they'd take her, and I don't know why they'd try to sell her off."

"Fred, even I can tell your boss is well off. Criminals are opportunistic," Luis added.

Fred looks at the floor and then back at Luis. "Now what?"

Luis swipes the gun from the desk and holds it at the ready.

"I only have the authority to detain you, and then I have to turn you over to the police. But... I also think that you need to have a conversation with Mr. Dee first. It'd be much better coming from you than from me. I can only give you twenty-four hours before I inform the authorities. It's better to get this out now before it gets worse for you and Grace."

Fred nods and picks up his phone. Luis keeps his gun on him.

He can hear Clifford's voice pick up.

"Hey Dee, I'm on the way now. There's something I need to fill you in on, but in person. Can we meet tonight before I link up with CBI?" Fred asks while looking at Luis.

Shoving the phone in his front pocket after the call, Fred turns to grab his jacket and reaches for the door.

Luis maintains his aim. "This sounds like it's getting way outta hand; you need to be careful."

Fred smiles, "I can handle myself."

Fred slides into the driver's seat of his car when he hears his phone vibrate. He glances down at the phone, and it displays a notification: "One message from Clifford Dee."

He opens the notification, which gives him the address, and says to report to the front desk for his room number. He programs the address of the hotel into the car's GPS and replies.

*Thx be there soon.*

Fred sets the phone down on the center console and drives off. He continues to Clifford as it becomes increasingly darker with each mile he leaves in the distance.

A car speeding up behind him on the single-lane road puts on its blinker and starts to pass. Fred slows down to allow, but the driver rams Fred's back tire, successfully performing the PIT maneuver. Fred's car skids sideways, then into a barrel roll as it litters the road with pieces of the SUV.

It's silent.

Fred, stunned from the accident, scrambles.

Bloodied, he unbuckles his seatbelt and reaches for a small .22 revolver strapped to his leg. He pushes open the door and crawls out of the wreckage. Grunting as he now can feel the pain of the accident, Fred looks up to see a shotgun barrel pointed at his face. He doesn't have time to utter a word. He doesn't even hear the shotgun fire. Just darkness, as his head splatters across the pavement.

# Chapter Thirteen

**As he's reading Fred's text**, Clifford walks Rox up to her apartment door and says, "Just stay inside and don't open the door for anyone. I'm going to head back to the hotel and wait for Fred. I'll come get you in the morning."

He looks at her when she doesn't say anything right away.

Rox stares blankly at Clifford's chest. "Same hotel as last night?"

"Mm-hmm. I figured it made sense."

"Stay here, please. Tell Fred to come here instead."

"I don't want you involved anymore than you nee-"

"And I don't want to be alone tonight," Rox replies, cutting him off.

Clifford admits to himself that he'd rather she be in his arms all night after everything she went through and compromises. "Okay, but I don't want you involved in this case. Wait in the lobby, grab a drink at the bar, and I'll call when Fred leaves."

"Deal! Can I pack an overnight bag and freshen up first?" She asks, standing back to look down at herself.

Clifford nods. "We should probably hit a drugstore for more bandages, too."

After running an errand, they head up to his room at the hotel. Clifford redresses the gauze on Rox's left arm from middle and ring finger up to her elbow.

"Hey, you should probably head down to the lobby in a minute. Fred will be here soon."

Rox pulls her sleeve down and says, "Trying to get rid of me already?"

Bluntly, Clifford says, "Yes."

Rox laughs and swipes the extra room key, shoving it into the back pocket of her jeans. "I'm taking this one," she says

Clifford smiles and nods.

"I'll be at the bar. Might flirt with some rando," she says as she heads out of the room.

Clifford laughs and says, "I hope you don't like him more than me."

She winks, says, "I won't," and heads out, down the hall toward the elevator.

Clifford plops down onto the bed and flips on the TV while he waits for Fred.

Rox exits on the first floor, bypassing the lobby as she scopes out a place to sit and wait. She continues until she spots the bar and wanders over.

The bartender heads over. "Hey sweetheart, what can I get you?"

"Old-fashioned, Woodford, please."

The bartender winks and heads off to make the drink.

A moment later, a gentleman walks up and asks, "Oh, you cut yourself?"

Rox raises her bandaged hand. "Tricky cuticle."

The man laughs and says, "May I get that drink for you?"

Rox smiles and politely says, "No thank you, charging it to my boyfriend's room."

The man smiles, nods, and continues on.

She was so used to the jerks at the club being extremely brazen that she almost forgot that there were actual true gentlemen in the world. After a moment, the bartender hands her the drink and says, "He insisted on paying."

She looks over toward the man, cocks her head to the side and smiles while raising the glass to say, "Thank you."

The man nods back and continues to drink.

She knows he's the subtle type that will try again, so she walks over toward the lobby area and sits in a chair, looking out of the glass doors into the parking lot. Clifford never described him, so she wants to play a game and try to guess which man entering the hotel was Fred.

She takes a swig of her drink and picks up the paper that's sitting on the large coffee table. It was from yesterday. She sets it back down and decides to people-watch, except very few people are checking in at this time of night.

Several minutes go by, and she is down to the final sip of her drink. She sets the glass on top of the paper and debates getting another.

She hears the ding of the front desk bell followed by the receptionist's voice, "How can I help you, gentlemen?"

"Hi, I'm Fred Polter. I'm supposed to meet Clifford Dee in his room. I believe he told you I was coming."

Confused, Rox looks over to see two men in suits standing by the desk.

One of them flashes a smile as the attendant types on their computer. She looks up and says, "Okay, I see a note that he's expecting you in room 625."

Something doesn't sit right with Rox. She stands up and walks over to a mirror in the lobby, and pretends to check her makeup in the mirror. She holds up her phone as if she were taking a mirror-selfie and turns the phone to snag a picture of the guys at the counter.

She sends the picture to Clifford.

*Fred? Who's the other guy?*

She grabs her empty glass and starts walking the halls.

Clifford comes out of the bathroom and plops on the bed. He notices the missed text on his phone from Rox.

He responds:

*NOT FRED!*

He then shoves his phone into his back pocket.

Unarmed, he has to make do with what he has. On the nightstand is his utility knife. Grabbing it, he heads toward the door. He can hear muffled voices talking in the hallway. He looks out the peephole and can see the same men from the photo Rox texted him standing outside his door.

Clifford backs away and heads into the bathroom. He turns on the water and tosses a bath towel into the sink, getting it soaking wet.

Returning to the peephole, Clifford watches as one man screws a silencer to a gun. The man behind him is holding zip-tie handcuffs.

He quietly backs into the bathroom, out of view. He's wringing out the towel when he hears splintered wood after three bullets hit the door just before one of them kicks it in.

The men carefully walk inside with only one gun drawn. Clifford, standing by the open bathroom door, waits, twisting the towel tighter and tighter.

Clifford snaps the wet towel just as the first man is fully in view, before he could point his gun. It strikes him on his Adam's apple.

The snap is so vicious; it breaks the skin, sending him flying backwards into his partner. A small trickle of blood runs down his neck. His partner, who was holding the zip-ties, loses his balance, causing both to stumble and fall onto the wet floor.

Clifford kicks the gun away from their reach, and as the other man tries to stand, Clifford jabs him between the shoulder blades with his utility knife.

He falls again, slumping forward over the side of the first man, pinning him down. Clifford hurdles both men as they struggle to stand. He sprints down the hallway and down the six flights of stairs.

Once on the main floor, Clifford pulls his phone from his pocket, seeing a missed text from Rox:

*Tell me you're okay.*

Dee texts back:

*I'm okay. Where ru?*

He waits for her response.

*ur car.*

He sprints outside and toward his car when he hears Rox call out.

"Dee! Dee! Thank God!"

He runs over and crouches down, pulling her down with him.

He reaches into his jeans, searching one pocket after the other.

"SHIT!" he blurted out.

"What? What's wrong?" Rox asks.

"I left the fucking keys in the room!"

"Oh, shit!"

Clifford nods. "Yeah. Those guys are pissed."

Rox points over toward the front of the hotel and says, "Look."

They were staggering out, one holding his neck, the other in clear pain from being stabbed in the back.

Rox whispers, "What did you do?"

Clifford says, "Snapped one guy with a wet towel and stabbed the other in the back."

Astonished, Rox asks, "You bested a gunman with a towel?"

Clifford says, "I'm pretty resourceful."

One guy points in a different direction, and they split up. Clifford and Rox crouch-walk around to the other side of the car to avoid being seen.

The men flank the cars in the parking lot while looking around before realizing the search is futile.

The man holding his neck calls out to the other, "Just get the car. He's gone."

"Fuck! What should we do now?"

"Get the car. We still have one other loose end."

"Can we regroup and do it tomorrow?"

"For fuck's sake, Pete!"

"Dude, I've been stabbed!"

The two men meet each other a few cars away from where Clifford and Rox are still hiding.

Pete turns his back for the other to examine his wound. He moves his shirt and looks at it.

"Yeah, that don't look too good. You might need stitches."

Clifford's phone vibrates, and he pulls it out of his pocket. It was a text from Bailey.

*HR spiked again. Bartender? lol. Sara filled me in.*

Clifford responds:

*Nope. Bad guys.*

Bailey texts back:

*Oh shit! Update me later.*

# Chapter Fourteen

**Once Pete** and his partner drive out of the parking lot, Clifford and Rox circle back around the hotel and head toward a side entrance. Clifford tries the door, but it's locked. "Shit!" He says in frustration.

"Sweetie," Rox says in a calm tone, and pulls out the key card from her back pocket. She winks, stepping forward to swipe the card. "After you," she says as the door opens.

Clifford kisses her forehead as he walks past.

At the front desk, a frustrated Clifford rings the bell, and the clerk appears from the back.

"Hello, how can I help you?"

Clifford says, "My name's Clifford Dee. You sent two men to my room."

The woman behind the counter gives an incredulous look, knowing a complaint is on the way.

"Didn't you inform us to do that?" She interrupts, bracing for the confrontation.

Clifford huffs, "I guess you didn't check their identifications, because that was not who I was expecting."

"Oh my God, I'm so sorry. What happened?"

Clifford looks at Rox and winks before turning back to the woman at the front desk.

"They shot the door open. There may be some water damage, too."

He grabs Rox's hand and walks to the elevator, leaving a shocked desk clerk nervous-giggling as she picks up her walkie-talkie.

"Housekeeping to room 625. It's an emergency."

While in the elevator, Clifford sends a text to Fred:

*Tell me you're okay. Guys came to my room and used your name.*

He shoves the phone into the back pocket of his jeans.

As they reach the room, Rox gasps at the sight of the door. She pokes her head inside and sees a small bit of blood on the wall, a wet and bloodied knife on the floor, and puddles of water both inside the room and outside in the hallway.

"Oh, my God!" she says as she looks around.

Clifford finishes tossing his belongings into his bag, grabs his keys, and says, "Let's get the fuck outta here."

Rox follows a visibly upset Clifford out of the room and into the hallway.

When they reach the elevator, he mashes the down button several more times than necessary.

Rox places her hand on his shoulder. Clifford closes his eyes, draws a deep breath, and instantly calms down.

The elevator dings, and they both step inside.

Once the door closes, she grabs him and pulls him into her and says, "Stop being pissy. It's over."

Then, she plants a huge kiss on his lips.

He pulls away, and a huge smile grows on his face.

"Feel better now?" She asks.

"Mm-hm. Wait, no. You could've been in that room with me."

"But I wasn't. It was *your* idea for me to stay in the lobby. It all worked out the way it was supposed to. Had I stayed home, *you* could've been killed."

Rox smiles and kisses him again when he can't argue.

Out in the parking lot, Clifford uses the remote to open the liftgate on the back of the Bronco, and he tosses their bags into the back.

They walk to the passenger side, and Clifford opens the door. Rox climbs into the passenger seat and says, "Let's go to my place."

Clifford shuts her door and walks around the car, never taking his eyes off her. She keeps her eyes on him as he rounds the front of the car and opens the driver's door.

"Do you think going to your place is a good idea? If they found me here, they might find me there. I don't want your home compromised." Clifford asks.

"I'm not a target. No one's interested in... Wait, how *did* they find you here?"

Clifford shakes his head. "Not sure. Only you, Luis, and Fred knew where we were staying, and they used Fred's name. That worries me."

"Perhaps Fred or Luis' communications are compromised?"

Clifford says, "Maybe. Hopefully, because my brain is going dark."

"What are you thinking?"

"That Fred's dead."

"So, my place?" She asks again.

Clifford smiles. "I should update Agent Fulk with what just happened."

"Will he make you come in?" she asks.

"Probably."

"Tell him tomorrow."

# Chapter Fifteen

**Clifford** pulls into the designated visitor spot meant for Rox's apartment. Rox is looking down at her phone with a look of concentration as she reads a lengthy text.

"Fuck," she says to herself.

"What's wrong?"

"Club's closed indefinitely. I'm out of a job. Fuck."

Clifford rubs her back. "You've had an awful day. I'm so sorry."

Rox sighs. "*And* my place is a mess, cause I haven't cleaned in a few days."

"I think you might be spiraling. I literally don't care what condition your place is in."

Rox, frustrated with herself, says, "I know! It's just I don't want you to get the impression that I'm slobish or anything."

Clifford laughs and questions, "Slobish?"

Rox says, "It's a word. You don't have to look it up."

"You're adorable," Clifford says.

"Shut up!" Rox says, getting out of the car.

Clifford goes around back to collect their bags.

Rox opens her door to her first-floor apartment and turns the lights on. She directs Clifford to her bedroom to put their bags down as she grabs the key for her mailbox.

"I'm going to grab my mail," she yells over her shoulder before walking back outside to the cluster box unit.

Clifford walks back into the living room when he feels something rub against his calf. Glancing down, he sees an orange and white cat bunting his leg. He sits on her couch, and the cat follows, placing his front paws on Clifford's leg. Loud roaring purrs escape the cat as Clifford scratches his head between his ears.

"This cat's as sweet as his mom," Clifford says when Rox walks through the door holding a couple of envelopes and a small stack of junk mail.

She smiles at the pair on her couch. "I see you've met Baskets," she says as she drops the mail on her coffee table and joins them on the couch.

"Baskets?"

"Well, Whisker Baskets is his full name. I found him outside about a year ago, sleeping inside a decorative wicker bassinet near the dumpster. I was thinking Dumpster-Cat was a terrible name, so Wicker Bassinet became Whisker Basket and then Baskets."

She watches as Clifford and Baskets get acquainted. Rox looks somewhat bewildered. "He never warms up to people this quickly," she says to herself.

Clifford tries to hide his smile, but fails. Rox reaches over to stroke Basket's fur, and Clifford puts his arm around her. The three sit on the couch with only Basket's loud purrs filling an otherwise quiet room. Rox moves one leg over Clifford's and leans into him.

With a sigh, Rox asks Clifford to tell her about Bailey.

"He's our nerve-center and mother hen," he begins with a chuckle as he looks down at his watch. Clifford goes on to explain how Bailey's brain can engineer anything with electronics and tech. "I'll never understand how he can do what he does, but I'd be dead in the water without him. You'd love him. Don't let me forget to update him on what just happened."

Rox lays her other hand over Clifford's heart and calmly says, "Tonight's been one adrenaline rush after another."

"Yeah. It takes a bit, but we will crash from it soon. I've actually kinda gotten used to it."

Rox redirects the conversation. She's not ready to think about Clifford being used to such danger. "So, tell me about Sara," she requests.

"Oh! She's awesome. You guys would really hit it - wait, when did I mention Sara? Have you been on my company's site?" He asks while he looks back with a big grin.

"Actually, I have a huge confession to make," Rox says as she sits up and faces him. The posture change convinced Baskets to excuse himself from the couch and sit on the floor. Clifford looks down at Baskets and back to Rox.

The look of concern etched on his face nearly breaks her heart. She lays a reassuring hand on his leg. "The walls in the hotel were paper-thin. I heard your side of the conversation with her."

"Oh," is all Clifford can say.

"I never really needed a comb," she admitted.

Clifford's sudden eruption of laughter makes Baskets jump and scamper out of the room. He apologizes to the cat as he gets up and stretches his legs.

Rox stands up and moves toward the kitchen. "Let me see what I've got to eat," she says, putting a hand over her growling stomach.

Clifford follows her.

"Police station coffee, vending machine-snacks, and homicide was not the date I was hoping to have with you today," Clifford says as he watches Rox scan her fridge and pantry.

She holds up her bandaged left arm. "Really? It went exactly how I thought it would go," she says dryly.

Clifford chuckles. "Yeah, you and Sara would definitely hit it off."

"She seems like a good friend."

Clifford's quiet for a minute. "I think she may be my best friend, actually."

Forgiving the scare and finding them in the kitchen, Baskets is bunting Clifford's leg again. "When do you feed Baskets?"

Rox turns to him. "Not until I go to bed. And text Bailey," she reminds him as she pulls out ingredients to make sandwiches for them. "Then, you can tell me more about your team, and maybe we can finally relax."

Clifford kisses her forehead and walks back into the living room to contact Bailey.

He sends a quick text to Luis first.

*Any idea where Fred is?*

Clifford knows the timestamp will fill in some blanks. Noting the late hour and adding another two, Clifford texts Bailey next.

*Are you up for a call?*

Within seconds, his phone vibrates, and he fills Bailey in on what happened at the hotel.

"What the fuck's going on with this case?" Bailey asks in frustration.

"I don't know, but I have yet to hear from Fred. I think he may be dead," Clifford surmises.

"Or he's involved somehow; sent those two idiots after you," Bailey suggests.

Clifford shakes his head at the thought.

"What would his motivation be to have Hadley taken? You didn't see him with Grace. I can't believe he'd do something like this to her."

"You'd know better than me. I think everybody looks suspicious as fuck. Need me to send Dan out? 'Specially now, since you've been playing house with a pretty bartender?"

"Thanks B, but I think I'm good," Clifford says, chuckling as he watches Rox carry a tray with sandwiches, drinks and chips into the living room. "I'll keep you posted," he says before hanging up.

"Forgot one other thing. Be right back," Rox says as she goes back to grab a bottle of ibuprofen. "Is this going to become one of my major food groups if I keep hanging out with you?" she asks as she sits next to him.

Luis' text comes through.

*Sorry. None. Look into it in A.M.*

Clifford hits the thumbs-up emoji and turns his phone over to activate its do-not-disturb function. He wants to give his undivided attention to the conversation he knows is coming.

He helps himself to some of the ibuprofen. "THC helps. I'm actually surprised you didn't bust that out instead," Clifford says.

"First of all," Rox begins after she swallows a bite of her sandwich. "Not everyone in Colorado has it on them. Secondly, if I *did* have any, Redacted would be here more frequently, and thirdly," she stops to take a breath. "I'm so glad to hear you aren't against it."

Clifford looks confused. "Why would you think I'd be against weed?"

Rox wipes her mouth and tries to explain. "Well, you've been on government cases, and that gives off a whole uptight-DC-vibe. Like you try really hard to uphold the law, so to speak."

Clifford's grin is slow. "First of all," he begins. "Look who's judging now? And secondly, you *have* been on my company's site," he accuses.

Rox laughs at his smug grin. "Well, work was slow before all the murder and mayhem," she quickly admits.

"So how'd you meet Sara?" she asks before taking another large bite of her sandwich.

She's hungrier than she thought.

Clifford clears his throat. "Sara and her girlfriend, Tracy, were my neighbors in Kentucky. I'd recently started my company; it was just me and my extreme organizational skills." He pauses, taking a sip of his water, when she chuckles at his description.

"They were as in love as two people can be. Sara was so happy and full of this light. Like, she was bubbly, ya know?"

Rox nods. "Oh, yeah, I do know. I take it that life beat her down? What happened?"

"I can't go into specifics, but it was a case I was on. Sara and Tracy... They just wanted to help." Clifford stops to clear the lump in his throat, and Rox turns to face him. Her hunger forgotten.

"Liam fucking Stacey," Clifford says the name, letting the weight of it hang in the silent room.

"A psycho, who actually worked the case with me, murdered Tracy."

"Oh, my God!" Rox says as her hand covers her mouth.

Clifford nods. "Liam got exactly what he deserved in the end."

"How did he go from working the case to killing a friend of yours?"

"He got a lot of shit twisted in his mind. Ego, narcissism, and cocaine... It's not a good mix."

"That's pretty fucking heavy, Dee."

"I blamed myself, and Sara was a mess for a long time. If you didn't really know her, she seemed fine. It's been amazing watching her heal and grow," Clifford says.

"She's in therapy?"

Clifford nods. "We all are. The last case made me realize how vital my team's mental health is. Mine, too."

Rox smiles. "What's she like?"

"Smart, funny, honest, strong, empathetic. She really loves being underestimated."

Rox picks up a chip. "You're right. Sara does sound awesome," she says.

Clifford's thoughtful for a moment. "It's funny; Bailey hardly trusts anyone, and Sara sees value in most people. She's actually the one who convinced me to bring Daniel on."

"Was he not a good fit at first?" Rox asks before putting the last bite of sandwich in her mouth.

"When we met him, he was barely an adult and in over his head trying to be a drug dealer. The poor kid had to drop out of college to help pay for his mother's medical expenses after she died."

"That's awful."

"He was lost, scared, and being preyed upon. Sara swooped in like an eldest daughter protecting her baby brother," Clifford says, before allowing a soft chuckle to escape him.

"I guess you could say we adopted him."

"How's he doing now?"

Clifford smiles with pride. "He's still learning, but intelligent. His youth is a strength, and in other ways, a weakness. He's back on his meds, and working on his first solo case."

Rox rubs his back. "It sounds like he has incredible people in his life to help guide him," she says.

"Well, he can't screw up too much with Bailey hovering... and he likes to hover."

Rox sits with all the information Clifford has given her. She didn't realize how much danger Clifford and his team put themselves in. The excitement of it all is very alluring, but the danger is very real.

Clifford stands up, pockets his phone, and carries the tray of empty plates and trash away. "Would you like me to change your gauze one more time?" He asks from the kitchen.

The sound of water running and the trash being gathered surprises her. Rox goes from inspecting her arm to looking over at Clifford washing the small plates. Too curious to see what he'll do next, she sits back, relaxing into the couch.

"Bleeding's stopped. I think I can switch to the smaller Band-Aids and finally wash most of the dried blood off... I just need to keep the stitches dry for another day. I'll do it in a bit," she says, suddenly feeling a little lazy.

She continues watching Clifford dry the plates and search for the proper place to put them. He then pulls a new trash bag up and over the lip of the garbage can.

"Be right back," he says as he strolls past her to take the trash to the dumpster at the end of the parking lot. He snags her keys and jiggles them in front of her. She acknowledges him with a laugh before he locks the door as he exits. She looks over at the tidy kitchen with its light now off.

With the trash bag tossed, Clifford turns to walk back to Rox's apartment when he sees an Acura drive into the lot and stop perpendicular to the Bronco for a moment before pulling into a different visitor's spot. Clifford continues walking toward Rox's door but keeps his eye on the car.

The man he now recognizes as Redacted gets out of the Acura and begins walking towards Clifford's vehicle while looking at him.

"Hey, is this your car?" he yells over at Clifford. "It's in my spot."

Clifford says nothing, but takes his hands out of his pockets and redirects from the apartment to his vehicle.

"We both know that's not your spot," Clifford says when he's only a few feet from Redacted.

The tall, skinny man with a bent nose folds his arms and widens his stance. "Who the hell are you?" He asks with disdain.

Clifford stays relaxed. "I'm Rox's... friend."

As if on cue, Redacted takes a swing with his right fist. Clifford catches the fist and uses momentum to swing Redacted up against the Bronco. He bends Redacted's right arm behind his back as far as it will go without snapping. He uses his other hand to palm Redacted's skull, keeping his left cheek firmly against the rear passenger window.

Before Redacted can react, Clifford kicks the inside of one of Redacted's feet, forcing him into an uncomfortably wide stance to keep him off balance.

He's at the mercy of Clifford's grip.

Redacted struggles to move, but only snot and spit come flying out.

"I don't know you," Clifford says in a low, calm voice. "And I'm not the problem here."

He feels the skinny man relax. Clifford releases his grip, but stays ready for another attack if Redacted's as stupid as he believes.

He takes a few steps away from Clifford. He rubs his shoulder, moving his arm around to ease the pain.

Clifford notices his grease-stained attire. "Mechanic?" He asks.

"Damn good one, too," Redacted says quickly, trying to salvage his dignity.

Clifford purses his lips, nodding. "Why did you try to fight me?"

"She's my girl. I mean, Rox and I have a thing goin', ya know? I don't know you either, dude, and I sure as hell don't know what *you're* doin' with her."

"Let me get this straight, you're a 'damn good' mechanic and you care about the woman in that apartment right there?"

Redacted looks at Clifford with confusion. "Yeah," he states.

Clifford can't help but chuckle. "Then explain why you're so comfortable letting her drive around in that?" He asks, pointing at Rox's car. "Hell, man, at the very least you could've made sure she had jumper cables."

Before Redacted can muster an answer, Clifford continues. "And a *man* who cares about a woman would never make her feel that staying the night with a complete stranger is more comfortable than going home."

Redacted looks stunned. He blinks rapidly and Clifford wonders if he's rebooting.

"That bitch doesn't need to be taken care of. Rox can take care of herself," Redacted adds, thinking feigned feminism can win the argument.

"You're angry. I get it, but if you call her a bitch again, I will rip your windpipe out," Clifford says, giving Redacted a minute to weigh his situation. "You're missing the point entirely," he continues. "A little unsolicited advice, man to... well, you?"

Redacted huffs with a smirk, which Clifford takes as permission. "You're gonna live a lonely and angry existence if you don't grow the fuck up."

Redacted's jaw clenches. He goes to say something when the familiar sound of a door's hinge draws his attention past Clifford.

"Go home, Tristan," Rox says, using his real name, from the doorway.

"If I leave, I'm never coming back, Rox!" he yells.

Rox tilts her head. "Yeah. That's the point."

Tristan stares at her in disbelief.

"The lady's told you what she wants," Clifford says, drawing his attention back to him. "Let's not be stupid, Tristan."

Tristan angrily retreats to his car. Tires squeal as he turns onto the main road.

Clifford, ignoring the second vibration from his cell phone in his pocket, finally turns to face Rox. The pathetic sound of his Acura's gears switching echoes around them.

"Hello, gorgeous," he says, closing the distance between them. "Even his car sounds like it's having a temper-tantrum."

Rox laughs at the silly grin on Clifford's face. "Did you enjoy manhandling him?" She asks, laughing.

He places his hands on her hips and kisses her. "What I just handled wasn't a man. I think you know that."

"Oh, I do," Rox says, leaning into him and feeling a funny sensation. "Uh, Dee... you're vibrating."

They go back inside, and Clifford finally looks at the three missed texts from Bailey.

*HR spiked. Lasted 2 quik. U good?*

*Did u fall asleep?*

*Update pls!*

Before Clifford helps Rox clean off her arm, he replies to Bailey.

*Random punk in the p-lot. Handled.*

After texting, Clifford follows Rox to the bathroom. It's the first time he gets a full look at each cut.

"We were lucky the paramedic could do simple sutures on the scene," Clifford says.

Rox focuses on the smaller cuts on her hand and wrist.

"Why's that?" she asks.

"Well, based on the casualties there, alleviating the hospital's ER in any way they can is a smart decision. It also saved us a long night of waiting."

"Hmm, can't imagine Agent Fulk being as cuddly asking me questions in an ER," she says with a yawn.

The circles under her eyes have grown darker. Clifford knows she's moments from the crash he mentioned earlier. He puts her to bed with little protest.

"What do I feed Baskets?" He asks her as he tucks her in.

Clifford spends the next few minutes making sure the apartment is secure, the cat's fed, and he has a plan to start the next day. He joins Rox, making sure she lays against him on her right side. Clifford gently guides her left arm across his chest to keep her from rolling onto it in her sleep. He kisses her head and settles in to let sleep take over. Just before it does, Baskets jumps on the bed. Eventually, settling between Clifford's legs.

# Chapter Sixteen

**Agent Fulk** arrives at the security lodge just after six in the morning, after having been working on the case for nearly twelve hours. He smooths his coffee-stained tie under his winter coat and promptly heads inside.

He finds the ranger, Luis, on the phone. Luis looks up from his call and raises a finger, indicating he would be with him in just a moment.

Fulk acknowledges and sets his badge on the desk for him to look at.

Luis nods and quickly concludes his conversation.

"Hey, Agent Fulk. What can I do for you?" he asks as he hangs up the phone.

Fulk, who was looking around, turns back to Luis.

"Ranger Ramos, a man by the name of Fred Polter, had this location in his GPS. Do you know him?"

Luis nods, "Yeah, Fred was here yesterday. His employer's daughter is missing. He went to meet with an acquaintance, Clifford Dee, just south of Estes Park."

Agent Fulk nods. The information tracks so far, which makes Fulk happy.

"What time would you say he left here?" Fulk asks, hoping the timeline matches as well.

"Not long after we got news of a shooting that got the, well, your agency involved. He was going to meet with you after he had a face-to-face with Dee."

Again, Fulk nods. "What's your part in all of this?" he asks.

"Dee directed us to a vehicle accident location. After some time, we uncovered the body of Raymond Pollard."

"The father of our kidnapped victim?"

"Yessir. So, you mentioned Fred's GPS, and Dee texted me he never showed up last night... Is Fred dead?" Luis says bluntly.

Agent Fulk rubs his eyes as he sits down in front of Luis' desk.

"Well, we believe Fred's dead."

"What do you mean by, you believe?"

Fulk sighs heavily. "Well, we're trying to confirm the identity of the body. He had Fred's wallet on his person. He was driving a car that belonged to his employer, Grace Dillenger, who's probably getting notified as we speak, but what the body didn't have was a face."

Luis looked confused. "I'm sorry?" he asks.

Fulk elaborates, "Someone shot him at very close range in the face with a twelve-gauge shotgun."

Luis' eyes grow wide and he says, "Jesús, María y José."

Fulk nods. "Yeah. It's not pretty."

Luis, still thinking about Fred, put his hand up to his own face in disbelief.

Fulk exhales again. "I should find Dee. Get him up here."

"Already on it." Luis says, putting his phone to his ear.

***

Clifford opens one eye and feels the warm breath of Rox on the nape of his neck. He smiles and pulls her into him. He hears a rhythmic hum and realizes his phone is ringing on the nightstand. As quickly as he can, Clifford carefully slides away from Rox and grabs his phone on his way into the hallway.

Clifford answers his phone. "Hey, Luis. Were you able to find Fred? I'm worried, man."

Agent Fulk's abrupt voice takes him by surprise.

"Clifford Dee? This is Agent Fulk. I really need you to come meet me at the lodge as soon as you can."

Luis cuts in, "There's been a development, Dee."

Clifford understands he's on speakerphone. "Fred?" he asks.

"It's best that we discuss it here," Agent Fulk interrupts.

"I'll be there in a few hours."

"Text your address to Ranger Ramos. I'm gonna arrange a police escort. Let's get you here as quickly as possible."

Before Clifford can protest, Luis says, "See you soon, Dee," just before ending the call.

"Shit," he says to himself.

"Bad news?" Rox asks, coming up behind him.

"I've gotta go back to the lodge," he says, turning around in time for her to walk straight into his arms.

"Okay," she sighs. "Let me get dressed."

"Oh, no no no. You're staying put. You're safer here with Baskets."

Rox turns and walks back to the bedroom. "I'm safest with you!" she yells over her shoulder.

"Oh, I don't think that's correct," he argues, following her to get dressed.

Rox pulls her jeans up over her hips. "If you think that I'm going to stay here ruminating, you're sorely mistaken."

"You've gone through a lot," he says, buttoning his shirt. "You need time to rest."

"Didn't you say you had a room at the lodge?" She asks, pulling her long-sleeved t-shirt down to tuck into her jeans.

"You want to stay at the lodge?" Clifford asks, tying one of his boots.

"Only for the time you need to be there," she says, putting her arms through a hoodie and sliding it on before continuing, "I can stay somewhere safe wherever you need to be."

"There's no way to change your mind?" he asks, pocketing his phone and wallet.

Before she can answer, there's a heavy knocking sound at her front door.

"Fucking Redacted!" Rox says in frustration.

"That's probably our escort. Fulk's way of reminding me of who's in charge," Clifford explains.

"Well," Rox walks past Clifford to answer the door. "This will be fun, then."

She answers the door and promptly tells the young officer from the local PD that they will be out shortly before shutting the door in his face. She walks into the kitchen, feeds Baskets, and grabs bottled water and protein bars from the pantry.

Rox places the provisions in a bag and hands it to a silent but watchful Clifford, as she passes him in the hallway.

"Go warm up the car, dear. I'll be out in a minute."

He hides his smile and walks over to Baskets, eating his breakfast. He bends down and scratches the cat's back. "Hope I see you again, buddy," he whispers before leaving to warm up the car.

Before the windshield can fully defrost, Rox exits the apartment and walks over to the patrol car. Clifford gets out of the vehicle and watches as she talks to the officer through the window. She hands him a bottle of water and continues toward Clifford with an overnight bag and a big smile.

He takes the bag and helps her into the passenger seat before placing her bag in the back. The amused officer nods to Clifford before turning on his lights and making his way to the entrance of the parking lot.

Once he pulls behind the officer, ready for the escort, he asks Rox why she approached the officer.

"I apologized for my behavior and offered an olive branch. Hurrying out of my home before the sun's up without coffee makes me cranky, apparently."

***

Warming back up in the security office, the lights of the patrol car catch Agent Fulk's attention as it pulls into the lot in front of the Ranger's office.

He steps outside in time to see a dark Bronco veer toward the lodge instead of pulling up to the ranger station with the police escort.

Fulk walks outside to thank the escorting officer, and asks, "What's he doing?"

The cop says, "He's with a woman. Probably dropping her off at the lodge."

Fulk nods and says, "I see."

He sends the officer back to his precinct and gives Clifford Dee some grace before he blows up his phone with accusations of impeding a case.

After a few minutes, Clifford opens the door of the Ranger's office and steps in. He's out of breath. Fulk, already standing, looks over to Clifford and says, "Mr. Dee, nice to see you again."

"Fred?" he asks, already knowing the answer.

Luis shakes his head.

Fulk says, "Someone shot him. Point-blank range."

"Fuck," Clifford says under his breath.

Fulk gives Clifford a heavyhearted nod and says, "Luis caught me up on everything. Including something that never made its way to you."

Clifford turns quickly toward Luis, confused.

"Dee, Fred was on his way to confess to you. I think he was... silenced," Luis says first, before catching Clifford up on the rest.

Clifford, in disbelief, says, "Unbelievable how he thought putting Hadley in danger was a smart thing."

After Clifford's moment of reflection, Fulk reaches into his pocket, pulls out his phone and opens a photo of the shotgun shell, and sets it on the desk.

"This was found at the scene. It has a Green Beret symbol on the side."

Clifford swipes the phone and looks at the picture. As he zooms in on the symbol, the words, "Son-of-a-bitch!" escape his lips.

The symbol resembles the Green Beret. It's also very familiar to Clifford.

Fulk cocks his head and looks over to Luis, who also looks intrigued.

Looking back toward Clifford, Fulk says, "Does that mean something to you?"

Clifford hands the phone back to Fulk. "That's not a Green Beret symbol. That's Cold Steel, an SMU within the Green Beret."

"SMU? Cold Steel? How do you know this?" Fulk asks in rapid succession.

Clifford nods. "Special Missions Unit. I was on a tactical team called Cold Steel. We were over in Afghanistan and ordered to take out a terrorist cell that was using a mosque as a stronghold. Dropping bombs on a religious structure would cause a PR nightmare, so they ordered us to go in on foot to take out the threat."

Clifford pauses.

"Somehow, they knew we were coming. While traveling, we got separated from the rest of the caravan and then ambushed in the desert. I was captured and later rescued. That's when I found out the rest of the unit was killed. Cold Steel was disbanded."

Clifford breathes a heavy sigh. "Apparently, that was bad intel."

Fulk's eyes narrow. "You were a P.O.W.?"

"Yessir."

Fulk pockets the phone and asks, "So, would this military unit you were in, Cold Steel, would they target civilians like this?"

"Absolutely not. Well, at least not back then," Clifford answers.

Fulk asks, "So, like I said before, maybe some people researched the group and are playing army, using the symbol?"

Clifford shakes his head no. "When the Army disbands an SMU, they remove all knowledge, including names, symbols - everything. No one would have known about that symbol unless they were in Cold Steel."

Fulk looks over to Luis and back at Clifford.

"How many people were in the unit?" Fulk asks.

"Twelve, including me."

Clifford runs his hand through his hair and continues, "I'll get you a list of names. Oh yeah! I was attacked last night by two guys at the hotel I was supposed to meet Fred at."

"Let me guess. At the Aurora Peak Inn?" Agent Fulk asks.

"Yeah, Aurora Peak Inn," Clifford says.

"Yep. That address was in Fred's GPS. So, they killed Fred and came after you."

Clifford swipes his brow and says, "Damn it."

"I sent a car to update Grace about Fred," Fulk says.

Clifford replies, "We should go talk to her as well. He had an office on her estate."

"I'll drive," Fulk says

**On the way**, Clifford sends a quick text to update Rox, and she responds, telling him to be safe.

Grace, notified by her security when they arrive, meets Clifford and Fulk at the doorstep when they walk up from the car.

"Clifford, the police just left. Who's this?" Grace asks with an uneasy demeanor. She looks as though she's just finished crying.

Fulk makes his own introduction.

"Agent Fulk of the CBI. I joined the case last night."

Grace lets out a dejected sigh and looks away, lips trembling.

Fulk looks to Clifford for some help.

"Grace, Agent Fulk is actually doing more than joining. The CBI has taken over the investigation."

Grace gives Clifford a concerned look and questions, "Oh, he is? Why is - How did Fred-"

She couldn't even get one question completely out before her brain moved on to the next question. "They never even told me how. Just that he was deceased."

Clifford places his arm around her and says, "Let's go inside and we'll properly brief you. "

He recalls the story that Fred shared with Luis, and Grace listens intently.

Clifford first asks Grace if she would like to give Fulk the full details about how this started.

She does.

Fulk fills her in on the rest of the story, and afterward, Grace breaks down and starts to cry.

"This has gotten so out of hand. We agreed we would confront him about his gambling *after* this trip, but Fred told the guy to do it anyway?"

Clifford nods and says, "It surprised me too."

Fulk sips his seltzer water and asks, "Do you know anything about the men Fred hired?"

Grace says, "No. He just said he knew someone. I was out of the loop."

Clifford leans closer to Fulk.

"It makes sense that Fred would protect her by keeping her out of the loop."

Fulk nods in agreement as he pulls up the file with the morgue pictures of the men killed at Wild Willies.

She looks at the phone and shakes her head. Fulk swipes through the photos, showing each to Grace.

"I don't know them."

Fulk locks his phone and stuffs it into his jacket pocket. "Okay."

"Would you mind if I took a look at the bodies?" Clifford asks Fulk.

Fulk reaches for his phone, and Clifford stops him. "I mean in person."

He nods and says, "Yeah, sure. Why?"

Clifford shakes his head. "If Fred's killer is from Cold Steel, and Fred hired these guys, I just want to look at them to see if there's a link."

Fulk nods. "Sure, we can go up there in a few. First, Grace, I was told Fred had an office on the property. Could we take a look around?"

She nods and says, "It's this way."

Clifford walks into the hall and flags down Spencer. "Excuse me, could you grab me a few plastic sandwich baggies and bring them to Fred's office?"

Spencer nods and hurries away.

Grace shows Clifford and Fulk to Fred's office. As they look around, Grace steps away. Clifford spots a small shelf with over a dozen police challenge coins and one coin from the 2nd Cavalry Division of the U.S. Army. As Fulk continues to look around, Spencer returns with a box of sandwich baggies. Clifford takes one and offers it to Fulk, who declines.

Fulk buries his head in a filing cabinet. "Doesn't look like much here. There are some files in his cabinet that I would like to get a closer look at, so I'm going to call some people to bag some things up."

Clifford says, "Okay" and uses the baggie to snag the military coin from the case. He closes it and puts it in his pocket while Fulk's still looking at the files. Clifford browses some of the decor on the walls and checks out his Police Academy graduation photo. "Class of 1984, wow," Clifford says.

Fulk looks up and asks, "What's that?"

Pointing at the picture, Clifford says, "Fred graduated the academy in eighty-four. I didn't think he was that much older than me."

Fulk nods and shrugs it off.

Grace walks up to the door of the office and asks, "Did you find anything?"

Fulk mentions taking his files. "We might need access to his computer files as well. Every bit of information will help us locate your daughter. For now, we're going to head over to the morgue. I'll have some officers come by for Fred's things."

Clifford looks back at Grace. "We'll find her."

***

Clifford follows Fulk back to the precinct to view the bodies and escorts him to the morgue.

Harry Sampson, the Chief Medical Examiner, looks over at them. "What can I do for you guys?"

Fulk says, "Doctor Sampson?"

He smiles and says, "Please call me Sam."

"Hey Sam, I'm Agent Fulk of the CBI, and this is Detective Clifford Dee. Mr. Dee wants to see the guys from the club."

"Oh, sure. One sec."

He walks over toward the body storage unit. Essentially floor to ceiling filing cabinets with giant drawers. He pulls open a drawer and exposes a body covered by a sheet.

He walks two rows down and opens two other drawers.

Finally, he opens a fourth drawer and says, "These are the perps from the bar. All I can say about these two is that they're from a European sovereign country. I was told to keep them on ice until their country can send someone to claim them."

"Have you ID'd the other guys yet?" Clifford asks.

Sam says, "Oh no, not yet. These two are still J.D.'s at the moment. Their identification was fake, but we believe they're American."

Sam pulls back the sheet, and Clifford looks over the first of the bodies. The first thing he spies is a small tattoo just below the clavicle.

He points it out and says, "Look here."

Fulk narrows his eyes. "What am I looking at?"

Clifford says, "Second infantry division."

The other body has a big red one tattooed in the same spot.

Clifford nods. "They were both infantrymen. First division and second division."

Fulk asks, "So we have a special forces symbol on a shotgun shell and two infantry symbols on dead bodies. Are these guys all ex-Marines or something?"

"Not Marines, ex-Army," Clifford clarifies.

He pulls out his phone and starts taking photos of the men, their scars, and tattoos. He texts the pictures to Bailey.

*Uploaded pics of the kidnappers. They're dead. Military tats. Can you run a check?*

Bailey texts back.

*On it.*

Clifford looks over to Fulk and says, "I have my guy on it."

Fulk scoffs, "We have pics of these guys being run against the largest criminal database in the country. We even have the FBI over in Denver looking into it. We don't need your guy."

Clifford smiles assuredly and says, "Wanna place a wager that my guy gets a lead first?"

Fulk laughs. "Seriously?"

Clifford replies, "My guy's the best."

Fulk scoffs in disbelief. "Yeah, okay. Sure."

Fulk gets a message on his phone and smugly says, "We got a hit on one of the names you gave me- from your unit."

Clifford looks up from the body. "No shit, which one?"

"Kyle Somers. Apparently, a guy checked into a hospital in Kentucky a few years back and then disappeared."

A memory flashes through Clifford's mind of when he escaped capture from the Tye Brothers after they tied him up and left him in an old decaying church. He used Kyle's name as an alias in the hospital.

He shakes the memory from his mind and says, "Ah-that's nothing."

Fulk asks, "How can you be so sure?"

"Well, that was me. I had to use an alias, and so I chose my old Army buddies' name."

A chuckle escapes Fulk. "I'd like to hear more about that story later."

The notification of Bailey's text interrupts the men.

*Both guys were infantry frm basic Ft. Benning, Georgia, 2006.*

*Christopher Louis and Troy Rockman.*

Clifford smiles at the texts. He sees that Bailey's still typing as he reads the current message to Fulk.

Fulk says, "He got something that fast?"

The next text comes in.

*2008 in separate units.*

*Louis= Second Infantry Div.*

*Rockman= First Infantry Div.*

Clifford looks over at Fulk and asks, "Do you remember what Rox said their names were?"

Fulk replies, "Yeah, she said Louie and Rocco. Sounds like the names of cartoon characters."

Clifford smiles and points at one body. "Christopher Louis. AKA Louie."

Then he points at the other. "Troy Rockman. Louie and Rocco must've been their nicknames for each other."

Fulk shakes his head. "How did he get that info?"

Clifford says, "I can ask."

He puts it on speaker, and the phone rings.

"What's up, Dee? You get those names?"

"Sure did. How'd you come across them?"

Bailey quickly retorts, "A magician does not reveal his secrets, Dee!"

Clifford replies, "Bailey, this is serious. Fulk needs to know for legal reasons."

Bailey sighs and replies, "Okay, fine. I took the images you sent and ran them through an app I developed that uses AI to de-age faces. Then, I used that image to drag a military-friend finder website. Found a platoon photo from basic training that had them in it. Same platoon. Their names are underneath the photo. So then I used their names to do a broader search and found they went to different units after training. The weird thing is both men went MIA during a field mission in 2010."

Clifford looks up at Fulk and smiles. "Thanks, buddy. Let me know if you find anything else. Oh, and send me that basic training photo."

He ends the call.

Fulk shakes his head. "Well, shit. I guess I owe you a Coke or something."

Clifford says, "Now that we have their names, can you do a more extensive search?"

He looks at his phone as the photo he requested from Bailey comes through.

Fulk nods and says, "Yeah, probably, but if they went MIA in 2010 and your guy can't trace them after that time frame, it might get difficult."

Fulk picks up his phone and places a call while Clifford reviews the image of the basic training platoon Bailey sent.

"Hey yeah, two of the Wild Willies John-Doe's have names," Fulk says into the phone. After a brief pause he continues, "Christopher Louis and Troy Rockman. See if you can find anything."

He hangs up and sticks the phone back in his pocket.

Sam chimes in. "Could I also have a copy of that information? We'd want to link their dental records."

Clifford says, "You got it."

Fulk, feeling good about the direction of the case, says, "Okay, we have some good information to go on. Tell your guy, Bailey - was it? Thanks. Let's see if we can find something in the morning."

Clifford, still looking at the photo on the phone, remains silent.

"Everything okay, Dee?"

Clifford looks up from the phone and says, "Kyle Somers was in the same training unit as these guys."

"What does that mean?" Fulk asks.

Clifford shakes his head. "I have no idea. At least not yet."

Leaving the morgue, Fulk continues to talk with Clifford as they traverse the hallway.

"Do you think Kyle joined these guys?" Fulk asks. "He was in your Cold Steel unit. The symbol was on that shotgun shell, and he was in their training unit. This is too much for just a coincidence."

Clifford shakes his head. "No. Kyle died with the rest of my unit. I heard his screams..."

His voice trails off as he says, "I still have nightmares about it."

Fulk shakes his head and says, "Alright. It just seems strange. All of it."

Clifford nods. "Yeah, I know. It really does."

He pulls out his phone and sends a text to Rox:

*OMW back to you soon. You okay?*

Rox texts back:

*Hungry. Bring food!*

Clifford smiles and replies:

*Totally!!*

Fulk, seeing Clifford absorbed in the conversation on his phone, asks, "Everything okay?"

Clifford shoves his phone into his pocket and says, "Sorry. Rox's back at the lodge. I'm checking in."

Fulk smiles, impressed. "So you *really* know the bartender?"

Clifford purses his lips in slight awkwardness. "We've hit it off."

Fulk says through a grin, "Mm-hmm. Oh! That actually reminds me. That bouncer at Willie's you wanted the update on?"

"Yeah?"

"He's alive. Still in the ICU with a long road of recovery ahead of him, but alive."

"Rox will be relieved. Thank you."

Fulk shrugs and smiles. "Well, now that we're all caught up to speed, I say you shouldn't keep a beautiful woman waiting."

A junior agent walks up and says, "Agent Fulk, we might have a lead."

Fulk asks, "What do you mean, might?"

He says, "The police here said it's Wally. He gave a statement the oth-"

Fulk shakes his head, cutting him off. "No. Hell no. We are not following that lead."

Clifford perks up. "Who's Wally?"

Fulk sighs. "He's our cherished transient who cries wolf. All the law enforcement around the area know the name. He's in and out of shelters and sometimes will report a crime just to get out of the cold and drink coffee. If we book him for filing a report, he gets locked up, which usually offers more than a shelter."

The junior agent cuts in. "He was hanging around Park View a few days ago; tried to report he saw two guys moving a girl against her will from an apartment building to a waiting vehicle."

Clifford asks, "We should talk to him."

Fulk sighs. "The location is a few blocks from where the casinos are, and the situation fits. Fine. Go eat, and I'll try to locate him. It might be a little while."

# Chapter Eighteen

**Clifford** reaches the lodge and heads up to his room. Before he can knock, Rox swings the door open. "I haven't left the peephole since your last text," she admits.

He's hiding a bag behind his back and slowly presents it. "Burgers and fries?"

Rox smiles and says, "You read my mind."

"Matt's gonna pull through, by the way," he says, walking inside.

"Oh! I'm so relieved, thank you."

The two sit at the small table next to the kitchenette, and he fills her in on what he can. Rox feels frustrated, but understands that she can only know information suitable to the public.

"I think what makes me the angriest is how those guys treated me. I don't want to imagine what they've been putting that scared girl through."

"What do you mean, how did they treat you?" Clifford asks.

She could still feel the gross hand trying to grip her thigh. "Sometimes men get a little... handsy. One of those creeps pawed at me."

She places a hand on top of Clifford's balled fist. "I handled myself. I just hope they left Hadley alone."

Clifford seethes under the surface. He wishes he could bring Rocco and Louie back to life just to kill them all over again.

"How's your arm?" he asks, dipping a fry in ketchup.

She proudly raises her arm. "Down to one Band-Aid and one bandage. I'm going to need your help in the shower though; I really want to wash my hair."

Clifford smiles, not feeling bothered by the task. "I have a better idea. Be right back," he says, getting up and walking out of the room.

Rox finishes her meal and cleans up when she receives a text from Clifford:

Rox feels intrigued at first, but then errs on the side of caution. She reaches into her overnight bag to grab her trusty serrated-blade pocket knife and hides it in the sleeve of her hoodie before following the instructions she hopes Clifford really sent her.

She finds the beautiful, quiet salon on the third floor. She spots Clifford chatting with a young woman who's clearly a salon employee. Clifford looks up and smiles. "Hey gorgeous," he says, walking up to her.

"What's going on?" Rox asks, smiling politely over at the woman.

"We're getting you washed, dried, and styled. What's the point of staying at a resort if you can't enjoy the amenities?"

She moves her knife from her sleeve to hide in the front pocket of her hoodie. Clifford leads her over to a chair where Cassie, the salon stylist, is waiting.

Rox looks up at him wide-eyed. He kisses her forehead before turning to leave. "I'll be back in about twenty minutes to escort you back."

Agent Fulk texted earlier that someone had found and brought in Wally. Clifford walks out of the salon and texts for an update.

Within minutes, Agent Fulk calls.

"So, Wally says he saw two guys with a girl. Said she looked drugged, but what piqued his interest was that she tried to fight 'em. I showed him her photo, and he ID'd Hadley as the girl. This broken clock is right on time for once. We're headed over to the apartment building he saw 'em come out of. It's one of those rent-by-the-month places."

"Where's this apartment?" Clifford asks.

"Now, now. I've sent someone to pick up the landlord for a chat and another to canvas the building to see if we can get any other eyewitnesses."

Clifford sighs. "Maybe we should make our way back to Rox's since it's closer."

"Or you can stay put tonight and let me question them. This *is* my case now, Dee," Agent Fulk politely reminds him.

Clifford peeks into the salon to see Rox's eyes closed as Cassie massages her scalp. The shampoo lather covered her long dark hair.

He knows Fulk is right. Driving back tonight made little sense. Clifford walks away from the salon towards the steps.

"Tell ya what, let's meet back here tomorrow morning. Say, nine?" Agent Fulk asks.

"I appreciate it. Have you gotten any sleep?" Clifford asks.

Fulk chuckles. "I'll see ya tomorrow morning," he says and hangs up.

Clifford walks around the lodge and sends a text update to Bailey:

*I'm in for the night. Meeting Fulk in the AM.*

Bailey responds:

*I wont ask abt HR unless it stops.*

He eventually makes his way back into the salon. Rox is talking with her back to Clifford. Cassie looks over at him and smiles. Rox turns around. "Hey," she says.

Clifford stops in his tracks. She looks radiant despite everything she'd been through in the past twenty-four hours.

"Damn," he says breathlessly.

"You're right," Cassie begins. "Curling it would've been a waste of time." She winks at Rox. "You two have yourselves a good night."

"A little pampering and a blowout do wonders," Rox says in the elevator. "Thank you so much, Dee," she says as she leans into him.

"Anytime," he whispers. Clifford kisses the top of her head, and waits for the doors to open on their floor.

"Are you okay with spending the night here tonight?"

Rox puts her hands on her hips and looks around. "Hmm, am I okay with staying in a luxury hotel with a sweet, sexy man?"

Clifford laughs. "Will Baskets be okay tonight?" he asks.

"Seriously? Sploosh!" Rox says with feigned exasperation. "I planned ahead and set up his auto-feeder."

Clifford thinks back to how she took charge that morning at her place. "I have noticed how you think ahead," he admits, impressed.

He pulls her into him. "Um, Rox, is there something in your pocket or are you just happy to see me?"

She steps back, laughing. She pulls her pocket knife out. "I was like ninety-five percent sure that you sent that text to go to the third floor, but..."

Clifford tilts his head. "Do you know how to use it?"

Rox looks at the closed knife in her hand, confused. "Well, open it and get stabby. Am I right?"

Clifford moves some furniture and starts teaching her a few of the same basic self-defense techniques he taught his team.

Breathing heavily, he chuckles. "Ya know, I told Bailey we were in for the night. He probably thinks we're doing something else."

Rox jumps on his back. "Then, let's prove him right. Take me to bed, Dee."

***

Agent Fulk sits down to talk with Terry, the landlord of the six-unit building. He explains that they're investigating an abduction and that they believe the missing girl was in their building at some point.

"I have a few photos I need to show you. Two of them are from the morgue. We beli-"

"Wait, you're gonna make me look at dead people? Why?" Terry interrupts.

Agent Fulk gives a tight-lipped smile. "Well, we only have these photos of the men, and as I was about to say, we believe they rented from you. We're hoping you can I.D. them for us."

"Did they die in my apartment?!" Terry asks, wide-eyed.

Fulk rubs his hand over his face. "No, at Wild Willie's," he says as he looks into his near-empty stained coffee mug.

"Oh, I heard what happened there. You think that was them?"

"We do, but need to confirm," Fulk pauses to place the morbid images of Rocco and Louie on the table. "Did they rent from you?"

Fulk concentrates on Terry's face as they scan each photo.

"Mm-hmm. A couple of weeks back, they wanted a unit for a week. I told 'em I only rent month to month. They said fine. I met them in the parking lot later that day. They handed me a stack of bills. I gave 'em a key."

Fulk huffs. "You didn't find that odd?"

"Odd? I thought it was suspicious as fuck, but I don't ask questions. Terry likes plausible deniability."

Fulk sighs as he sets down two recent photos of Hadley. One was her most recent professional school picture. Grace took the other photo on the day of the trip with Raymond.

"How about her? Did you see her with these guys or anywhere on your property?"

"Is she the missing girl?" Terry asks.

Agent Fulk nods his head.

Terry shakes theirs no. "I want to help, but I've never seen her."

"Are there security cameras around your place?"

"I can give you footage."

Fulk sits back in his chair. "How'd they get in touch with you?"

"There's a sign on the building with a phone number to call. It gets forwarded to my cell."

"The phone number they called from. Do you have that?"

Terry nods, scrolling through their phone as Fulk turns a legal pad of paper around and plops a pen on top for Terry to transcribe the phone number for him.

# Chapter Nineteen

**Clifford** and Rox arrive before nine with several boxes of pastries and two carafes of coffee from a local coffee shop.

Agent Fulk laughs at the slack-jawed officers in the small town precinct. "You always this nice to local law enforcement?" he asks.

Rox interrupts, "You should see how much he tips waitstaff."

Agent Fulk raises an eyebrow, shakes his head, and waves his hand for them to join him in a quiet room.

"So, I sent everything to the department techs after I sent it all over to you last night, but they haven't gotten back to me yet," Fulk says as he sits down.

Clifford, who'd been looking at his phone, says, "Hey Bailey, you're on speaker."

"Dee, that's another burner phone. It's different from the other one that pinged near the casino, but get this - I was able to use it to do a ping-trace on the cell-towers. According to this info, the phone was only active for forty-eight hours. It pinged all over Denver, and then I ping-traced it back to an area up in the mountains. There's only one building near there."

"Jesus, how many pings does it take to get to the center of a Tootsie Pop?" Rox mutters loudly enough for Bailey to hear over the phone.

There's a brief silence.

Rox looks contrite, but Clifford smirks and winks at her to ease the tension. Fulk hides a smile.

Clifford says, "You did say 'Ping' a lot there, buddy."

There's another brief silence before Bailey says, "So anyway, that building is a private gun club. Like one of those militia, survivalist-type clubs."

Clifford says, "Great, send me the details, please."

"I'll ping it to ya... Ping!" he says and then hangs up.

Fulk nods and says, "He's good."

Clifford smiles and replies, "He's the best."

"Funny, too," Rox says.

Clifford smiles. "I have a great team."

A second later, an officer walks in and says, "Fulk, we have a report on the number."

Fulk looks over at Clifford.

"So close." He turns to the officer and says, "Lemme guess, it's a burner phone that traces back to a gun club?"

The officer looks at the report and starts to re-read it. He looks up from the paper and says, "Yeah. That's it."

Fulk says, "Well, let's get a warrant."

A while later, the officer returns and says, "Judge says there isn't enough for one."

"Fuck!" Fulk blurts out in frustration.

He looks over toward Clifford and Rox, who both look disappointed.

Fulk says, "Let's just drive up there and ask some questions. We don't need a warrant for that."

"Bad idea!" Clifford says sternly. "If they do have her and suspect we're onto them, they might just opt to kill her instead. We need a better plan."

"Could you send someone in to act like they may want to join the club? Maybe ask for a tour and get the lay of the land?" Rox asks.

"It's not exactly *that* type of club. Where anyone can walk in and join," Clifford explains.

Silence fills the room.

Clifford shakes his head. "Fucking red tape! I don't care about a God-damned warrant, we need to get the girl!" Clifford shouts.

Fulk looks sternly at Clifford. "We're trying, Dee!"

"You and I both know the type we're dealing with here, Fulk. Women and girls are considered property, and that's just surface-level hell for her if she's there."

An officer's knock halts the argument. Agent Fulk swings open the door, agitated. "What?!"

"Uh, sorry. A name just popped that's tied to your investigation. They found a park ranger named Luis Ramos with a GSW to the head. He was found in his car on the side of Route 125."

Clifford jumps to his feet as Fulk grabs the printed report from the officer.

"God-dammit!" Fulk exclaims.

Clifford bites his lip in frustration, remembering the picture of Luis' wife and kids he had at his desk at the Ranger's lodge.

"It has to be the same guys who got Fred and came after me in the hotel," Clifford offers, his anger beginning to mingle with grief.

Fulk looks up from the report. "Says it was a twenty-two cal, not a twelve-gauge shotgun-"

"They didn't come at me with a fucking shotgun, either. I think Fred got special treatment," Clifford surmises.

Rox is confused. "Who was Luis Ramos?" she asks.

Clifford grabs his jacket from the back of the chair he was in, knocking it over. "I need to get outta here."

Rox stands and tries to say something, but Clifford shakes his head and says, "And Fulk," he says with a pause, "please call me when you get something."

Rox grabs her jacket and follows Clifford just before Fulk tosses a pencil across the room in frustration.

***

Rox finds Clifford near the Bronco by the passenger door, on his phone. She folds her arms and stands in front of him while he asks someone about picking up a purchase he made days ago.

He pockets the phone. "Luis Ramos was a Ranger from the lodge. He had a young family." Clifford stopped to clear his throat. "I need to go pick up some things I've been waiting for. It could be awhile. I'll drop you off at home."

Rox narrows her eyes as she examines his demeanor. What he said was clearly not open for discussion. She drops her arms to their sides.

"Okay," she says.

Clifford opens her door and helps her into the car. "You're not fighting me?"

He stands as Rox puts her seatbelt on before facing him. "Doesn't feel like a good idea right now," she responds.

The ride back to her apartment is quiet. Clifford parks and gets their bags out of the back as Rox unlocks her front door. He brings the bags in, continuing to the bedroom. Rox immediately grabs her mail key and leaves. He picks up Baskets and carries him into the living room to wait for her return.

"I'm sorry if I made you uncomfortable back at the station," he says as she walks back in.

Rox drops the mail and her key onto the table and sighs. "I thought you had to go pick something up?" she asks.

"It can wait. I need to make sure you're okay first."

"I'm not sure what okay is right now. We've been connected at the hip through some pretty fucked up shit - and, I know... I know I'm to blame for that, but I just..." she catches her breath and swallows hard. "I just really wanted... to be around you, but I think we should take a beat, ya know?"

Clifford sets Baskets on the couch. "I want to be around you, too. I'll get my bags. I'm so sorry, Rox."

She offers a smile. "I think it's just that I'm not used to being around someone with such great work ethic."

"I've never been accused of slacking off," he says, taking a cautious step forward.

She takes a step. "That makes sense. I've yet to experience you slacking off, Mr. Dee."

They stand directly in front of one another. Rox tilts her head up, and Clifford brushes her hair back and over her shoulder.

"You don't have to stay anywhere else tonight. Just... take your time on your errand. I wanna work some things out in my head."

Clifford kisses her forehead, and then the tip of her nose before looking down at the cat. "Baskets, I'm gonna need you to be the bestest boy for your momma, okay?"

He turns back to Rox and gently tugs her hair until she's looking up at him again. He gives her a soft kiss and whispers, "For the record. I *really* like being around you, too."

Clifford jumps into the Bronco, ringing Bailey as he hurries off.

"Hey Dee, what's up?"

"Can you control a drone in Colorado?" Clifford asks, navigating the roads back to the gun shop.

"Sure can. Just get me the make, model, and serial number. Wait - why?"

"I'm gonna need your help with something."

He pulls into the parking lot of the gun shop, jumps out of the car and heads inside.

He rings the bell on the counter, and the owner steps out from the back.

"Ah, Mr. Dee, right?"

"Yep!"

The man heads back to the rear to grab his order.

Clifford looks around and when the shopkeeper returns he asks, "I see you have old Army surplus. Can I get a pair of the Army Battle Dress Uniforms and those black jungle boots?" He looks around and points at a knife through the glass. "That boot knife, and the drone too."

He also grabs a pack of nylon cord and places it on the counter.

The shopkeeper totals the items and hands Clifford a pair of elastic boot blousers.

"Those stretchy boot cords will help keep your pants in your boots. They come free with a pair of boots." The cashier offers.

Clifford smiles and says, "Thanks," knowing exactly what they were.

He stops before walking out of the shop. "Is there, like, a nicer restaurant around here?"

The man looks confused. "There's the steak place up the road," he tentatively says.

Clifford smiles. "If you took your wife there for an anniversary, would you get in trouble?"

The man laughs. "Oh, you want *Burton's*. Need a reservation."

# Chapter Twenty

**After he finishes the errand,** Clifford continues to give Rox the space she requested, but sends a text asking her out to dinner, which she accepts.

He knows the suit he travels with will be good enough for the restaurant, but goes into Boulder for a new tie and some other requirements for a proper date.

He feels nervous and out of his element while standing in front of her door. He shifts the bouquet of pink roses to his left hand as he knocks softly.

She opens the door, and for a moment Clifford forgets how to speak. Rox stands in front of him in a burgundy off-the-shoulder dress with long sleeves and a pencil skirt that goes just below her knees. The pointed nude heels are a tasteful touch, matching the handbag she holds. Her hair is parted deep on one side, with a pearled comb keeping the hair behind her ear. The rest of her long, dark, curled hair cascades over the shoulder that isn't bare. The only jewelry she has on are the gold hoops in her ears. Her neck, arms and fingers are bare.

Clifford notices and almost regrets the roses, wishing he'd looked for a fine jeweler instead of a florist.

Rox's eyes grow large. "Is that a whole dozen?"

Clifford looks at the long-stemmed roses with the greenery and baby's breath tucked into a couple of layers of tulle with a long pink ribbon tying the bunch together. He wants to ask if he's the first man that ever gave her roses, but knows the answer might make him want to hunt down every man who'd ever let Rox down, beginning with Redacted.

Instead, he smiles warmly as he hands them to her. "I picked pink because I thought you looked prettiest in pink, but now..." Clifford takes a step back to look her up and down. "I don't believe there's a color you aren't the prettiest in."

Rox blushes. "Camel," she blurts out.

"Oh yeah?"

"Yep, washes me right out," she says with a grin as she steps back to allow Clifford into her apartment. He chuckles as he shuts her door.

She lays the bouquet on her coffee table before turning to wrap her arms around his shoulders.

"Hi," she whispers.

Clifford puts his hands on her hips. "Hi," he whispers back.

She leans in. "I've missed you- Um, what's crinkling in your jacket?"

"Oh!" Clifford leans back to reach the interior pocket. "The guy at the pet store said that these Churu packs are the best treats for cats. I thought Baskets would like 'em."

Rox takes a step back and puts her hand to her mouth as she looks over the pack he's handing her. She takes a long, steady breath and smiles.

"Let's find out. You feed him one while I put these in some water," she says, as she hands them back and reaches for the flowers.

Baskets had already made his way down the hall from Rox's bedroom at the first mention of his name. Rox moves around him as she walks into the kitchen and grabs the only vase she has, which was filled with old wine corks. She dumps them into the trashcan from the clear vase and rinses it before putting the flowers inside.

"It's time to admit you're never going to make that corkboard, Rox," she whispers to herself as she adds water.

Rox returns to the living room to see Baskets climbing all over Clifford on the couch to get to the treat.

"It looks like he's a fan," she says.

They reach Burton's early enough to sit at the bar for a drink before their table is ready.

Clifford orders a Woodford Reserve old-fashioned with a lemon twist after Rox orders the same, minus the citrus.

They make small talk as they people-watch. Clifford pushes aside his unease over keeping something from Rox, but he's determined not to talk about the case tonight. For just a few hours, he wants the world to stop spinning so he can enjoy something amazing.

Rox can see something is weighing on him even as she catches him gazing at her.

She feels herself blushing again. "It really sucks that Fulk couldn't get that warrant. I know it must be frustrating."

Clifford nods and says, "It is. But I'd really like to concentrate on you tonight."

She smirks, "You say such swoon-worthy things. It's really irritating to know you're leaving when this is over."

Clifford wants to toss out the idea of her leaving with him, but knows they're not ready for that conversation.

Before they can get into a debate over ordering a second drink, they're notified their table is ready.

After ordering, Clifford looks across the table at her and smiles. He inhales a deep breath and lets the air slowly leave his lungs as he appreciates the beauty before him.

"Rox?"

She smiles as she looks over. "Hmm?"

"I am *so* thankful I walked into Wild Willie's that day."

Rox almost does a spit-take while she sips her water.

"I don't think anyone's ever said that before."

Clifford chuckles. "Lemme try this again. Um, Rox?"

Her face is bright with amusement. "Hmm?" she repeats.

"I think we have something special here," he says, taking her hand.

Rox's eyes widen, and her cheeks flush with color.

Clifford notices. "I'm getting mushy. I'm sorry."

"No-no-no," Rox instantly says. "It's just... No man has ever treated me like you do. You treat people right, Dee. It's pretty amazing, actually."

Clifford smiles. It's his turn to blush.

"It's just a little overwhelming, but in a good way. When you're used to the bare minimum, you drop all expectations. You're not being mushy. Not one bit. Whatever time I get with you, I'm going to cherish."

Clifford nods. "Here's to more time."

He raises his glass, and she meets it with hers.

# Chapter Twenty-One

**Sometime around midnight**, as Rox sleeps soundly, Clifford kisses her gently and slips out of the bed. He sends Bailey a text asking for a map of the area.

Bailey texts back almost immediately.

*Way ahead of u*

Clifford gets a file from him with several pictures, property lines, and overhead footage of the property.

Clifford smiles and slides into the bathroom.

Two hours later, Clifford, parked on the side of the road just outside the gun club property, is along a dense wood line. He loads up the gear in a small pack, straps the guns onto his back, and heads into the woods.

Bailey has been operating a drone and surveying the area for over an hour.

He closes in on the property, and it's surrounded by a chain-link fence.

Bailey was a voice through the radio in Clifford's ear. "Hey buddy. I got eyes on you. Shutting the power to the fence off now."

Clifford clicks his radio and says, "Going silent."

It takes only a few seconds before Bailey has all the alarms connected to the fencing shut off.

Clifford snips the chain-link fence and enters the property. He scales down a small hill at the back of the firing range and dashes out of that area, to cover.

He finds a spot closer to the gun-lodge that's shrouded by a thicket of trees and shrubs.

He spies the giant metal shipping container in the back that was seen on the footage Bailey sent, and perches on a small tree stump in the area to scope through binoculars.

He spies a man opening the door and flipping on a light inside. The light cast a slight shadow outside the metal door of several people moving inside. He could hear the muffled screams to stay away.

Bailey radios in, "Dee, I got it. She's in there. She's not alone either."

Clifford hears the man say, "Shut up! In a few hours, you'll be His Majesty's problem!"

He leaves with a bucket and dumps it in a small water-drainage creek about twenty yards away.

The man belts out a quick, "Woo, that's gross." Confirming to Clifford that he was emptying a waste bucket.

He takes the bucket back toward the shipping container and heads back inside.

Bailey says, "Dee, go. We have the proof. Let's go to Fulk."

Clifford heads back into the woods and circles the property. He turns his radio back on.

"We need to get them now. No time."

Bailey replies, "I don't think we should, Dee. They'll have enough for a warrant, and can be here in the morning."

Clifford continues to make his way around to the front.

"The guy said they were shipping them out in hours. So, you can help me rescue these kids, or we can go to Fulk. We can't do both. They'll be shipped out before Fulk has that warrant in his hand."

Bailey sighs, knowing Clifford's right. "Be careful. Try not to kill anyone, okay? We're the trespassers."

Clifford radios back, "I'll try not to kill anyone, but I'll need you to create a distraction."

Clifford climbs a tree and secures the rifle between a branch and its trunk. He loops the nylon cord around the gun and around the trigger.

He takes the cord and tosses it over a higher branch, pulling it down to his canteen cup, which was resting on a lower branch. He smiles at the fortuitous gift as he uses the elastic boot-blouser cord to tie the cord to the canteen cup.

Clifford takes the canteen and punctures a small hole in it with the leather punch tool on his utility knife. He shoves a piece of the nylon cord into the hole, plugging it.

He runs the cord down to the canteen cup, which causes the water from the canteen to slide slowly down the cord and drip into the cup.

He ties another piece of cord to the canteen cup and tosses an enormous length of the parachute cord to the ground, and jumps out of the tree. Thirty yards to the left, he props the shotgun up onto a rock. He loops the cord tightly around a tree and uses the other boot-blouser to hook around the trigger of the shotgun, tying it to the cord.

He tests it to be sure it's taught.

Clifford heads back to the tree to check how much water has dripped into the canteen cup so far, empties the cup, and notes the time.

Quickly, he disappears into the shadows of the wood-line and hurries away to the rear of the building toward the storage container.

Clifford finds a place about twenty yards away where he can see the building and the container. He sits ready.

Bailey radios in, "That was an interesting set-up you did out there."

Clifford smiles.

After a few more minutes, the canteen drips enough water into the cup to weigh it down just enough to slide it off the branch.

The cord pulls the trigger of the rifle first, sending a round toward the gun club entrance. The elastic boot-blouser causes the cup to bounce, releasing the trigger of the rifle and tightening around the trigger again, which fires a second shot.

The cup continues to the ground, which triggers the shotgun via the second string. This sends birdshot sprinkling across the front of the building.

Clifford sees flood lights come on, and the property illuminates. He watches as several men fire into the woods in front of the building.

After sprinting to the container, he pulls a crowbar from his pack and pops the padlock.

The metallic door lets out a loud creak as he tugs it open.

Inside were two young boys and four girls, including Hadley.

They're screaming and crying, chained to the back wall with their legs affixed to a shackle. The inside of the container had spray soundproofing-foam.

"I'm here to help. Stay quiet."

Pressing his back against the wall of the container, he pulls the door shut as he hears two men rushing toward him in a panic.

"Get the little shits and meet me at the Jeep," one of them says as they approach.

Clifford hears one man sprint by while the other slowly walks up to the door.

"What the fuck?" He says as he spots the door partially open.

Clifford waits for the man to get closer, then kicks open the door, smashing the man in the face.

Stumbling backward, the man raises his semi-automatic pistol to fire, but Clifford runs up on him and disarms him with a swoop of his left arm, and pulls him to the ground, wrapping his arm around the man's neck, he squeezes until he passes out.

Clifford zip-ties his arms and legs together and drags the body to a nearby bush, relieving him of the shackle keys.

He sprints back to the container to free the children.

***

Rox rolls to her side and reaches for Clifford only to find a cold, and empty bed. The only light coming through the windows is from the parking lot. She lurches up, trying to hear or smell anything from the kitchen, but discovers the disappointment of silence and a realization that Baskets just used his litter box. She rubs her eyes, and groans.

"Dee?!" she calls out as she swings her legs over the side of the bed.

Rox walks through her apartment and looks out the front window to see that the Bronco is no longer in its parking spot before sending Clifford a text.

Willing herself to think back on their conversations from the previous night, she searches her memory for a clue where he could be.

She stares at the pink roses. The longer she waits for a response, the bigger the pit in her stomach grows.

"Please don't be doing something stupid," she says, looking at her phone, hoping for a sign she'd made contact.

Rox spends the next few minutes pacing, wishing she knows how to contact Bailey. If anyone knows where Clifford is, he would. She finds the business card he gave her the night they met. If Bailey's the nerve center, Rox figures the odds of him answering have to be in her favor.

They aren't. She's asked to leave a detailed voice message. Instead, she hangs up and quickly gets dressed.

She chews on her lip as she scrolls through her phone and presses the call button.

"Hey, sorry to wake you, but I think Dee may be on his way to that gun lodge," she says as she grabs her keys and heads to her car.

***

Bailey radios to Clifford, "The back is clear. I am flying toward the front to see what's going on up there and will report back."

Clifford takes a little longer than he wants getting the kids from their chains. After the last is free, they head out of their prison.

"Look out!" Hadley yells.

Clifford spies an attack over his shoulder. He reaches up and twists the knife out of the attacker's hand from overhead. This exposed his front leg, which Clifford stops down on just above the knee, causing it to bend backwards, tearing ligaments.

He lets out a blood-curdling scream, which gains the attention of the men in the front.

The man lurches forward, forcing Clifford to stumble toward the ground with him. Clifford reaches for the crowbar, but his hand lands on the waste bucket. He pulls the bucket toward him and slams it over the man's head as he is screaming. Clifford stumbles to his feet and gets a firm grasp of the crowbar. He swings and hits the side of the bucket hard enough to knock the man out.

It was too late. The others hear the screams and begin circling back toward his position.

He tells the kids to run and hide in the woods.

"Over there!" He points. "Stay together!" He shouts as they run towards the cover of trees.

Hadley, the oldest, acting as the other children's guide, shushes them as they hide.

Bailey flies the drone back toward Clifford. He flies across the faces of an angry mob as a distraction while he radios in, "Dee, there are six more guys coming your way. Get the kids out of there."

Clifford shouts to them as they run toward the trees, "Stay there, I'll come back for you."

Two men fire their pistols at Clifford, and he takes cover behind the container.

He unmutes his radio and calls Bailey. "Hey B, I need eyes on the targets."

Bailey responds, "There are six, in pairs. Two behind the dumpster toward the side. Two are by the woodshed, and I am not sure where the other two are. They could be trying to flank you. I'll find out."

With that, Bailey flies the drone off to check the surroundings.

Clifford pops around with the semi-automatic he confiscated from the first man. He fires three rounds towards the woodshed, where two of the men left their safe cover in their approach.

The first two shots strike the ground just in front of one man's feet, and the third hits the second man's boot, sending both men scrambling for cover.

Clifford crouch-runs toward the woods, staying under cover of the brush and surrounding debris in the yard. He meets back with the children.

"Now what?" Hadley asks, soothing one of the little boys.

"Through the trees is a fence. Try to find the hole in it and run. I'll keep them away."

Clifford sprints toward the back of the lodge and slows as he takes cover, spotting another stealthy man rounding the building near him.

Engulfed in shadow, Clifford eyes him like a hawk.

The man signals to someone inside the wood-line, which compromises the plan for the kids to find the hole in the fence.

Without a sound, Clifford breezes behind the man like a shadow, and grapples the man, choking him unconscious, while pulling him from visibility. Crouching down, he watches for movement in the woods.

He spots a branch moving.

Relieving a M16A4 rifle from the man he just rendered unconscious, he switches the lever to 3-round-burst, and aims toward the movement in the brush. He fires several bursts of rounds while on the move, causing the men approaching the children to flee in the opposite direction.

Buckshot scatters across the trees toward the back of the lodge, narrowly missing Clifford. He drops to the ground and crawls to a larger tree stump for cover.

Another man coming up the side near the building with a hand-gun spots his movement. He fires at Clifford and misses. Clifford rolls over and fires the rifle, but it was empty.

The man smiles at his fortune, but Clifford drives his boot into his shin, sending him to the ground just before using the butt of the rifle to knock him out.

Clifford hears a shotgun ring out twice, but not at him. A moment later, Bailey radios in, "Dee, I'm hit. Going down."

Clifford pulls his earpiece out and shoves it into his front pocket. Hearing the clacking of the shotgun shells being inserted into the gun, Clifford takes this moment of opportunity, jumps to his feet, and sprints toward the corner of the building, where he crouches and waits with his back firmly against the structure.

Clifford spies the shadow of the shotgun-wielding man peak around the corner. He slowly rises to his feet and pops around with the rifle and pulls the trigger to be met with a loud click.

It's jammed.

He looks at Clifford and smiles a black-toothed grin.

Clifford lurches towards him just as the man squeezes off a round. The gun's barrel shifts, causing it to miss its mark.

The shooter, knocked off-balance, loses his grip and drops the gun. As he gets his feet under him, Clifford throws a punch across his chin, sending the man in the opposite direction.

The man stumbles backwards, but again, regains his composure quickly.

He squares up, and Clifford tightens his fists. The man throws a punch, but Clifford grabs it, rolls around him and kicks the back of his leg, sending the man to his knees.

In the same motion, Clifford gets a good chokehold of the man with the crook of his elbow and leans back, adding pressure and leverage with his foot on the back of the man's knee so he cannot straighten or stand. The pressure of the chokehold causes the man to black out and fall to the ground.

In the distance, Clifford can hear sirens. He knows they're coming for him.

He goes back toward the children in the woods.

He sprints toward the back wood-line and hears shots ring out.

As he finds cover in the darkness of the trees, he spins around to see several more men taking cover as they're still following him.

Suddenly, a squawk comes across the radio in the distance.

A man's voice shouts, "Cops are almost here. Move out!"

They all jump to their feet and retreat.

Clifford doesn't stop to watch them run to an old shack near the woodshed. Moments later, as he reaches the children, he turns to see a Jeep crash through the swinging doors of the shack and drive around the front of the building. A few more men jump into the back.

The Jeep speeds off and hits a dirt trail and drives away from the sound of the police cars driving up the main entrance of the gun lodge.

Clifford pants, "You did great, Hadley. Nice job keeping everybody calm."

Hadley places herself between Clifford and the other children. "How do you know my name?"

Her expression is fearless even as her voice shakes.

Clifford raises his hands. "You can call me Dee. I'm a friend of your mom."

"Then, what's the goddamn password?!"

"Whoa, language, *Smarty Jones.*"

Her entire body relaxes, and her smile beams just before the tears take over. Clifford reaches out to steady her.

Hadley wipes her face with the back of her hand.

"Which way, Dee?" she asks as she picks the scared little boy up, resting him on her hip.

Clifford smiles proudly at her. He signals to the kids. "Okay, guys, stay with me."

Hadley encourages them along. "Come on, guys. We're going home. Stay together."

He leads as they follow closely behind, rounding the side of the lodge.

A swarm of police awaits them.

One officer spots them.

"Freeze!" he yells, drawing his weapon.

Fulk swipes at the officer's gun. "Don't shoot! That's Dee!"

# Chapter Twenty-Two

**In his office,** a furious Fulk reprimands Clifford.

"What the fuck were you thinking?"

Clifford says, "They were moving the kids this morning!"

Fulk shakes his head. "It was dangerous, not to mention outside the confines of the law. Judge Warrenton is *not* going to be happy when he gets in this morning."

"You know my job was to get the girl back, and that's what I did."

Fulk glares at Clifford. "It's my job too, Dee! You could've at least kept me in the loop."

Clifford looks away. "I just wanted to look around when I saw the container and heard a girl screaming. Then I heard them say they were moving the kids this morning."

Fulk nods sincerely. "I get it, Dee. I get it."

"So, what's going to happen?" Clifford asks.

Fulk drops into his chair and forces a huge breath of air out of his lungs.

"Well, the Captain's been briefed. She's on her way in. Same with Judge Warrenton. They'll talk and probably want my input, seeing as I'm lead on the case. So it's hard to say, Dee. You attacked eight people."

"In self-defense. And, I didn't kill anyone," Clifford adds.

"It's not self-defense if you were trespassing in the first place! But... there are a lot of other factors to consider here."

"Including trafficked children?" Clifford asks.

Fulk sighs, "Yes, that'll be factored in."

Captain Jennifer Gates leans against the doorframe of Fulk's office. "Mr. Dee, my office."

Clifford stands and follows her out.

Her graying hair is up in a messy bun, and she has a button-down shirt tucked into a pair of blue jeans.

She rounds her desk and plops into her chair.

"Sit," she says, gesturing to the seat at the front corner of her desk.

Clifford slides into the chair, letting out a quick breath.

"I'm actually more upset at being called in before six in the morning than anything. This is going to be a long day."

Clifford speaks but gets put in his place with a look.

"Before you say anything, you *will* get your chance to give an official statement," she states firmly before continuing.

"We don't go rogue here. As much as you were right in saving those kids; as much as you feel justified going in there and getting them, the way you went about it is what's going to be the problem here."

Clifford nods. "Yes, Ma'am."

"We are a nation of... laws, Mr. Dee. They're in place to keep us safe. From the good guys, too! You cannot trespass on private property. You cannot take the law into your own hands. You cannot use illegal surveillance by any means. Not only could I have your licence pulled, I could throw you in jail for a very long time. Do you know that?"

Clifford nods. "Yes, ma'am. I understand."

Captain Gates sighs and eases up. "I have to talk to the judge about the legality of all this. We don't want to charge you if we don't have to. I appreciate you saving the children. I really do. But you broke laws. Their lawyers will argue for protection of private property."

Clifford nods again and says, "I understand."

Fulk taps on the door and says, "Capt'n, the Judge is here."

Captain Gates says, "Go wait in Fulk's office," as she pushes away from her desk. She walks out of her office and points at a cop near the front desk. "Make sure he stays in Fulk's office," she says, nodding toward Clifford.

A little less than half-hour passes, and an officer taps on Fulk's office door. "Dee, Captain's office." He lets out a huge huff of air as he stands.

In the office, Fulk sits in a chair near the desk. Judge Warrenton and Captain Gates are huddling near a phone on speaker.

Clifford asks, "What's going on?"

On the speaker was a familiar voice, "Clifford Dee! Should I be surprised you got yourself in trouble?"

"Sims?"

FBI Special Agent Tal Sims worked with Clifford's team on a case in Northern Virginia when the assassination of a sitting US Senator led to a corrupt US Government official and weapons trafficking ring.

"Yeah, it's me. I just briefed them; you were under my direction. It's okay to tell them you were working for me."

Clifford looks over at Fulk, who nods, understanding what's going on.

Sims says, "They gave me a list with several charges here; illegal surveillance with a UAS, illegal search and seizure, reckless endangerment of minors, illegal operations of firearms, and more. Oh, and I was told that you modified a rifle and shotgun to self-fire. What's that about?"

Clifford responds, "Drip rifle. A tactic created by a desperate soldier in World War One to create ground cover so all the allied troops could escape. It was taught as part of my advanced combat training when I joined the special forces. I'll show you later," he adds.

"Jesus Dee," Sims says in disbelief.

Clifford exhales hard. "Okay, let's rip the band-aid off. What's going to happen now? I needed to act before they moved the children."

Judge Warrenton speaks up. "Special Agent Sims, if I may?"

Sims says, "Of course, your honor. Please."

"Mr. Dee, I would like you to give us your official statement of what happened this morning. Leave no detail out. It's important."

Clifford spends the next several minutes laying out his entire plan for surveilling the property. He explains it was just to gather evidence at first. He also explains the plan only changed when he learned they were moving the children before he could have the authorities notified.

After hearing his statement, the judge speaks up.

"Clifford, never in your statement did you say you were working in conjunction with the FBI. So, now I'm going to ask you directly; were you working under the direction of Special Agent Sims?"

"A simple yes is all you need to say, Dee," Sims voice cracks over the speakerphone.

Clifford looks around the room. It occurs to him that his friend is willing to take a professional hit for him. "Before I answer, may I have the room to speak privately with Sims?" he requests sternly.

The judge looks over to the captain, and the captain nods in acknowledgment. Fulk opens the door and allows them to walk out first. Fulk looks back before shutting the door behind him. "So you know, Rox called me. She's in the waiting area. She's not happy."

Clifford nods, looks down, and waits for the door to close.

He picks up the phone receiver and asks, "What's the deal, Tal?"

"My friend, you stumbled on a case file we've been having a hard time gathering intel on," Sims admits.

"No shit. So, saying I've been working with you on a consultant-basis, does what, exactly?"

"We need to take down this cell. If I loop you in on 'Operation Ghost Hunt' now and you help bring the entire organization down, I may get a slap on the wrist," Sims pauses and sighs. "But you'll get prison time if I don't."

"So, I act as though I've been here for that purpose all along?" Clifford whispers into the phone.

"No, not all along. You were working for your client to find her daughter. That's all still true. Through my communications with Bailey, I made the connection between your case and the cell's ranch compound," Sims states.

"The gun club," Clifford surmises.

Sims continues. "Yep. They either killed or recruited the owner and slipped in there sometime within the last week to hold the kids. We're learning more about it thanks to your actions tonight. Other than that, all we know is that the leader goes by Skyler Mose. He's a ghost. We don't know what he looks like or even the gender, honestly. We're positive the name's fake. An informant was embedded with the cell, but we do not know if he made the move to Colorado."

"When was the last time you heard from the informant?" Dee asks.

"According to the file? Longer than anyone's comfortable with. Contact is very limited, however.

"This group is professional; most definitely military trained, and very off-the-grid. There's a good chance the informant can't safely break away."

"Fuck," Clifford mutters.

"You'll have full resources and the full support of the FBI. What do you say? Should I notify the Denver bureau? I have a few things to tie up here in D.C. But afterwards, I'll meet you in Denver."

"I was so close to being done with this," Clifford moans.

Sims sighs again. "Dee, they'll hit you with everything I listed, and it will stick. You already know prison's on the line. You'll lose your business; the team will be disbanded... and most likely monitored."

"Fine. But I want full utilization of my team."

Sims says, "Consider it done. I'll contact Bailey right now and fill him in on everything."

Clifford hangs up the phone, opens the door and waves everyone back in to finish the conference.

After his statement, and pledging cooperation with the FBI, he's free to leave. Clifford walks up to Rox, who's sitting on a bench just inside the police station doors. She stares at the ground while her bouncing leg reveals her anxiety. The dark circles under her eyes tell a tale of sleep deprivation.

Clifford doesn't have any regrets about how he handled the extraction of the children, but he knows he mishandled Rox. His remorse sucker punches him in the gut when she lifts her gaze to meet his eyes.

Once again, he's stopped in his tracks by her. Clifford watches as the expressions dance across Rox's face from worry to relief, and then finally to anger.

"I'm sorry," he says, standing yards away.

She stands, folding her arms as she narrows her eyes. "What exactly are you sorry about, Dee? Hmm? I wanna hear where *you* think you fucked up?"

Clifford's throat goes dry. He'd rather be interrogated by terrorists than be on her bad side.

"I'm sorry... that I put you in an impossible situation. I should've communicated better, so... you didn't worry."

Rox raises her eyebrows. She's used to men running away from accountability. Clifford is definitely a breath of fresh air, even if he isn't completely correct.

She smirks. "Well, it's a good start," she says as she pulls her keys from her pocket and turns toward the door. Clifford follows behind her.

He gets into the passenger seat of Rox's car, and they sit as the car struggles to heat; both of them missing the luxury of the Broncos heated seats.

"Was the whole point of last night a *'goodbye'* in case you didn't make it out alive?" Rox asks, breaking the silence. "Cause see, I thought you took me out on a date to put the case behind us so we could... see if there's something real here that's worth exploring. But then, after you left... and the more Agent Fulk talked about what you were probably doing..."

She lets her voice trail off as she continues to stare through the windshield. Clifford blows his hot breath into his clasped hands while he listens.

A car horn startles both of them. Clifford turns to glare when he feels the car shift.

"The police station's popular first thing in the morning," Rox mutters as she puts the car in reverse and backs out.

"I'm so sorry, Rox. I never even thought..."

Rox looks in her rearview mirror and narrows her eyes.

"What?" Clifford asks.

She shakes her head as she focuses on pulling out of the lot before turning onto the main road. "I felt helpless, Dee. The thought of never seeing you again knocked me right on my ass."

Silence fills the space. Clifford knows that now isn't the time to fill her in on his new, and very dangerous assignment. "For the record, I *know* there's something real between us," he says confidently.

"My life, though... it'd be selfish to ask you to explore this, but it's what I want more than anything I've ever wanted before."

Rox, realizing she cannot stay mad at him, reaches for his hand as they stop at a four-way intersection. "Clifford Dee? This is crazy, but are we... falling in love?"

The light turns green. Rox's gaze lingers on Clifford's face. His eyes twinkle as his own realization creates a boyish lopsided smile.

The car behind them honks. Rox squeezes his hand before turning her attention back to driving. Pressing down on the gas pedal, she glances in the rearview mirror as she slowly rolls through the intersection.

Before Clifford can muster the courage to answer her, a large truck with a massive grill guard speeds through the intersection on their left.

There's no time to yell out a warning or even brace for impact. Rox's car launches to the far side of the road, rolling twice before landing on its roof. The sounds of metal twisting and glass shattering dissipate as the vehicle slides in the snowy grass well beyond the asphalt.

# Chapter Twenty-Three

**Bailey** puts his phone in his lap after ending the call with Special Agent Sims. He rolls toward his keyboard and starts looking at his monitors. Clifford's heart rate spiking catches his attention. He reaches for his phone to check the GPS location of Clifford's phone.

He sees that Clifford's only a couple of miles away from the police station. Bailey looks through the scanner app for the zip code and hears an emergency call for a vehicle accident at the same location.

"Shit!" Bailey switches to his contacts.

"Agent Fulk," he answers.

"Fulk, it's Bailey. There's a ten fifty-two right down the road from you. It's Dee!"

"Bailey? How the hell do you know this?" Fulk asks as he stands and grabs his coat. In the background, sirens wail.

"Man, I'll explain while you go to him. I monitor his vitals through his watch while he's on mission. His heart rate spiked, so I checked his phone, GPS location an-"

Bailey abruptly stops talking when he loses the signal to his watch.

"Shit!"

Fulk asks, "What?"

"I lost his vitals. Get there *now!*"

A quick drive later, Fulk meets the paramedics at the crash site. He rushes up to one of the EMTs and asks, "How are they?"

"They? Only one patient was recovered. She's in the back," he replies as he smacks the side of the ambulance.

"Her name's Rox. Is she okay?"

"Unconscious, but vitals seem stable. We'll know more when she gets to the hospital."

As Fulk watches the ambulance drive away, he makes his way over to the wreckage.

The driver's side is totally wrecked. The windows are all broken, and the windshield is covered in spiderweb cracks. Someone had forced the passenger door open.

Fulk peeks inside the car and looks around for a moment. He notices a small, dried, oddly shaped piece of dirt next to the car. He straightens his posture and looks around at the people at the scene.

A man in a strange, non-badged uniform that Fulk doesn't recognize catches his attention.

Aware that he's caught Fulk's interest, the man turns and walks towards a patrol car. Fulk follows.

The man looks back and sees Fulk walking in his direction, and picks up his pace.

Fulk notices that as well. The man climbs into the driver's seat of the patrol car. Slamming the door shut, he starts the car.

"Hey!" Fulk yells.

Another officer closer to the man looks over, and Fulk commands, "Stop that officer!"

The officer jumps into action, but the imposter pulls away in haste as they get closer to the patrol car. Fulk looks for the identification number on the car, but it's painted over. "Shit!" he yells.

The officer looks over at Fulk with a confused look.

Fulk asks, "Did you know that officer?"

The officer shrugs and shakes his head.

Fulk rolls his eyes, then feels his phone vibrate.

He pulls his phone out and answers it.

"Fulk."

"Hey, it's Bailey. What do we know?"

Fulk scoffs, "We?"

"That's my partner out there. So, yes, *we!*"

"Dee and the driver of the other car are both gone. Rox is being transported to the hospital. She's unconscious right now."

"Gone? What do you mean Dee's gone?" Bailey asks.

"Gone! As in not here. Vanished. Vamoose. Gone!"

"So you don't know what happened to Dee?"

Fulk sighs, "I don't. It looks like he was pulled from the wreckage. Rox's car was rammed on the driver's side by a truck equipped with a deer killer on the front. The impact flipped her car a few times. She was in the driver's seat, but the passenger door was pried open. Drag marks in the snow, come back to the road near the collision. The truck was used as a battering ram."

Bailey says, "I gotta make some calls."

After the call ends, Fulk shoves his phone into his pocket. Something catches his eye on the opposite side of the road. He steps over and finds Clifford's shattered smartwatch.

# Chapter Twenty-Four

**Clifford Dee** regains consciousness to find he is in extreme pain. He attempts to sit up from the bed he's in, but quickly realizes he's cuffed to it. Pulling them tight, the cold shackles on his wrists clank against the metal rail of the bed as they tighten. He lets out a tremendous groan as he feels bruises on his back and legs.

Fragments of the accident enter his mind. *Rox?*

He slowly opens his burning eyes as they connect with the sunlight emanating from a small window on the other side of the room. It is the only light source he can see. He blinks rapidly as the burning fades.

"Hello?" he calls out, not expecting an answer.

Slowly, he pans the room, taking in his environment. It isn't a hospital room. It has the feel of an old Army infirmary. His bed has a sheet, half drawn, partially separating it from the rest of the room. He can see two other beds across from him and a shelf with supplies in the corner.

He takes a few calming breaths and slowly exhales.

He pushes his feet down against the bed and tests his leg muscles. He can feel slight pain, but can tell that nothing's broken.

Clifford rotates his shoulders and feels the pain in his upper back and neck. He is sore from the accident, but it doesn't feel like he has any major injuries.

He notices his watch is gone. He is pretty sure that they either took his phone or it smashed in the wreck.

A few minutes go by, and he hears a door open. The light changes, and the next sound is footsteps approaching.

He goes limp and shuts his eyes, feigning sleep. The sound of the footsteps tells Clifford more than one person is approaching.

"Looks like he is still out."

"Boss'll be here tomorrow morning. Leave him be for now."

Clifford listens as they leave.

He quietly tests the cuffs again, but they are sound.

He focuses on the light. He can time the frequency of their checks by the position of the light on the floor; a mechanism he learned out of necessity when he was a POW.

Clifford can feel the drowsiness creeping in again. His eyes grow heavy. After a few long blinks, he passes out.

——

**US Army outpost, south of Kandahar, Afghanistan, 2005:**
"Hey Sergeant Dee, have you heard?"

Staff Sergeant Clifford Dee looked up from his radio. "Heard what?"

"They're activating Cold Steel. We're moving out to Darwisan tomorrow," Specialist Kyle Somers said.

"Darwisan? Why?" Dee asked.

Somers said, "Dunno, it's about the fucking Ali-Babas. They're taking refuge in a mosque, and we're gonna raid it. SFC Barr mentioned it in formation just now. Where were you?"

SSG Dee looked up and said, "I needed to get this radio fixed. I thought that was more important than formation. They say the same damn shit every day, anyway."

Somers asked, "Still avoiding Barr?"

Dee scoffed, "I'm not avoiding him. Why? Does it seem like I'm avoiding him?"

Somers laughed, "Yeah, you're totally avoiding him. Oh yeah, and that's not all. I passed the board. I'm getting E-5. They're gonna pin it on at Darwisan after the raid."

"No shit! Congrats Sergeant!" Dee says, proud of his soldier. "So what about the Haji you were saying?" He asked.

"Yeah, they drove them out of Kabul. Need us to pack up and relocate before driving them out of that mosque."

"What about the rest of Charlie Company?"

"Charlie's stayin' here, and we're movin' out to re-org under Delta," Somers said.

Dee shook his head. "Shit. I really like Captain Hamilton. Who's going to be our new C.O.?"

"Looks like we're going to be under Captain Ranch."

Dee smiled. "Ranch is cool. Good guy."

"Yeah, but..."

"But?"

"They're moving Burr under him, since he just got his E-7. He will be our new NCOIC."

Dee set the handset of the radio down and gave Somers his full attention.

"That little shit's going to be our NCO?"

Somers nodded. "Yeah. I knew you'd love that news."

"Fuck. That shit-for-brains? He's going to get more people killed out here."

Somers laughed. "Yeah, probably. He's a hater. Our unit makes him look bad. Especially you."

"He doesn't need any of my help looking bad. When do we move out?" Dee asked.

"Tomorrow morning, zero four hundred."

Dee shook his head. "Early morning drive. Gotta love it."

"Well, you'll love this more. There's a haboob warning. We've gotta take the main drag monitored by the Taliban."

"What?" Dee asked with concern.

"They said there's no way we can drive through the beach."

"Fuck me! Are you serious? Why move us during a sandstorm?"

"Yessir! They believe the Taliban will be hunkered down. Honestly, I think it's perfect. Well, I mean, no need to drive through the desert tomorrow. Because it's hot, sandy, and no ocean...just like you hate it."

"Don't quote Major Mackenzie. He'd like that too much."

"Well, I thought it was fitting seeing that it was his order."

The next morning was chilly. SSG Dee, the squad leader for the Cold Steel special missions unit, had his soldiers prepare several canteens of water each, and instructed them to load their gear in the troop carrier before 3am. Dee was issued a Humvee with a fifty-caliber weapon mounted on top. Two benches on the inside walls sat five troops each, and two in the cab made room for twelve troops and their gear.

Dee retrieved his vehicle from the motor-pool and pulled up toward the convoy near the gate. Newly promoted Sergeant First Class Burr walked up to Dee and said, "Hey, you're bringing up the rear. Back of the line."

"I thought I was running point today?"

Burr whipped around and gritted his teeth. "Dee, I don't need this shit. Back of the line!"

"Okay, sure." Dee replied.

SFC Burr narrowed his eyes. "Okay sure? Is that how you address your NCO?"

SSG Dee inhaled deeply. "I'm Sorry Sergeant. Moving the vehicle now, Sergeant."

"Thank you, *soldier*." Burr said disdainfully as he walked away.

Dee smiled through his contempt as he faced his troops while they load up their gear. He tapped his assistant squad leader, Sergeant Young, and said, "Why don't you take TC?" She smiled and asked, "You want me to be the Transport Commander?"

Dee smiled and nodded. "You gotta get those leadership hours somehow if you want to get your E-6. This should get you through the rest of them. I'll submit your promotion packet tomorrow."

She smiled. "Sergeant Dee, you're the best."

Somers ran up toward Dee and asked, "Can I run TC and navigate?"

Dee shook his head. "Nope. Already gave that to Young."

She winked at Somers and said, "It's my turn for once."

Dee also knew she had a thing for Williams, who volunteered to drive. Besides, he never minded taking a back seat to further his troops' advancement. Letting his team have leadership experience was why they were the best. He was under the school of thought that a unit is only strong as its weakest member, and he wanted all his troops expertly experienced.

Somers grunted and said, "Fine."

He stepped over toward the back, jumped in, and shouted, "But I got top first!" as he climbed up to take control of the fifty-caliber gun on top of the Humvee.

Dee turned to two of his other soldiers and said, "Tank, Jonesy, go grab the others from the smoke pit. We roll in five."

Just after an hour of slowly driving in the back of the convoy, Corporal Smith tapped Somers on the leg and says, "Shift change."

Somers was reluctant at first, but Smith said, "Dude, c'mon," to hurry him along.

Somers said, "Yeah, okay."

Smith took the gun as Somers climbed down into the back. He took Smith's seat to rest. He tapped Dee on the shoulder and gave him a thumbs up. Dee nodded.

Somers turned away from the front and becomes reacquainted with the back of the vehicle. Next to him was Ershadul, their civilian linguist and trusted guide.

"Hey Dee!" Smith yelled from the gun to get his attention.

Dee leaned back to get a better visual of Smith and asked, "What's up, Smitty?"

"I can't see the caravan anymore."

Dee started looking around, trying to get a view out of the back of the Humvee. He finally looked back at Somers and said, "Did you see the caravan up there?"

Somers said, "Yeah, it was just there a minute ago."

Dee leaned toward the front to look at Williams. "Will, are we lost?"

"I don't know. We're off the road. It was covered in sand, so I followed the tracks. We went over a dune and then nothing. I don't see any tra-."

From the gun, Smith yelled, "HABOOB!"

Young looked over toward her right. "SHIT! On your right!"

Dee leaned back into the cabin and yelled, "Keep going in the same direction! How long do we have?"

Smith said, "It's coming fast! My guess is five or ten minutes."

Young replied, "Sergeant Dee, we need to get back on the road! There's nowhere to shelter!"

She looked around and shouted to Williams, "Look ahead! Tracks! I bet the convoy saw the haboob and went into the desert."

"Okay, follow them!" Dee yelled.

Young looked over to Williams and said, "You heard him, turn left."

After a few minutes, Young spotted something in the sand. "There, look! It's a soda can. I think we're on the right track."

Williams scoffed and said, "Leave it to Americans to litter the desert."

They climbed another dune and could glimpse a small cloud of sand in the air. Tapping the roof of the Hummer, Smith said, "There! Ten O'clock." referring to the cloud.

Young looked over and asked, "Is that the caravan?"

Williams replied, "What else would it be?"

He steered toward the cloud of sand in the air and said, "They must have diverted to avoid the dunes. That's how they got so far ahead."

Dee said, "Okay, let's catch up."

Young yelled, "Smitty! To your left!"

Smith looked over and can see a different caravan approaching. "SHIT!" he yelled as he rotated the fifty-caliber weapon toward an enemy convoy.

An explosion rocked the vehicle as an RPG struck the sand just before it. The Humvee lost traction in the sand as it veered up onto two side wheels. They slammed back down on all four tires, and it caused a plume of sand to fill the cabin and back of the vehicle.

Williams floored it, and the wheels just spun in loose sand. Young looked over and saw them approaching quickly.

"Smitty! Fire!" Dee orders, but nothing happened. He could hear bullets collect across the side of their Humvee. He tugged on Smith's leg, but he collapsed into the back with a thud. They rolled him over to find a round struck him in the side of his neck, severing his spinal column.

More rounds littered the side of their vehicle.

"Let's GO!"

Williams said, "I can't; we're just spinning!"

"Shit!" Dee exclaimed.

Williams pushed his door open and climbed out. "Hand me a weapon!" Young grabbed her M16 rifle and handed it to Williams as she climbed out of the driver's side behind him.

She ran around back to open the Humvee to let everyone else out. As she pulled the hatch down, there was a loud explosion, which threw Dee from the vehicle.

The Humvee rolled onto its right side, wheels facing toward the enemy. With blurred vision, Dee could see Williams screaming, crushed by the upset vehicle.

He tried to shake the blur from his vision and the ringing from his ears as he heard his name being called through the tinnitus. "Dee! DEE!" Somers cried out.

Somers continued to yell, but the ringing was too loud to make out any coherent words.

Dee stood up and called over to Young. She returned fire, exposing herself to the enemy.

"Young! Get back!" She looked over toward Dee just as several bullets struck her side, knocking her to the ground. She scooted herself behind the smoldering Humvee wreckage next to Williams, and away from danger, leaving a trail of smeared blood in the sand.

Two shots hit the sand behind Dee, forcing him to dive behind a small dune of loose sand for cover. He returned fire, giving Young more time to get fully behind the wreckage.

Ershadul was on his knees pleading to the enemy in their native tongue as a man walked up and popped a round in the center of his forehead, then spit on him as he fell into the sand.

Dee spied an enemy combatant pop out of the back of a truck with a rocket launcher trained on his position. "Oh, shit!" escaped his lips as he abandoned his position and ran toward Young, behind the wreckage.

The rocket hit just behind Dee, and the explosion knocked him forward onto the ground, forcing sand into his face, nose, and mouth.

The ringing continued.

Dee looked up, shaking the sand from his face. With his eyes hurting and his vision compromised, Dee saw someone fire two bullets into Young, and she fell next to Williams, still pinned under the vehicle. Williams reached for her and cried out in sorrow, as losing her hurt worse than his crushed legs. A single shot rang out, silencing Williams. Dee could barely hear the sand moving under the boots of his attackers.

He realized that no one else had survived the vehicle explosion, which destroyed his hope of salvation. Although deafened from tinnitus, Dee could still hear the Humvee tires burst from the heat of the fire that's now engulfed the vehicle.

His vision cleared for a moment as he looked over, spotting an enemy with their weapon on Somers, walking away. Somers looked back at Dee and nodded as he continued walking from the wreckage.

A kick to his stomach rolled Dee over into the sand as he tried to scramble to his feet. He looked up and pleaded as he heard more gunshots ring out. "Please don't."

The stranger spat in his face and struck him in the head with the butt of a rifle, sending him into darkness.

***

Shrouded in a cloth sack, Dee awakened in pain. He grunted as he felt his heartbeat in his head, pounding violently. His hands were bound behind him, tied to a chair. He tried to shake the hood off, but not only was it secure, his injuries forced him to rethink shaking his head too much. He heard voices speaking in Arabic, but he could barely make out any of the words, especially words he might understand.

Ignoring the pain and determined to get the sack to slip off, he eventually moved it to a spot with a hole, and could get an idea of his surroundings. His eyes still felt irritated, and the hole was small.

He was in a cage inside what seemed like a bunker or hollowed out cave.

The walls were stone, and in the corner was a video camera.

He heard faint screams in the distance, and then silence, and could only imagine what torture he would endure when they found him awake. As he heard footsteps approaching, he slumped down, pretending to still be out.

Dee felt the cloth ripped off his head and a splash of liquid hit his face. He opened an eye to see his captors holding a bucket. It was then he realized it wasn't water. The foul, musky, ammonia-like smell led him to believe it was animal piss, most likely from a goat, that drenched him.

He puffed air through his lips to keep the liquid from entering his mouth, then juddered the piss from his hair and face. He glanced up and noticed one of them had a camera and was recording.

Dee reacted. "FUCK YOU PIGS! FUCK YOU!" he shouted at them. He continued shouting until one captor struck him on the side of the temple, sending even more reverberations through his skull that shook him to his soul. He slumped down into the chair again and passed out.

Day turned to night, and in between conscious states, he surmised a few days have passed.

Dee finally awoke, but in tremendous pain. His head was still throbbing, and he felt drugged. After a few minutes, he realized it was the longest he had remained awake since his capture.

"One, two, three, four, five, Clifford Dee is still alive." He kept repeating that phrase until he was fully conscious.

Just as he started to get used to the pain, he could hear footsteps approaching the cell.

"OVER HERE!"

Dee could hear someone yelling in English. Then he heard gunshots in the distance, and more voices.

They were American troops.

"One, two, three, four, five. Clifford Dee is still alive!" he said again in a more joyous tone.

"We're gonna get you out of here, soldier. Sit tight!"

Dee smiled through the pain as he was soon to be free.

—

Clifford startles himself awake, saying, "One, two, three, four, five! Clifford Dee is still alive!"

He was dreaming.

The thought and memory of his capture never really leave. It just hides until he becomes stressed. He looks around the room again, and the cuffs clank as he moves his hands, sounding like alarm bells, betraying his alertness.

He can hear voices, and one of them says, "I think he's awake now. Go get the boss."

"Fuck!" Clifford whispers to himself.

The outside looks much darker. He must have been out for almost a full day.

The door to the infirmary opens, and he hears footsteps approaching.

"Wakey-wakey!"

There was no use in feigning sleep now that they know he's been moving around.

Clifford turns his head to get a better look.

The man whips the curtain back and looks him in his face. "You don't look so tough without your guns."

He looks over as his partner approaches and says, "Boss is coming in a minute."

Clifford narrows his eyes as they land on a small bandage on his neck. He remembers them from the hotel when they attacked him.

He grabs Clifford's face, looks him dead in the eyes, and says, "He's been waiting patiently to talk to you." He roughly slips his hand from Clifford's face, causing him to jolt backward.

"Hey, how's the neck? Didn't need a gun then, either," Clifford growls.

"Fuck you," the man says with a smile.

Clifford asks, "It's Pete, right? Do you tell people a towel split your neck open?"

His smile fades, and he abashes silently. "Tim, Pete was the other guy."

A moment later, Clifford hears more footsteps. Again, he can hear whispering as they approach. The footsteps continue, coming up from beside his bed, and they circle around the curtain.

The other man Clifford recognizes from the hotel incident says, "Mr. Dee, meet our boss, Skyler Mose."

Clifford looks up and stares at the slightly recognizable face of a man with jet black hair and a full black beard showing sprinkles of grey.

The realization finally hits Clifford like a giant wrecking ball to his gut when Skyler slowly leans down and says, "It's been a really long time, Sergeant Dee."

Clifford, taken aback in disbelief, blurts out, "Kyle Somers?"

# Chapter Twenty-Five

**Rox** realizes she's in a beautiful dream that she doesn't want to leave. Kate, her dear friend, appears healthy and vibrant as they enjoy the warm afternoon sun at a cozy bistro.

She struggles to listen to Kate's sage advice as her blissful dream dissipates. The sounds from the busy hospital hallway come through the paper-thin walls. Realization of where she is, triggers memories of a CT scan tunnel and uncomfortable x-rays.

Rox takes a moment before fully opening her eyes. The meds in her system make her feel loopy, but do very little for the pain. She remembers overhearing her injuries being listed from one tech to another.

*"Mild concussion, a couple bruised ribs, whiplash..."*

She braces herself for the fluorescent lighting as she slowly opens one eye; she's confused by the level of darkness in her room.

The neck brace she's wearing restricts her movements as she becomes conscious of it. Her attention becomes more focused. Rox spots a young woman near the window out of the corner of her eye.

"I closed the blinds," the woman says, rising from her chair. "I figured you'd prefer it dark with that concussion."

Rox swallows, her dry throat reminding her how thirsty she'd gotten. "The lights?" she asks weakly.

"I dimmed them. Do you need me to make it brighter?"

Rox shakes her head and regrets it immediately.

The woman lays a reassuring hand on Rox's shoulder. "Ooh, try not to move too much. I'm Sara. Dee's friend. Do you feel any nausea?"

"I... don't think so. Just really thirsty."

Sara grabs the water bottle from the side table and holds the straw still, so Rox can take a sip.

"I'm all too familiar with concussions. It's a journey," Sara begins with a soft smile. "We're in a bit of a time crunch, Rox. Are you up for some questions?"

Rox studies Sara's face. "Where's Dee?" she asks.

Sara pulls the chair she was sitting in up to Rox's bed and sits again. "That's what we're trying to figure out. Do you remember the car accident?"

"Some asshole ran the red light."

"Mm-hmm. You were T-boned. What's the next thing you remember?"

Rox closes her eyes as she struggles to make the fuzzy details in her brain clearer.

"Well, we flipped... a boot." She opens her eyes again and focuses as best as she can on Sara.

"I remember a boot by Dee's door and the car rocking back and forth."

"The entire car rocked?" Sara asks.

"I thought we were being rescued, and they were using something to get Dee's door open. The rocking was from their... efforts, I guess."

Sara's eyes narrow as she remembers Bailey relaying the details of the accident from Agent Fulk.

"Can you tell me more about the boot?"

Rox shrugs. "Tan. It was caked in, like, a reddish-clay mud. I must've been in a weird position because I can't remember seeing Dee at all. I just felt the car rock, saw a boot, and then..."

Sara can see the irritation building in Rox as she struggles. She lays a hand on Rox's leg. "Hey, hey, hey. Let's try something else," she suggests as she waits for Rox to gain control, and calmly offers her more water to sip.

"What can you tell me leading up to when you were hit?"

Rox's eyes dart back and forth as she struggles. "Um, we were talking, and the car behind me... it..."

Sara leans forward. "What did the car behind you do? Can you describe it?"

Rox blinks rapidly. "I think... when we were leaving the police station...I wanted to talk so... we sat in the parking lot," she says as tears well in her eyes. "A black... Explorer? I think, honked like they wanted my spot. Their plates were different, like not from Colorado."

Sara's brow furrowed. "That sounds like something that happens in a mall parking garage during the holidays, not a police station."

"Mm-hmm. I thought it was weird, too, but... I was more focused on the conversation."

Sara wants to revisit Rox and Dee's conversation later, after she clarifies some timeline details. "So, what'd you do next?"

"I pulled out, and we turned left out of the parking lot. I stopped at the red light..." Rox pauses as tears spill over. "I didn't notice the light change... I was looking at Dee... I heard a honk behind me... and it's the same SUV."

"The same SUV? The one that looked like an Explorer in the parking lot?"

Rox chokes on a sob. "I'm sorry. Yes. I... I thought it was strange, but the light was green and the horn made sense this time."

Tears stream down her face. "I'm so sorry, but... I can't remember anything else!"

Sara stands up and gets a tissue. "You did great, Rox," she says.

"I wish I knew why I'm so fucking weepy right now," she says in frustration.

"Adrenal fatigue. It's common with all you've been through," Sara says matter-of-factly.

"So, we don't know where he is or who took him?" Rox asks between sniffles.

"Not yet," Sara says, helping to adjust her pillow. She looks at Rox and gives a smile of assurance. "But we will. I need to go talk to some people waiting on this info, but I'll be right back."

Sara squints as she walks out of the darkened room into the brightly lit hallway. Dan, the youngest member of the team, is leaning against the wall, trying to engage in small talk with Agent Fulk, who's sulking.

"Going in alone was a good idea," Sara says. "Rox has been through it, and she's worried."

Dan looks pleased with himself while Fulk grunts, annoyed that he didn't question Rox.

"Did she give you anything useful?" Dan asks.

Sara's hitting the call button on her phone. "Not sure yet," she mutters. "B!" she exclaims when Bailey answers on the first ring.

"Whatcha got for me, Baby Girl?" he asks over the speaker-phone.

"Have you tapped into any street cams between the town's police station and the intersection yet?" she asks.

Fulk pulls out his phone to see if the local PD has done the same.

"I'm working on it. What'd Rox tell you?"

Sara relays everything Rox told her to Bailey, Fulk, and Dan. "She could be confusing memories and dreams. You know what brain injuries can be like."

"The same SUV honked twice at her... In my experience, rushing someone is manipulative. This sounds like it was a coordinated attack."

Fulk and Dan nod their heads in unison.

"We're all in agreement on that one, B," she says.

"Okay, Baby Girl. I'll do some diggin' and update Sims."

"Chat later," Sara says, and hangs up.

Fulk sighs, "Well, I'm going to go back and see if we have any info on that SUV. Will you please keep the local PD and me apprised?"

"Of course!" Sara says with a big smile as Fulk passes her.

Agent Fulk leaves, and Daniel asks Sara, "What's the plan?"

Sara sighs as she slides down the wall and sits on the hard floor. "Bailey's trying to figure things out on his end. We just have to -"

She pauses for a second before continuing. "Detect. We're detectives."

Dan sighs. "When is Sims going to be here?"

Sara shakes her head. "A day, maybe two. I need coffee. I'm too jet-lagged to think."

Dan looks flustered. "I'm gonna go find a decent coffee place around here. You stay with Rox until we know what the plan is," he says, holding out his hand to help Sara up off the ground, as he continues. "Just give her a heads-up that she'll be meeting me when I get back."

Sara pops to her feet with his help and says, "That's a plan."

Before Sara goes back into the room, she runs to the gift shop a floor down.

Sara rejoins Rox again. "Dan's going to get us some coffee. Do you need anything? I can text him."

Rox attempts a smile. "Just Dee. Safe and sound."

Sara sees Rox is sitting more upright. "We're working on that, Beautiful. You're trying to rally. I respect that. Do you mind if I sit with you?"

"Not at all."

"I've been dying to meet you, actually," Sara says as she opens the bag with her gift shop purchases.

"Ditto. I hate that it's this way."

Sara pulls out a pair of dark, oversized sunglasses.

"For when the doctors forget about the dimmer switch on the wall. Because they will."

Rox chuckles and winces. "Thank you. I've never been around so many thoughtful people at one time."

Sara hands the glasses to Rox and sits in the chair again. Rox lays the glasses on the bed next to her.

"So you two got close, huh? You really care for Dee?"

Rox smiles, then replies with a question of her own. "Did you know he considers you his best friend?"

Sara chuckles. "The man's got good taste. So... do you?" She asks, circling back to her question.

Rox tries to take a deeper breath and winces. "The conversation... we were having when... Dammit!" she says, reaching for another tissue. "I swear I don't normally cry this easily."

"It's okay." Sara uses her other hand to pat Rox's leg.

Rox wipes her nose. "I was angry with him. He slipped out after I fell asleep and took it upon himself to rescue Hadley and the others. Right after the most amazing night. I accused him... I *thought* he gave me that perfect night to say goodbye to me. Like he knew he wasn't coming back."

Sara shakes her head. "Nah, you were right if you went off on him. Don't blame you for that."

"It's like, I *just* found him, ya know? I just want to be in his arms again."

Sara gives Rox's hand a light squeeze. "Do you need more to drink?" she asks.

"No, I'm okay. You know, the last thing I remember before," Rox hits her right fist into her left hand, showing the accident. She winces. "Oof, forgot about the ribs for a minute," she whispers.

"Take your time," Sara says gently.

"I asked him if we're falling in love, and the look on his face..." Rox's expression goes from joy to sorrow in the blink of an eye. She met Sara's gaze. "I love him. I'd never believe it could happen so fast if it wasn't happening to me, but... hell, even my cat loves him."

Sara can feel a smile tugging at the corners of her mouth. "Love at first sight isn't a myth," she says, thinking about Tracy.

"Yeah, but does loving Clifford Dee always hurt like this?" Rox asks, almost sarcastically, as she lifts her arms until she winces again.

Sara picks up on Rox's concern. She takes a moment to choose her next words carefully.

"To love him is to love everything that makes Dee... Dee. He's a protector, and he inspires others to protect. This job... this *life* can get dangerous. But it's his calling, at least for the time being. I've had the best and scariest adventures with him."

"I can tell he's loved," Rox says, reaching for Sara's hand.

"Who do we love?" Daniel asks as he enters the room with a cardboard tray of takeout cups.

"Rox, Dan. Dan, Rox," Sara says as she reaches for the coffee Dan's handing her. "Who's the third one for?"

"Well, I know coffee has too much caffeine. So, I asked a nurse, and she said that peppermint tea is okay," he says, handing the tea to Rox.

"I love peppermint tea, thank you. That was, once again, you guys, very thoughtful," Rox says, slightly exasperated.

Sara takes the silicone straw from the water bottle and helps Rox take a sip of the hotter beverage. "Dee's a heavy influence on thoughtfulness," Sara says. "Watch this." She raises her voice to direct her next question to Dan: "Was there a tip jar on the counter?"

"Yep, left a ten-spot," he says.

Rox chuckles and winces. "The tipping practice is company-wide, huh?" she says.

"Dee doesn't want anyone to feel unappreciated," Dan says with a smile as he gets adjusted in another chair closer to the door.

"So, tell me something awful about him," Rox requests. "There has to be a red flag I'm missing, right? Is his place disgusting? Does he do finger guns when he drinks? Follow models and porn stars on social media...?" She looks back and forth between Sara and Dan. "Maybe even DMs them? C'mon, give me something!"

Sara looks at Dan, and they both start laughing. "Dee's a bit more evolved and emotionally mature," she finally says.

"What kinda creep follows porn stars on the internet?" Dan asks. "As far as the finger guns... I've never seen him do them, but I don't know what he does in the privacy of his own home."

"Which," Sara interjects, "*is* clean, by the way. He has a weekly service..."

"Yeah, that he *tips* generously," Dan says, hiding his smile behind a sip of coffee.

Rox blows air through her lips and says, "Of course he does. Full-circle convo, guys. Love it."

"The only problem with Dee is his inclination to piss off dangerous people," Sara says with a shrug.

"You know, I've picked up on that," Rox says dryly. "Oh, did Bailey fill you in on the guys who tried to kill Dee at the hotel he was supposed to be meeting that Fred guy at?"

Sara stands up. "I forgot about that! Fucking jet-lag..." She walks out of the room, scrolling on her phone for Agent Fulk's number. Dan follows close behind.

"Fulk, it's Sara. Did you ever pull security footage from the hotel Dee was attacked in?"

# Chapter Twenty-Six

**Special Agent Sims** looks down at his ringing phone.

He answers, "Hey B, what's the news?"

Bailey relays to Sims what Sara told him.

Sims says, "Okay, that's a start. I'll swing by the hospital when I get there tomorrow, after I check-in with the field office to see if Rox can remember anything else."

While on the call, Bailey notices a flashing light on his computer console.

He says, "Hey Sims, I think I have an issue?"

"What do you mean?"

Bailey moves quickly. "I have unexpected company!"

He switches the computer to the feed from his security cameras to see someone quietly picking his front door lock and silently walking toward his command center.

"What do you need?" Sims asks.

"Backup!"

Bailey reaches under his desk and pulls out a double-barrel shotgun, placing the barrel on the left armrest so he can cover his back as he gets to safety.

Watching the camera, Bailey spies his uninvited company rounding the corner into the room. He brings his right arm across his abdomen to pull the trigger, sending buckshot across the back of the room.

The point man, hit, is pulled from the room by the man behind him.

Bailey smacks a button on the top of his desk, and a 9mm Ruger handgun springs up. He grabs it with one hand as he spins himself around with the other. He fires two rounds at the door and smacks another button, which activates a metal lock across the door.

His computer systems go into a contingency mode, and everything except his security cameras and their respective monitors lock down. All his tools and network systems go offline.

***

Bailey's cousin, JJ, who became the head of the Kentucky Mafia circuit after Clifford Dee dethroned E. I. Bandoni, is in a meeting with some local associates. She looks down at the vibrating alert on her phone.

*"JB Systems Offline."*

One of her men notices and asks, "Ma'am, what is it?"

She glares at her phone for a moment and says, "Excuse me for a second," before deciding to send a text.

***

Bailey wheels over toward the wall shared with the living room. He grabs an aerosol can from a drawer and sprays foam into a giant 'x' on the wall and a square around the 'x'. After a few seconds, the spray hardens and turns a yellowish hue.

Bailey unloads another shotgun shell toward the locked door and then reloads.

He looks at the monitor and sees two people near the door and one over by the front.

A man pulls out a small metal-cutting torch and starts to cut through the locks on the door.

Directly across the room from him, on the other side of the wall, is his in-apartment elevator.

He pulls the trigger of the shotgun, which causes the foam he sprayed onto the wall to explode, creating a giant hole, big enough for him to wheel out. He pushes forward and fires the last shotgun shell toward the door, hitting one man, sending him into the guy with the torch. The torch falls and ignites the man's pant leg, and he vigorously pats at it to put it out.

The third guy, by the front, opens fire but misses. Bailey aims his pistol toward him and unloads several shots as he wheels to the elevator door.

He presses the button and enters.

The metal doors close when he hears several shots scatter across.

One man shouts, "FUCK!" The other says, "Upstairs now!"

Inside the elevator, Bailey pulls the stop button. He presses another hidden button that opens the back of the elevator. Praising himself for having the door installed after he found out Clifford built a secret small armory behind his elevator.

Inside the secret room, Bailey turns on another monitor. He can see the two men upstairs trashing his room and looking around. One guy keeps mashing the elevator button and finally says, "He stopped the elevator."

The other man says, "Pry it open."

Hearing the gunshots inside the condo, the three other men waiting in a van outside grab their weapons, ready to storm the building, when they spot a dark Chevy Tahoe speeding into the parking lot. They freeze and take cover around the side of the building when the SUV drives up onto the sidewalk and swerves, cutting off their path to the door.

The men look at each other and decide to investigate the car instead of heading inside. They cling close to the building until they reach the corner. The point man holds up a fist, and the following two men stop and wait.

The point man peeks around the corner and stops. His body leans against the corner and goes limp, but does not fall. The man behind him tugs his shoulder back, and the point man falls backward with a boot-knife lodged in the front of his skull.

"Shit! Fall back!" he shouts. He picks up his radio and calls, "Team Delta, we have a man down."

They both start moving backward in haste, pointing their weapons toward the corner where their colleague lost his life.

The man in the rear turns around and spots a shadow. "What was that?"

The other man turns and asks, "What?"

"I saw something!"

"Where?"

"There!" He points just as shots ring out, striking them in the chest. Both men fall.

One lay on the ground in agonizing pain. He picks up a radio and calls, "Team Delta.."

A black man with greying hair approaches and fires another round into him, this time hitting his head.

The rest of the team inside the condo hears the squawk across the radio, and calls back, "What's going on out there?"

There's no reply. The men JJ called to action were gone as quickly as they arrived on site.

The man prying the elevator stops when he hears sirens in the distance.

"Shit. Cops!"

They abandon the elevator and head out of the condo. The first man heads out, steps over a dead colleague, and takes a direct line to the van.

Two cop cars swoop into the lot, and he runs. He opens fire on the approaching police car, and it screeches to a halt. The cops jump out and fire. He covers behind the van for a moment. He pops out to fire, but another cop fires first and hits him between the eyes.

The second man watches from the breezeway of the condo and heads back into Bailey's. He throws a chair out the back window, breaking it open, and jumps out. He heads toward the woods when he hears, "Freeze! Don't move!"

Two cops circle around him, and more police swarm from the other direction.

He drops his semi-automatic weapon and raises his hands.

***

Special Agent Sims arrives at the station, and an officer escorts him to the interrogation room.

He pops into the observation room first to talk with the lead detective.

Glancing at the name on his badge, Sims asks, "Detective Campbell, has he said anything yet?"

Campbell shakes his head. "Nothing. He hasn't even asked for a lawyer."

Sims sighs, looks through the two-way mirror at the perp and asks, "Mind if I take a crack at him?"

Campbell gestures toward the room. "Be my guest."

Sims slips into the room. The man looks up and then away as he steps up to the table.

Sims says nothing at first.

He slips his FBI badge from his pocket, opens it, and sets the badge in his eyeline.

The man looks at it and then at Sims.

He shrugs, unimpressed.

"You tried to kill a friend of mine."

The man sighs deeply and looks up at Sims again.

"I'm patient."

"Bite me!" he says, and bites down on a false tooth that makes a loud cracking sound.

Sims asks, "What was that?"

The man swallows hard and sits back with a stupid grin on his face. Sims grabs him and pries open his mouth to find nothing inside.

He pushes him backwards and says, "Please don't tell me you did what I think you did."

He hiccups and says, "Fuck you pi-" His voice trails off as he looks sick. He hiccups again, and foam forms around his mouth.

Sims stands up quickly as the perp falls to the floor with his arms still chained to a handcuff ring in the center of the table. A mixture of vomit and blood spews from his mouth and splatters across the table and floor.

He vomits again, and this time it produces more blood.

Sims takes a step back as the medics rush in.

"Can you save him?" Sims asks.

One medic checks for a pulse while the other tries to clear the airway. Another minute goes by before they announce the time of death.

# Chapter Twenty-Seven

**Skyler Mose** basks in Clifford Dee's disbelief.

"Surprise!"

Clifford looks him up and down. "How are you here? I saw you die!"

Mose asks, "Did you? Think about what you really saw."

Clifford stammers. "-I. I'm not so sure now."

He pulls up a chair and leans into Clifford's eyeline.

"You see, back in the desert, I was making less than two grand a month. Remember when I asked the Army for assistance? Remember when my request to go back stateside was denied? Well, my mother was in Philly, recovering from cancer, with the bills piling up."

Mose sighs. "I was desperate. I was angry, and that's when I found out that mercenary work was just as dangerous as life in the US Army, but the pay was so much better."

Clifford says, "You could have talked to me. I would have helped you."

Mose shakes his head. "I tried, Dee. You always had other concerns. In-fighting with Burr, trying to get Young promoted. You didn't have time for me. But I still idolized you. You were like a brother to me."

Mose leans in closer and continues, "You see, I learned the U.S. government makes so much money moving things from place to place. People, weapons, hell - even toppling governments for profit. So I thought I could do this freelance."

"It started small. I did a few jobs. Minor stuff. Selling ammo, gear, anything really. Then they asked for something bigger. Dee, I got fifty grand just to tell a few people where we would be and when. I only had to make sure that we got lost, and they did the rest."

Clifford looks at him with disbelief. "What? *You* sold us out? That day in Kandahar?"

"I had no choice, Dee. Not only was I scared back then, but I was desperate for money, and black-market work pays really, really, well."

Mose raises his hands and looks around.

"Since then, I've built my own team, a *massive* following, I create my own missions and approve my own work. And I'm good at what I do. I am not that scared, desperate little boy anymore. I'm Skyler Mose."

Clifford shakes his head. "What the fuck, Kyle?"

He strikes Clifford across his face. "Kyle Somers is dead!! I! Am! Skyler! Mose! Don't forget that!"

Clifford licks blood from his lip and looks up at Mose, glassy-eyed from the hit. "So you just *play* soldier now?"

Mose laughs. "I could have let them kill you in that raid in Afghanistan. I told them to bring you along unharmed. That's why I yelled over to point you out. That's why you were in the bunker, but Badger had to call in a rescue mission." Skyler grins while recalling the past.

"I honestly had no idea what happened to you until I saw the headlines from Kentucky. Nice job taking out that gilded turd of a Mob boss, by the way."

Clifford shakes his head in disbelief but remains quiet.

"Kudos, really! But when I saw that you and Kevin Burr were at each other's throats again, and right in our nation's capital of all places, I grabbed my popcorn and thought, 'I gotta see how this plays out."

"What you didn't know is that Burr, fucker that he is, found out about my dealings almost immediately. He was actually a client for a bit until he cut me out, thinking he could handle the Ethiopians himself. The egotistical prick didn't realize how difficult it would be, and he decided to take a train out of town. Trash really does take itself out sometimes, doesn't it?"

"So you've been watching me for years?"

Mose laughs. "You make it sound like I am obsessed with you. No, not watching. That's creepy, Dee. I've been... keeping tabs."

Clifford scoffs, but Mose ignores him and continues, "I always wanted to loop you in, Dee, because I always wanted you to work with me. But, you know how it is with long-lost pals, right? There's never really a good time to reach out."

Mose sighs. "However, I did *not* know you were going to be here looking for that kid. I had no idea that you would have raided my compound back in Colorado. That... was just a really delightful co-incidence. A sign!"

Clifford licks his sore lip again, mentally noting the statement '*back* in Colorado', and asks, "So... now what?"

Mose smiles. "I figured I'd give you an option... work for me. You're one hell of a soldier, and that's undeniable. I could use a guy with your talents."

Clifford sneers. "Or what? You kill me?"

"Oh, no. I wouldn't kill you. I'd leave that up to Barajas here. He's a lot like us. Special forces trained with a non-stop motor. He knows how to make it painful."

Barajas chimes in, "Just say the word, boss. I'll give him a nice smile, ear to ear." He makes a slow swiping motion across his neck around his jawline and smiles at Clifford while suggestively raising his eyebrows.

Clifford gives him an incredulous look at his over-the-top villain sidekick vibe. "What about my team, Kyle?"

Mose clenches his jaw hearing his old moniker. "The bimbo-les-bo, the cripple, and Ritalin kid? Left alone. It's obvious how much you care for them. If you agree to join me, and call me by my proper fuckin' name, of course."

Clifford sighs and shakes his head.

Mose smiles as he continues. "We'll make it look like you're dead. Just like we were trying to back in that bunker. Oh, and don't worry, I'll make sure you look heroic."

Mose laughs at his statement and asks Clifford, "How do you want to look dead? This could get fun. Make it a whole guy's night. We can catch up."

"Yeah, a guy's night with someone who tried to have me killed twice will be a real hoot!" Clifford says.

Mose laughs loudly. He feigns wiping a tear of joy and says, "Dee, God! I missed your sense of humor! Always so funny." He sighs and continues, "If I wanted you killed, I would've killed you."

Clifford looks around at the people flanking his bed, and turns back toward Mose with an irritated look as he continues, "In fact, I could have you killed now. All I have to do is snap my fingers."

He raises his hand with his middle finger resting on his thumb.

Clifford remains silent.

Mose leans in and says, "Dee, I'm offering you the world here. You have no idea how big we are, the people I control, the things I know, the connections I have. I operate in nearly every country in the world and have made a lot of prestigious friends. You'll see what I have in the works real soon."

He leans away from Clifford and looks around.

"The only thing I ask is that you remain loyal to me. Everyone here is a loyal subject, isn't that right?" He asks the room.

Every man nods. One man says, "Yes, sir."

Mose looks over at him. "Jacob, you are a trusted friend."

"Thank you, sir."

Mose looks back and glares at Clifford. While locked on his eyes, he continues.

"Jacob, how long have you and Steven known each other?"

"Since I was six years old."

Mose nods, still holding eye contact with Clifford. "Kill Steven."

Jacob pulls a gun from his holster and points it at Steven, who begins to object, "Wha-"

A single shot rings out, hitting Steven in the temple. He falls with a thud.

Clifford flinches, and Mose smiles, seeing his point coming across loud and clear.

"Steven wasn't loyal. He was colluding with the FBI. For three weeks he was feeding them information about our operation. Do you know how I know?"

"Some of the people you control are Feds?"

"Ding! Ding! See? You're *smart*. I don't have to spoon-feed you." Mose paces. "Loyalty is all I ask of you, and loyalty is what you'll get from me. We'll be partners. Equals." He spreads his arms wide. "We're all equal. Right, gentlemen?"

Jacob and Barajas both say, "Yes, sir!" in unison.

Mose waits for an answer, but Clifford remains stoic.

"I guess you need some time to think."

He backs away and leans toward Jacob and says, "Watch him. We'll come back after the service. That's plenty of time for him to think things through."

Mose radios on a walkie-talkie and says, "Get someone in the infirmary for a large cleanup."

He gestures, and Barajas turns with him. They walk out together, leaving Jacob behind with Clifford. A moment later, three other men come into the room with cleaning supplies, a body-bag, and a mop with a bucket of water.

Clifford watches in disgust as they swiftly bag up Steven and start cleaning the blood, brain, and skull fragments off the floor.

He watches two men pick up the bag and a third, wring out a bloody mop into a bucket, and set it on the floor in the corner.

Once they're alone, Clifford looks over at Jacob. "So, can I bill this to my insurance, or?"

Jacob glares back and then rolls his eyes.

Clifford pulls his handcuffs tight and adjusts his weight in his bed. His hands still have a bit of dried blood on them. He grimaces, feeling the tightness and pain in his back as he rolls his shoulders.

He's still very sore from the accident.

"Stop moving!" Jacob demands.

"C'mon, man! I was literally hit by a car. Imma bit sore."

A smile grows across Jacob's face, and Clifford notices.

"That was you?"

Jacobs' smile grows bigger.

"Damn, man. You really got us good. Where's the woman? Is she here?"

Jacob shrugs.

"Is she dead?"

Jacob shrugs again.

Clifford thinks for a second. "You left her, didn't you?"

Jacob tries not to react, but his brow lifts, betraying him.

"Did you at least call her an ambulance?"

Jacob huffs and shifts his eyes.

Clifford sighs, "I guess that's a no."

As he tries to engage, Clifford pulls at a small sliver of metal stuck in the palm of his right hand. He rolls his shoulders again to mask the pain of the last tug, to free it from his flesh.

"Jesus, this hurts," he acts, and he pretends to rub his bad knee.

"Could you get me a glass of water? Maybe a Motrin?" Clifford asks.

Jacob says angrily, "I said stop moving!"

"Come on, man, I'm in pain here."

Jacob shakes his head. "No meds 'til you give Mose an answer."

"Fine. Can I at least have some water?"

Jacob huffs, but he walks away toward a storage cabinet.

Clifford takes the opportunity to pick at the lock of the hand-cuff on the bed. Jacob returns and tosses a bottle of water at Clifford, hitting him in the chest and then rolling off the bed.

"Little help?"

Jacob shakes his head. "Fuck's sake, you're pathetic."

As Jacob bends down, Clifford pulls the chain of cuffs tight and swiftly wraps the chain around his neck, choking Jacob.

He pulls a pistol and fires a shot in desperation, trying to hit Clifford but misses. Clifford pulls the looped chain tighter, causing Jacob to gurgle spit from his throat until he collapses, falling like a ton of bricks.

Clifford loosens his strangle-hold and begins picking at the key-hole in the cuffs.

After a minute, he hears a click and the sliver of metal breaks inside the cuff on his wrist. He's unable to pull his hand out.

Clifford slides out of the bed. He bends down and lifts Jacob off the floor, putting him in his place. Clifford covers Jacob's face with the sheet. He stands up straight, revealing he truly is weak in the knees, stumbling from the instability. Clifford relieves Jacob of his pistol and limps over to the mop. He unscrews the wooden mop handle and uses it as a crutch.

Clifford limps toward the shelf to look for supplies.

He looks back and sees Jacob is gone. Clifford heads back toward the bed when Jacob jumps out and swings a wooden stool at him, knocking the gun from his hand.

Clifford loses his balance for a moment and falls backward. He scurries backwards on the ground as Jacob swings again and misses, hitting the ground and breaking the stool into pieces.

Clifford crawls on his back, and Jacob swings a large piece of wood from the stool, narrowly missing, striking between Clifford's legs just below his crotch. Both men stall for a moment, in shock that he missed. Clifford looks down at the wood plank and back up at Jacob. This prompts Clifford to place a swift kick to Jacob's knee. It buckles and sends him to the floor. His face hit first, splitting his lip.

Jacob pushes himself up, and Clifford swings his left hand, not to punch, but for the loose handcuff to swing wide. The cuff hits Jacob in the face, sending a stream of blood against the wall.

He crumbles to the ground on top of his gun.

Jacob pops up and quickly trains his gun toward Clifford, but Clifford's deceptively quicker.

He places a well-targeted jab to Jacobs' face with the mop handle, striking his nose squarely.

The strike causes him to step backward and trip over the rest of the broken stool.

Clifford skirts around him, and stomps on his face, knocking him out. Clifford, using the mop-handle for help, picks up the gun and fires a round into Jacob's head.

"Shit!" he says to himself, not happy that he just shot an unarmed man, but also about the easily discoverable mess that he will not be cleaning.

He releases the magazine from the pistol and counts the bullets.

Four, including the one in the chamber.

He puts the magazine back in and secures it in the back waistband of his jeans.

Clifford drags the body into the cage, toward the bed, muscles him back into it. He raises the sheet back over Jacob's bloody head. Just in an undershirt and pants, Clifford removes Jacob's sweater and slips into it. Next, he takes his boots and finds the size slightly off, but close enough, as he gets his own feet into them.

Clifford reaches the door, but it's locked from the outside.

He takes time looking at the supplies in the room, on the shelves, and in the cabinets, when he spots a large door in the back of the room.

Clifford opens the door to reveal a large storage closet. In the back, he spots a switch. Throwing the switch causes the back wall to open to an elevator. He steps inside and presses the only button inside.

It goes down.

The elevator doors open to a row of isolated cells, divided by concrete walls. Clifford thinks the place is purposed for temporarily keeping trafficked people. He enters the room, proceeding carefully. The metal cages on the right are unoccupied, implying the occupants were either moved or killed.

Continuing past, hobbling slowly, he uses the mop as a crutch.

He turns a corner and spots a wooden stairwell at the end of a long hallway.

Slowly creeping up the stairs, he spots the soundproofing foam on the walls and door.

He now knows for sure it's a hidden room.

As he reaches the top of the stairs, he realizes there's no door-knob. He feels around, finding a button, and presses it.

The door slides open to a brightly lit room.

# Chapter Twenty-Eight

**Special Agent Sims** pulls up to Bailey's condo, taken aback by the destruction.

He steps out of his car and spots Bailey talking to an insurance adjuster.

"Hey Bailey, this looks terrible."

The adjuster says, "I'm going to take another look inside and be on my way."

Bailey smiles. "Sure, thanks." He turns toward Sims. "That punk you took in, he say anything?"

Sims shakes his head. "He's dead. Had a suicide capsule in his tooth."

"What? Like World War II Nazi spies and shit?"

"Like World War II Nazi spies and shit."

Bailey shakes his head. "Unbelievable."

Sims says, "I changed my flight to tonight. I am actually on my way to Dulles right after this, and I fly out in two hours."

Bailey asks, "I guess I'll try to get my comms back up. Everything's pretty much destroyed."

Sims says, "Well, I -uh, I made arrangements for you."

"Arrangements? I am not your elderly grandfather, Tal! I'm fine here."

Sims grimaces and frustratingly says, "I'm starting to think we know nothing about this group anymore. If they came for you once, they'll come again, and watching these guys suicide themselves to keep secrets? That..." He shakes his head. "That takes the situation to a whole other level."

Sims takes a moment and continues, "You're not safe, B. There's an FBI offsite in Chantilly. You can stay there. They've got small dorms, you'll be granted temporary access to the building, including the command center, and you should be able to access some of your online tools from there. Just until we get a better hold on this situation."

Bailey shakes his head in objection and breathes in sharply, but knows that it's probably the best idea, and gives in. "Fine," he says after thinking for a moment.

Sims says, "Grab a bag of essentials. I'll have the guys get you what they can as you need it. A car is on its way."

Bailey says, "Couldn't I just take my van?"

Sims nods. "Sure. I actually forgot you tricked out your van."

Bailey smiles and says, "I'll follow you there."

After the quick trip, they arrive at the Chantilly FBI site. Bailey follows Sims though the gate and parks in the very back of the parking lot.

Sims pulls up next to Bailey and rolls his window down.

"They know who you are, and why you're here. The guy at the desk will get you a temporary access badge and give you instructions."

Bailey wheels toward the building, then he turns toward Sims. "Hey Sims...Thanks."

Sims nods, "Don't mention it. I'll reach out once I land."

***

Bailey wheels into the command center in the FBI building in Chantilly. Agent Minh begins a brief tour.

"Over here is Network Operations. Over there in that section is IT Support, and finally, this office in the corner is for you. We made sure that you have access to the Internet, but you're not authorized to have access to our internal network."

Bailey smiles, conspiratorially. "Scared of what I might find on there?"

Minh stammers, "Uh, no, well. No, you don't have the clearance to get on that network. The FBI doesn't hide anything. We investigate."

Bailey purses his lips and narrows his eyes. "Mm-hmm."

"Well, that's your office over there, for the time being. Should I show you to the living quarters?" Minh asks.

Bailey's smile fades, and he sighs.

"Sure."

Minh points down a side hall and says, "That way is the café. It's small, and they mostly have sandwiches, snacks, and drinks. It's pretty nice, but everything's pre-cooked."

Bailey remains quiet and unimpressed with what he's seen so far.

Finally, they arrive at a small room. Minh pushes open the door and reveals a room with a TV, a small twin bed, and a dresser.

"This is it. It's not much, but it's something."

Bailey wheels in. "It'll do."

"You have a phone next to the bed. My number's written down next to it. Call me if you need anything."

Bailey nods and says, "Thanks."

Minh turns and walks off as Bailey shuts the door.

He wheels over to the bed and lifts himself onto it.

Lying down, he stares at the ceiling and lets out a sigh.

He doesn't want to be here.

He pulls a vibrating phone out of his jacket pocket. It's his cousin JJ.

"Hey, J."

"B! Thank God. What's going on? My guys said you were under attack."

"I think we all are, cuz. Right now, I'm in an FBI building in Chantilly. I'm okay, just really worried about Dee."

"Where was he last?"

"Just outside of Boulder, near Longmont, Colorado. There was a car accident. It looks like it was meant to stun him to be taken with little resistance. Dee had someone in the car with him. She's in the hospital. Sara and Dan are with her."

"Okay, I have some people near there. I'll send them to the hospital to coordinate with Sara. Do you happen to know which hospital?"

"It's on Riverbend Road," Bailey says, looking at the location-sharing app.

"Are you good? Do I need to come get you?"

"Nah, Cuz. I'm good here, lying low. If I need you, I'll reach out."

"Don't fuckin' hesitate," JJ says.

Bailey smiles at her sharp tone. "I won't. Love you, too."

# Chapter Twenty-Nine

**Clifford** looks around the room — a typical, generic office of some sort. It comprises a desk, cabinets, a closet, and even shelving with tchotchkes.

The air in the room smelled stale, but not old and musty like the basement he was just in. It gave the impression that the office was not used very often, and seldom cleaned.

He hears a 'whooshing' sound behind him. He turns to find that the door he stepped through is disguised behind a full wall-sized religious triptych-style painting, the center panel being the door. The center panel closes, revealing three words in Latin inscribed on the bottom:

*~ Redivivus · Vivifica · Renascentia ~*

Clifford walks toward the desk, finds a pen and jots down the words on a small notepad. He shoves the paper in his pocket and continues to look around. He opens the small closet door in the corner of the room. Inside are tools inside a toolbag, several boxes, a big winter coat, and on the floor, he sees a box in the back corner.

It is partially open, and inside he sees a dark green metallic container with two round slots. The container has 'SMi-35 Schützen-abwehrmine' stenciled on the side.

His eyes light up. "Holy Betty!" he exclaims quietly to himself. "What are you doing in here?"

Clifford wraps the case inside the coat and shoves it under his arm before continuing out of the room into the hallway.

He looks at several religious paintings and other works of art displayed along the hallway walls. He pauses as he hears someone talking through a speaker. Listening, he can barely make out the words.

He moves around a corner, carefully checking for guards, but finds none.

Continuing down the hall, he closes in on the voice. The closer he gets, the more intensely he can smell a woodsy incense of earthy notes combined with citrus and spice commonly used in religious ceremonies.

He reaches a sanctuary where a sermon is taking place. The room's filled with people. Some with their heads bowed, others with hands raised, swaying.

At the pulpit, stands Mose, speaking passionately to his congregation, which holds the attention of every member.

Clifford changes course to find a way out.

He's lighter on his feet knowing that most of the people are all in one area. Clifford quickly makes his way to the back of the building and hears talking down another hallway. He stumbles upon a small storage area and heads inside.

Inside the storage area, there was a cabinet where he found several small back-packs, U.S. Army-issued "Meals Ready to Eat", and several bottles of water.

Attached to the wall is a box that has several individual packs of emergency thermal blankets.

He loads up a backpack with a few MREs, water, a spool of cord, a thermal blanket, duct tape, and a first aid kit. As he shoves the first-aid kit into his bag, he notices a small fire-starting kit in the corner. He quickly examines the kit to see it has a small knife, small fatwood sticks soaked in pine oil, cotton pads soaked with petroleum jelly, water-proof matches, and other necessities used to not only start a fire, but to keep it going for a while.

He puts it into the backpack.

He hears the talking in the hallway grow louder. He opens the door just a crack to peek out and waits for the voices to fade. On the back of the door, was a large canvas tote bag with drawstrings.

After the voices become comfortably distant, he opens the door and continues to search for an exit, with the German S-mines in the tote bag.

The sound of even more voices indicates to Clifford that the sermon is over. He picks up the pace until he can hear the buzz of an exit sign as he carefully rounds another corner. Without hesitation, he quickly travels through it.

Outside, the sun stings his eyes. Shielding them, Clifford looks around to gather his bearings.

A light frost is covering the grass in shady areas, and the ground is hard. He spots a small drainage tunnel along the barbed-wire fence at the very back of the property. He allows a smile, knowing he's found his way out.

Seeing his breath as he exhales causes him to suddenly feel the cold. The metal handcuff on his left wrist feels heavy. It's just loose enough to pull the cuff off his wrist, but not without taking off a few layers of skin with it.

He grits his teeth and does just that, tossing the bloodied cuff on the ground, and away from the church in frustration. He tries to keep the raw skin from touching anything until it has time to scab over by keeping it in the coat's pocket.

***

As Sara's on the call with Agent Fulk, a uniformed officer opens the door to Rox's room and peeks his head in.

"Roxanne Curry? I'm Officer Whittington. I was told to check in with you and inform you I've been posted at the door."

Sara smiles at the officer as she loudly asks, "Hey Fulk, did you send Officer Whittington to guard Rox?"

Dan takes a photo of the officer with his cell and texts it to a group chat with his name.

Fulk and Sara get the text notification at the same time. Fulk says, "Just got the pic, yeah that's him. Tell Rox, she's in good hands."

Officer Whittington keeps his smile in place and his eyes on Sara. "Will do. Thanks, Fulk."

Feeling better, leaving Rox with a guard, they say their goodbyes and make their way out of the main corridor to leave the hospital.

"Maybe we should get an Uber to the station and see that footage ourselves," Dan says as the automatic doors open and they walk out into the crisp air.

A car pulls up in front of them, and a man rolls down the passenger window and asks, "Sara? Daniel?"

Sara quickly looks around. "Yeah?"

"JJ sent us. Get in," the man says.

Dan's eyes widen, and Sara says, "Holy shit. She has people out here?"

"Ma'am, we're everywhere. We can explain, but you need to get in first."

Sara looks back at Dan with a quizzical look and opens the door behind him, sliding over so Dan can get in the same way.

As Dan closes the door, the passenger turns to face them in the backseat. "I'm Reese and this is Fabian. He doesn't talk."

The driver with a wicked thick scar across his throat nods as he maneuvers around the parking lot and back onto the main road.

"We're gonna help find your friend, Dee. We'll take care of everything you need during your time here." Reese turns to face the front as he continues, "In the center console are some weapons. They're clean. What info do you have about Dee's whereabouts?"

JJ's quick involvement when so much law enforcement is in the mix doesn't make sense to Sara. She waves her hands to disrupt.

"Hold up - wait. It's not that I don't appreciate any help we can get, but why exactly are you here? Like, why did JJ send you right now? Has something else happened?"

Reese glances at Fabian. "We don't know the full story, but something happened back east with her cousin. She sent up an SOS."

Sara gasps. "Is Bailey okay?"

Reese sighs, "He's fine; in an FBI safe-house, unfortunately. Now how about that intel on Dee?"

Dan pulls out his phone to text Bailey, feeling the need to check for himself, and mutters, "I bet B loves that."

Sara looks over the weaponry inside the console. "We don't know much, just that it was a coordinated attack to hit them broadside. The passenger with Dee said that one of the assailants was wearing tan boots that were covered in a reddish clay mud and an SUV with, possibly, out-of-state plates seemed to herd them into position for the impact."

She takes a sheathed knife and stuffs it into her boot, covering it with her pant-leg before continuing. "She said Dee was dragged from the wreckage and taken before anyone arrived at the scene. The truck that hit them was abandoned, stolen, of course - and there was no sign of the SUV with the weird plates."

"Bailey's good," Dan quietly says to Sara, as he pockets his phone.

"We have more shit in the trunk. We're kinda prepared for anything."

Dan looks over at Sara, and they smile at each other.

"What's in the trunk?" Sara asks with a grin.

Reese nods at Fabian, and he turns down a small access road with very little traffic. He drives for a minute and stops.

Reese gets out and says, "Let's have a little show-and-tell."

Sara and Dan step out as Fabian pops the trunk to reveal a small arsenal of weapons. Several rifles of different calibers, shotguns, pistols, semi-automatic weapons, knives. They even have throwing stars, sai, and other martial arts weaponry affixed to the underside of the trunk.

Sara's eyes narrow as she examines the cache. She grabs a semi-automatic pistol and clips it to her side. Dan does the same, then he swoops up three throwing stars and puts them in his pocket.

Dan smiles at Reese and says, "Okay. I think we're good now."

Sara gives Dan a look. "Ninja stars?"

Dan says, "I was really into Ninja Turtles. I practiced a lot."

Sara's eyes widen, "I am so glad I know that now."

Dan looks over to Reese and says, "I'm ready when y'all are."

Sara nods in agreement with a smug look on her face.

"Ma'am, if I may... you lookin' badass," Reese says with an approving smile on his face. Fabian nods in agreement.

Sara smirks. "I make it look good, don't I?"

***

Clifford makes a direct line to the drainage ditch, using the wooden mop handle as a walking stick. He makes his way to the edge of the building, which is about a hundred yards from the drainage pipe along the fence line. The first thing he notices is a huge snowy mountain peak jetting out of the skyline in the distance. He knows for sure that he's not in Colorado. Under his breath he questions, "Mt. Rainier?"

He regains his focus and can see two people around the side that might spot him, but they're facing away from him. He can hear people chattering as they're leaving the building out front.

People dressed in their Sunday best walk toward another building that looks like a dorm of some sort. As he continues to look around, he spots the main drag of a town.

He was in a functioning community.

Complete with different shops, stores, and a small business center. Everything has the same name attached to it. SledgeHaven.

A good distance away, along the other fence line, were small farms growing winter-hardy crops of kale, spinach, cabbage, leeks, and root vegetables such as carrots, beets, and turnips. They had a coop with chickens, as well as goats and dairy-cows.

A creek near the back of the property supplies the farm with water, irrigated by a small lake. The creek curves around near the drainage pipe he spotted. If he gets to the pipe, he can follow the creek and, most likely, find a neighboring town and call for help.

Clifford takes a deep breath and heads toward the pipe, hoping he won't be spotted. As he turns the corner, he runs into another man.

"Careful, brother," the man says to Clifford.

Clifford smiles at the man. "My apologies! I need to mend the hole in the fence before we lose any more chickens!"

The man looks unsure, but nods and says, "Must hurry then, brother."

He steps aside to allow Clifford to pass.

Clifford smiles back and nods as he hurries to the fence with his supplies.

At the fence, he notices there is a grate in front of the pipe with a padlock. He spots a decent-sized rock near the pipe. He uses the wooden mop handle to place behind the lock's U-shaped shackle, then uses the rock in a downward smashing motion against the body of the lock.

The lock doesn't pop, but it makes a loud, unique, rock-on-metal sound. He looks around to see if anyone notices before doing it again. This time the lock pops open.

He unhooks the lock from the grate and swings it open.

He climbs inside the pipe, latches the grate, and places the broken lock back on, concealing what he just did.

This will buy him time, but not much.

***

Skyler Mose heads into the infirmary to visit Clifford Dee, with Barajas behind him.

"Okay, Dee, I hope you've made your de-"

Skyler stops when he sees a small pool of blood on the floor and notices a broken stool pushed into the corner of the room. He hurries the rest of the to find the bed with a bloody sheet over a body. Mose looks over at Barajas before he grabs the sheet and rips it off to reveal it's not Clifford Dee.

He turns toward Barajas and with a voice filled with disappointment says, "Looks like we're starting a hunting party. Time to kill Clifford Dee."

# Chapter Thirty

**As they get back in the car**, Sara and Dan get a text message from Sims.

*I've landed. Meet at Denver FBI on E 36th Ave.*

"Hey guys, would you mind dropping us off at the FBI building in Denver?" Dan asks as Sara vigorously shakes her head at him.

Fabian glares at him in the rearview mirror as Reese says, "Hell no! We don't fuck with the feds."

Dan looks from Sara to Reese and states plainly, "We work with our contact, Special Agent Sims. We're supposed to meet with him. He's one of us."

Fabian looks over at Reese and gives him an incredulous look.

"So, that's what she meant by 'play nice about Sims'," Reese finally says.

He turns his attention to Sara. "Okay, we can drop you off at the corner of Quebec and 36th. You'll walk the last block. When you need us," Reese says as he hands her a card with just a phone number on it. "Text the word, Badass, so we know it's you."

Sara smiles and nods as she tucks the card into her back pocket.

On the way to the FBI office, Sara looks at Dan and says, "Nice work being so firm with those guys about the FBI. I was concerned at first."

The praise makes Dan blush.

"Sims is like family. I figure if Bailey can find a way to make it work, they can too."

They jog up a few steps, go inside the front entrance, approach the security guard, and say, "We're here to see Special Agent Sims."

They're directed to the Visitor Center and ask the woman at the window to page Agent Tal Sims.

The woman asks them to take a seat and picks up the phone. After a few minutes, she calls them back up and hands them temporary badges.

"Special Agent Sims will meet you near the elevators in the lobby. Go through the checkpoint, then turn left at the end of the hall, and you'll see the elevator lobby. Just make sure," she begins as she taps on a sign with her pen. "If you have any of these items, you need to put them in one of the lockers near the metal detectors."

"Is there a special place designated for weapons?" Dan asks innocently.

Minutes later, a hurried Sims finds his way downstairs to find Dan and Sara sitting on a bench in handcuffs.

Dan looks up and sees Sims exhaling a sigh of disbelief. He elbows Sara, who's looking out the front door. She looks over at Dan, then up at Sims, and slowly smiles.

Sims looks at the bin filled with various weapons. "You've been in town for less than a day. How'd you get all these?"

Sara smiles and shrugs. "Found 'em?"

Sims shakes his head and says with a smirk, "You know what? I don't wanna know, but - c'mon, guys, you knew better than to bring them into this building."

"Are you going to keep them?" Dan asks, not in the mood to be chastised.

Sims looks over at the guard. "Bag 'em."

He turns back to Dan and Sara. "You can pick them back up on your way out."

"Awesome. The pistol completed my outfit," Sara says, holding up her handcuffed wrists to be unshackled. "The bracelets, however..."

Sims escorts them down the hall and toward the elevator.

"We're still in the process of getting traffic cam footage of the crash. We're also going to get footage from cameras in the area and will try to find out at least what direction the car came from."

Sims presses the third-floor button followed by the button to close the door. "We have a committee set up to discuss our plan to find Dee," he continues to explain during the short ride.

"You'll meet the Special Agent in Charge, one of the Assistant Special Agents, the Senior Supervisory Intelligence Analyst, the Chief Security Officer, some Field Agents, and the Media Coordinator."

They continue toward a conference room where several people are sitting around a large table. "They just aren't clear on a few things," he whispers as he opens the door.

Sims ushers Sara and Dan to two chairs against the wall.

Sitting on the outskirts of the core group makes Dan feel like they aren't meant to have any input. He shares a look with Sara and knows she's noticed, too. Her eyes narrow at Sims as he moves to the front of the room.

"Thank you for waiting," he says to the group seated around the table. "Uh, ladies and gentlemen, let me introduce you to Sara Brooks and Daniel Watson."

A few in the room glance toward them while the others keep their eyes on Sims. Sara observes the people at the table appearing bored or irritated as Sims tries to summarize.

"They work for BluTrace Investigations, a team we trust and use often. BTI is based in Virginia and run by our vetted Special Consultant, Clifford Dee. Mr. Dee was called here to work a private, missing child case that unfolded into something much bigger. He stumbled upon the network we know as 'Operation Ghost Hunt'. Reference case number 8-6D97-12A"

Sims pauses as interest strikes the committee, watching as they shuffle through their copies of the report. Sims continues, hoping to avoid questions before he's done.

"Our special consultant was coordinating with Agent Nathan Fulk of the CBI in Lakewood on his case before I looped him into ours. Mr. Dee then found his client's child among the others he subsequently rescued on my order. He found them on Skyler Mose's ranch compound disguised as a private gun club just outside of Denver. Unfortunately, minutes after briefing the CBI and other law enforcement, Mr. Dee and his companion were subjected to a coordinated attack, in broad daylight. The other victim, Roxanne Curry, is stable but hospitalized. However, Mr. Dee was abducted, and at this time, we believe he's still alive."

Sims motions over toward Dan and Sara. "Ms. Brooks and Mr. Watson arrived earlier today and have already questioned the witness, Ms. Curry, but she was unable to provide much-"

"Special Agent Sims," The Special Agent in Charge, Mark Tanner, interrupts. "Are we supposed to believe that after all this time, and with very little traction, your civilian consultant just happened to stumble onto 'Ghost Hunt.' A top secret FBI operation?"

"That's exactly what happened," Sims says matter-of-factly.

One of the field agents speaks up, "Shouldn't we wait until the informant reaches out? If this special consultant is already dead, we shouldn't waste the manpower-"

Sara stands up, furious. The younger field agents both place their hands on their weapons, ready to draw as Sims steps forward. "Stand down, Agents."

They look to their superior and relax after he nods his head.

"Your informant is why you *haven't* gotten traction," Sara spits.

The same field agent Sara interrupted glares at her. "Our under-cover informant is-"

"Information about our informant is classified," Andrea Whit-beck, the senior supervisory intelligence analyst, cuts in before turning to Sara. "And, young lady, you do not have the clearance for that!"

Sara sets her jaw, her hands balled into fists.

"Clifford Dee is a vital asset to the D.C. bureau," Sims says loud-ly, to retake control of the meeting. "He's assisted us in capturing known criminals, assassins, and weapons smugglers."

Before he continues, he nods at Sara, and she reluctantly sits back down.

"He's important to all of us, including this office, because while working with Agent Fulk of the CBI, they uncovered several pieces of evidence that seem to tie into the background of a military unit that Dee is familiar with," Sims says.

"I'm sure you recall the shooting at Wild Willie's? Yeah, those gunmen were somehow connected, which ties into 'Ghost Hunt' too," he continues.

The chief security officer opens her government-furnished lap-top to freshen her memory of that incident.

Sims presses on through his hurried presentation.

"We know of a main compound, a much larger property. Unfor-tunately, we're not sure of the location, but we do know it's outside of Colorado."

"It sounds to me that the status of your consultant is unknown. And since Mr. Dee let almost everyone at the compound escape, couldn't the informant be on the way to their main encampment? Shouldn't we just stand by for contact?" Ms. Whitbeck asks.

"We're not twiddling our thumbs anymore," Sims says sternly.

Dan huffs and stands, placing his hands on his hips.

"You are all talking as if Dee is dead. He's not! And we're getting Dee back with or without your help. Marinate on that all you want, but it's a fucking fact!"

The room grows quiet, and they all look toward Dan.

Sims clears his throat. "I agree with Mr. Watson."

Sara looks up at Dan, and whispers, "I love you for what you said, but you should sit down now."

Dan slides his hands down from his hips and takes his seat.

Sara rubs his back. "Hands on the hips... very manly. Real power move, bud."

Dan looks at Sara side-eyed and huffs in frustration.

***

Clifford Dee stands with his hands on his hips looking at the drainage pipe from the other side, thinking.

The creek is extremely cold. In fact, a few spots near the bank are freezing, and chunks of ice are running with the water.

He opens his pack and pulls out a water bottle, scoops up some water from the small tributary off the main river, filling it an eighth of the way, and dries the sides and top. Clifford swirls the bottle and scoops up some rocks from the water's edge, dropping them into the bottle until they completely cover the water. He finds some bits of metal shavings left from the chain-link fence's construction, placing them in the bottle along with some metallic fasteners and twigs.

Clifford opens his pack and retrieves an MRE. After opening the Meal Ready to Eat package, he places the food aside and rips open the flameless ration heater pack. Squeezing the chemical into the bottle, Clifford works quickly but very careful not to get it wet.

In traditional use, an MRE heater placed inside a heavy-duty plastic bag will react with added water, boiling it to heat food.

Clifford closes the bottle, creating a tight seal. He then takes a small piece of cord and ties it to the neck of the bottle. He runs a length of cord across the end of the pipe and sets the bottle near the edge of the small stream on a large rock.

Clifford smiles and then walks with the flow of the stream to the river.

Reaching the river, a frigid wind picks up and cuts through his clothing. There's a spot across the river where he can enter a wooded area for cover.

He looks up and notes the direction the sun is moving, suggesting the river is flowing southeast.

He puts the sun and the giant snowy peak towering over the distant hills to his back and heads with the river. He climbs over a few rocks and travels deep into the woods until he's out of sight.

# Chapter Thirty-One

**Sims** walks out to the lobby of the building with Sara and Dan, apologizing for the rest of the team not sensing any urgency to help find Clifford.

"We'll find him, guys. I promise!" Sims says.

An agent rushes down the hallway. "Sims! Sims!" he shouts down a crowded walkway, navigating people.

Sims looks over and nods. "Hey, you got something?"

The agent rushes up.

"Sara, Dan, this is Agent Glen Arbor. He's trying to find out where the car that ushered Rox into the intersection came from."

"Utah," Agent Arbor rushes out with a smile. "The car came from Utah."

"Was it the same SUV that hurried her out of the parking lot?" Sara asks.

Agent Arbor nods before turning to Sims.

"Sorry, I missed the meeting, but this was what I was doing."

"You didn't miss much," Dan says, folding his arms.

Arbor hands Sims photos. "The tinted windows prevented us from getting a decent look at the driver, but we have a partial number on the plate."

Sims smiles, "Nice! Did you run it?

"I did! Oh, and it was reported stolen. So, both cars were stolen."

Sims looks disappointed. "Shit, that's probably the car."

Arbor smiles and says, "Special Agent Sims, never doubt me."

"You found the driver, didn't you?" Sims asks in astonishment.

Arbor's smile grows. "So, I looked at the report and noticed the car was stolen from outside a warehouse on the border of Utah and Colorado. I called the warehouse and got them to send me some stills from their CCTV security footage." Arbor pauses for a quick breath before he continues.

"One of the stills showed another car, also from Utah, and it's registered to an Erik Anderson.

Mr. Anderson is a small business owner, and his business is a place that has lots of mud all year round."

Sara's eyes light up. "You told him about the muddy boots?"

Sims raises his eyebrows in confirmation, and Dan smiles.

***

Erik Anderson lives on a vast plot of land. His residence includes a large workshop with equipment to dry out mud and a few pug and ball mills. One is used to crush dry clay to create a volcanic powder and the other to process the power to mix with supplements, oils, and other cosmetic grade ingredients that big named spas use for their exotic mud baths, masks, and other treatments that people love.

He loves his job. Working outdoors and in nature is an honor to him.

Erik is carrying two large buckets of unprocessed clay, his boots covered in mud, and his blue jeans are an ombre from a silvery clay powder to deep denim-blue from bottom to top.

Several SUVs and local police cars pull up to his property.

Erik drops the buckets and knows it's too late to run or fight, so he just stands and waits.

The vehicles pull up near him and strategically park.

Sims steps out of the back and pulls his badge. "Erik Anderson?"

Erik nods. "Yeah."

"Gonna need ya to come with me. We have a few questions to ask you."

At the local police station, officers walk Erik inside and directly into an interrogation room.

The deputies stop and watch as they're not used to seeing the FBI walk a perp into their station.

Sims steps into the interrogation room and sits on the other side of Erik, who sighs and looks toward the ground.

"It's almost as if you want to tell me," Sims starts in.

"Sorry?" Erik asks.

Sims shifts in his seat. "I can tell there's a lot on your mind. Let's talk."

"About what?"

"I'd like to talk about my good friend Clifford Dee. He went missing after a car accident. Hit and run. Know anything about that?"

Erik sighs deeply. "I do."

Sims leans back in his chair, surprised at his response. "Please continue. I'd like to know as much as you are willing to tell me."

Erik sighs. "Well, I was contacted and told it was my favor."

"Your favor? For what?"

"A guy named Skyler Mose saved my life and my business. For that, I owed him a favor. That was four years ago. A few days back, he told me he was calling it in."

"So did he text you or call? Write a letter or postcard... something?" Sims asks.

Erik lets out a slight laugh.

"Over the internet. I had to download this app on my phone, and it notifies me if I get messages. So I got a notification with a button to click. It opened a message. There were numbers; grid coordinates."

Sims nods. "Did you save a copy of the message?"

"No, I didn't. The app disables screenshots." He pauses.

"There was a countdown in the corner counting down from 60. Once it hit zero, the message disappeared. But I could copy and paste the coordinates into a text file. I googled it, and it was a pretty big field with a marker about thirty yards into it. I drove out there, got out of my car, and walked into the field. About thirty yards in, there's a small pile of rocks that looks completely out of place. I pull the rocks up and find an envelope. Inside was a typed note. Like, typed from a typewriter, not printed from a computer."

Sims looks intrigued. "Really? Still have it? The note?"

"Nope, I tossed it. So it said to meet a guy at an address. I went, and it was outside a public library. Then, the guy gets into my car and tells me I need to drive to another location. He never told me his name."

Sims asks, "Can you identify him?"

Erik shakes his head. "He was wearing a gator mask and hat. All I can say is he was a white guy."

Sims nods while Erik continues.

"We got to a warehouse, and he stole this big pickup truck, right? I asked if I was done with the favor. The guy said, 'No' and then told me we were going to get a guy in Colorado. I drove. He rode shot-gun, taking directions from someone on his phone. The guy pulls a gun on me and tells me to wait at an intersection. We sit through a couple of cycles of red lights. A crappy coupe pulls up to the right, and he tells me to floor it when they start to cross the intersection and ram their car. I did, and it flipped. I was a bit stunned, but the guy points his gun again and says, 'Go help pull the guy out'. I went and it took some doing, but pulled the guy out of the car, and we put him in an SUV that was behind the coupe. The guy I pulled out of the wreckage was pretty out of it, but once he was in the SUV, I saw one of the others jab him with a needle anyway. Said something like, 'That'll keep him out for the trip.' I assumed they were going to be driving for a while."

Sims shakes his head and says, "Wow! What a story. So what happened next?"

"I got in the SUV, they dropped me off at my car and told me to delete the app on my phone. Then, they left."

Sims looks a little disappointed. "So, you didn't travel back to where they took Dee?"

"Dee? Is that the guy's name? No, I didn't go with them."

"Can you ID the guys from the other car?"

Erik shakes his head. "Hats and masks, too."

"Why you?"

Erik shrugs, "I don't know. I was just told that's how I was to repay the favor. I didn't ask questions."

"We appreciate your cooperation. We're going to hold you for a few hours until we process this statement, but you'll be free to go afterwards."

Erik asks, "I'm not in trouble for hurting that young man?"

"From the statement you gave me, it sounds like you were a vic-tim too. You were forced into an accident. Then, forced to remove Dee from the car and place him in the other vehicle. Is that about right?"

"Exactly how it happened."

Sims says, "Then if this information checks out, you're good to go."

Sims turns and heads out of the room. He taps on the door of the viewing room, and an officer opens the door. He says, "We got all of it, and we are digging into it now."

212

Sara and Dan are waiting in the lobby.

Sims approaches and says, "We got a lot of info from that guy. It sounds like Mose wanted Dee alive. We're going to find him."

"Where do we start?" Sara asks.

Sims shakes his head. "I'm not sure right now. I have to vet his info, and then we go from there. But one thing is for sure, Dee is outside Colorado and probably further away than Utah."

Dan and Sara look at each other and stand up.

"Call us when you get something," Sara says.

"Where are you going to go?" Sims asks.

Dan smiles and says, "We are gonna go find Dee."

# Chapter Thirty-Two

**A woman** pleads with her husband as he is dressing for the harsh outdoors.

"I don't want you to go. Saul, you're a handyman, not a damn soldier. Hell, I'm better suited to go out there."

"Jessica, please. I need to help Skyler. I actually think I saw the guy earlier today. He was talking strangely about chickens and a hole in the fence."

"So what? You don't know for sure that was him. Also, what would Mose do if he found out you saw him?"

Saul shakes his head. "Why do you think I want to help? If I sit back and do nothing, it'd be worse."

Jessica breathes sharply through her nose. "Honey, please be careful."

A short time later, Skyler Mose turns to face a small platoon of men. Next to Mose are a few hunting dogs.

The men all dressed in winter gear to protect themselves from the elements. It was close to freezing, and the chill in the air told them it would only get colder as the sun set.

Mose bought only what he considered the best on the market.

He is equipped with a new thermal-lined jacket, waterproof boots, night-vision goggles, two sidearms, and a knife on his hip next to a hand-held radio.

He looks over his men with a scowl and says, "Who's ready to get that traitor who killed two of our beloved?"

The men harrumph in a loud uproar.

Mose smiles for a moment in pride and then motions for them to be quiet, waving down their enthusiasm.

"Men! Men!" he shouts for their attention. As they grow quiet, he continues, "We must find Clifford Dee and send him to be judged by his maker."

Again the men holler.

Barajas approaches Mose and whispers in his ear. The expression on Skyler Mose's face changes.

Displeased, Mose wipes the corners of his mouth and takes a deep breath.

"Did anyone here see Clifford Dee leave the compound?" he asks.

A hush falls over the crowd of men, and they look around. Saul drops his head.

Mose looks among the men and says, "Come on, let's hear your voices. Let each one of you speak the truth with his neighbor, for we are members, one of another."

Saul steps up through the crowd.

"I guess I saw him," he says with worry in his voice.

Mose closes his eyes, and a slight frustrated smile crosses his face, but he tries to hide it by licking his lips.

"Brother Saul, please stand by me."

Saul looks around and hesitantly walks toward Mose.

Mose places his hand on Saul's shoulder and spins him around to face the men.

"Brother Saul said he saw Mr. Dee before he left the compound. Did you recognize him, Saul?"

"No, Sir. He said he needed to tend to a hole in the fence."

"A hole? In what fence?"

"Yes, Sir. Over that way. So the chickens wouldn't escape."

Mose gestures to the crowd.

"He did not recognize him, yet accepted his lies and let him walk away."

He turns to Saul before continuing, "Is that correct?"

"I guess so, sir."

"You guess so?"

"Yeah. No. I mean, that's correct."

Mose nods and says, "And where did he go?"

Saul looks behind him and says, "That way, toward that fence."

Mose glances over and sees the concrete pipe and lets out an audible sigh before turning his attention back to Saul.

"He saw, yet did not speak. So, it's as if he did not see at all."

Mose clutches the back of Saul's head, who struggles. Barajas kicks the back of Saul's legs to force him to his knees. Barajas unsheathes a knife and places it against Saul's throat, waiting for a command.

Mose looks over at Barajas and says, "No, Brother. We will not take his life."

With quick pressure of his thumb, Mose pushes it into the struggling man's left eye and pops it out in one swift motion. "We take his eye! If you turn a blind eye, then it's no use to you."

He leaves the eye dangling from Saul's face so everyone can see. Saul screams in agony as Mose walks forward toward the men.

Barajas lifts Saul up and cuts the optic nerve, tossing his eye toward the dogs, then escorts him to the medics.

Mose raises his fist as his men cheer in his judgement. "Let's find Clifford Dee."

***

Sara and Dan head outside and turn their phones back on. Dan calls Bailey to update him on the meeting. Sara texts Reece as they walk toward the corner where they were dropped off.

Sara's phone rings.

"Hey, Girl. Where you at?" Reese says when she answers.

"Dan and I are going south on Quebec Street. Can we get a ride?"

Reese says, "Of course. Pulling up beside you now."

Sara looks over, smiles, and ends the call.

They drive to get some food as Dan talks with Bailey, who's still at the FBI field house in Chantilly.

"I gave him all the info we have, and he's going to work his magic. I don't know what he'll find, but he usually comes up with something."

Reese asks over his shoulder, "So where are we goin'?"

Sara asks, "Is there a place where we can sit down and eat? We need to regroup and go over things while we wait for Bailey to do his thing."

Reese looks back and says, "I know a spot. Ten minutes away."

***

Mose leads the group of men toward the drainage pipe at the rear of the commune. They follow him in three flanks of four.

As he gets closer, he spots the broken padlock on the latch.

He reaches out and takes the lock off and tosses it aside and shakes his head.

"Tisk tisk. I guess Dee doesn't think we would follow him through a pipe."

He opens the gate. "First squad, enter and secure for the rest."

After Barajas drops Saul off at the infirmary, he heads back to join the others in an all-terrain vehicle.

Mose spots him and smiles as he approaches. He jumps out of the vehicle and walks up toward the rest of the group.

Mose has an idea as he glances over at the vehicle and asks, "How long would it take you to circle the perimeter and join us on the other side by the creek?"

"Thirty minutes, maybe forty-five."

Mose nods. "Do it."

He points at Chris and Billy and says, "Go with him and get two others. We can use the vehicles to navigate the creek and catch up with Dee."

The men jump into the ATV and head off.

One man approaches Mose. "Sir, slight issue."

Mose turns from watching the ATVs speed off and irritably says, "What is it now?"

"The dogs won't go into the pipe."

He looks over to see another man struggling to convince the dogs to enter the dark enclosure.

Exasperated, Mose throws his hands in the air and says, "Fuck it. The dogs stay home."

Mose follows the second squad through the pipe, and the third squad follows directly after.

The pipe is only a few meters long. The water table is low, but the men's clothing still gets wet.

He pops out of the other side of the pipe, and two of his men assist him onto the stream's bank. Mose looks around and sees his first squad aiming their weapons toward the tree line. One man walks over toward the stream's edge and spots a suspicious water bottle on a rock.

He looks back at Mose and says, "Sir, he left a water bottle. Looks like there's pebbles inside."

Before anyone can stop him, his foot strikes the cord attached to the bottle, and it falls over. The MRE heater inside the bottle rapidly reacts with the water, and the plastic bottle fills with pressure and swells.

Mose shouts, "Get back!"

But it was too late.

The bottle bursts under the pressure, and it sends the pebble, metal, and silt shrapnel several yards in every direction.

One rock strikes Mose across the face, just above his beard, and causes him to lurch backward. He puts his hand up to his cheek as he feels the blood trickle down into his facial hair, slightly warming his face.

He regains his footing, dusts himself off, and looks around. He sees the two men closest to the bomb on the ground. One is screaming in agony and the other is not making any sound at all.

He rolls the quiet man over onto his back. He has a small hole in his neck, and he is gasping for breath.

The shrapnel caused his trachea to collapse.

Mose pulls out his knife and slits a small hole in his neck. He cuts the shoulder straps of the man's CamelBak drink system, cuts a length of drinking tube, and shoves it into the hole to allow him to breathe.

He drags him over toward the concrete pipe and grabs another one of his men by the scruff of his jacket in frustration and says, "Make sure he keeps breathing!"

Mose continues over to the man in pain and says, "Brandon, what hurts?"

Brandon, still in agony, lifts his arm, which is littered with holes, cuts, scrapes, and is most likely broken.

"Fuck!" Mose exclaims. He lets out a frustrated sigh, removes his hat and slaps it on his leg. He helps Brandon up while saying, "On your feet."

He helps him walk over toward the pipe and says, "Sit."

A few other men have scrapes and bruises, but nothing major.

"What should we do with them?" a man named Eddie asks.

Mose looks over and grits his teeth.

"Brandon can't crawl in the pipe with that arm, and that tracheostomy would probably fall out. We need to wait for Barajas to get here. He can take them back in an ATV."

# Chapter Thirty-Three

**Mose** can hear ATVs traveling up the wide bank of the stream. He walks toward the river to see if he can spot them, but can't see around the bend.

Mose walks back over toward the rest of the men and sits on a rock, waiting. He's struggling to keep his patience.

After a little longer, they arrive and spot the men huddled around.

Barajas pulls up and hops off the vehicle and says, "What's going on?"

Mose rolls his eyes and points over toward the injured men and says, "He didn't know what an MRE bomb looked like. But he does now."

"He fell for some basic-ass boot camp trickery?" Barajas asks.

Mose gives a sardonic laugh. "Yep. The one thing they tell you not to do when they hand you your first MRE," he says through gritted teeth.

Barajas rubs his chin and asks, "Should I take them back?"

"Not you. Him!" Mose says, pointing to Billy.

Billy hops off his ATV and says, "Yes, sir!" before turning to the men waiting for instruction. "You heard the man, put 'em in the back!"

Several men help the wounded over toward the ATV and assist them in getting in the dump-bed.

Mose pulls out a map and turns to the driver. "Look here! You get them to the infirmary and take the road up past where the creek meets the river. Clifford Dee will go with the flow of it. You meet us here," he says, pointing at a rendezvous point.

Billy asks, "How do you know he's going that way?"

Mose didn't have time to explain and didn't have the patience either. He looks him in the eye and, through gritted teeth, says, "Because he's smart, that's why!"

Barajas walks up to Mose and asks, "Where are the dogs?"

Saul is lying on a table with a bandage over one eye, in terrible pain.

His wife bursts into the room, and the doctor tries, but fails, to stop her from entering.

"Out!" Jessica yells as she grabs a scalpel from the table next to her husband. She holds it toward the doctor and gestures at the door.

The doctor raises his hands. "Easy, Mrs. McKinley," he says sternly.

As he angles toward the door, she pushes him out of the room, slamming the door before locking it.

She tosses the scalpel to the side, and she rushes to her husband.

"Saul, are you okay?"

"Hi Jessie," he whispers, unable to see her because of the cumbersome bandage blocking his view.

"What happened to your eye?" she asks, tears beginning to well as she looks over the bandage.

He turns his head to see out of his functioning eye, and flatly says, "Mose took it."

"Why!?"

Saul sighs heavily. "He said it's because I turned a blind eye."

Jessica grabs the tray holding the rest of the surgical instruments and throws it across the room.

"That fucking bastard!" she yells.

"Honey, please calm down." Saul begs as the doctor bangs on the locked door.

"I'm going to report this to Skyler, Mrs. McKinley!" he bellows through the door.

"Well," Jessica says, sweeping her hair off her face. "I guess I'd better make it worth my while then, huh?" she says a little too calmly.

"Honey, no, it was my fault."

"Oh?" she says, grabbing the stainless steel surgical table. "So your eye just popped itself out?"

Saul turns away in shame.

"Really, Saul? I told you following Mose was a bad idea."

She hurls the small but sturdy wheeled table into the drywall. The impact causes items from the cabinet above to spill out onto the floor.

She pants as a huge smile grows on her face. "This feels good!" she says as she looks at her astonished husband. "You should try it."

"Honey-" Saul pleads.

"Hey, Dr. Lans!" she yells at the door. "You can just charge me for therapy. How's that sound?"

"You'd better hope he's in a merciful mood when he gets back," the good doctor threatens.

Jessica rolls her eyes and shrugs as she catches her breath. "Saul, where did Clifford Dee go?"

"I- I don't know, into the woods, probably. He asked about the drainage pipe. So, through there, I guess. Why?"

Jessica thinks for a moment. "I'm gonna go find him. My brothers taught me how to track and hunt. I should put that to good use."

"Baby, Skyler is already going after him. We need to worry about your punishment when he returns."

Jessica scoffs, "If Mose wants that man so badly, there's a reason. I'm not gonna track Clifford Dee to kill him. He's gonna help put an end to all of this."

***

Clifford Dee, cold and wet, is staying close to the river's edge as he looks for any signs of human life. So far it's nothing but wilderness, and the sun's setting. Looking for any sign of where he could be geographically, he mentally takes a note of the river's milky-blue hue. He could only guess that he was near a mountain range that hosted glaciers, which were melting.

He's been hiking for hours, and the terrain is becoming rocky and severely uneven. Clifford stops for a moment. He can hear the ATVs in the distance as they echo along the bank. He turns toward the sound, but then stops. It's Mose with a hunting party, and they're gaining on him. His only chance is to head back into the thick, where the vehicles can't follow. This also gives him a chance to find a good place to set up camp for the night, and with any luck, dry his clothing.

Clifford travels away from the bank, toward a rocky incline. He spots an area where a small vehicle could pass and get closer toward the hilly wood-line. He kicks a few rocks, breaks a few sticks near the river, and scatters them in a place that he hopes Mose will notice.

As he gets to the pass, he takes off his pack and digs a small hole, using the mop handle and some flat rocks. Clifford smiles and grabs the tote bag.

After his task, Clifford continues into the woods until he can no longer hear the river.

He continues up the incline and tries to get as deep into the woods as he can.

Clifford spots a small cove inside a wooded glen that's surrounded by several large rocks. He figures this would be the best place to rest up for the evening.

Using his hand stretched out in front of him, he measures the distance from the sun to the edge of the terrain to determine that he has slightly over ninety minutes of daylight left.

Clifford, tired and worn, starts scavenging for twigs, sticks, and small branches. He digs into the remnants of his MRE pack and laughs to himself that he never paid attention to the food before making the bomb. The chili-mac had always been pretty decent.

He huffs at the realization that it won't be as good cold.

"Oh well," he says to himself as he sets it aside.

As his damp clothes against his skin remind him it's growing colder, he pulls out the napkins and matches that are still inside the pack. Working as fast as he can, he uses rocks and sticks to dig a small pit. Combining the napkins and sticks, he starts a "Dakota" fire inside the pit with the matches from the MRE.

The fire's concealed inside a hole and draws the oxygen from a smaller tunnel-connected hole. He sits next to the warm flames and digs into the chili-mac. After a few bites, he reaches back into the MRE bag and finds a pack of crackers. He viciously devours the crackers with the chili. Dumping the rest of the pack on the ground, he sees a large tube of peanut butter.

He laughs to himself as he realizes that's what the crackers were for, and not the chili. He opens the tube and squeezes a small bit into his mouth before deciding to save it for later.

In the distance, he can hear the ATV's growing closer.

Mose, in the lead of the other two vehicles, is moving along the riverside at a quick pace.

He is sitting directly behind Barajas when he spots a footprint on the muddy riverbank.

He taps Barajas on the shoulder and says, "Stop here."

Mose steps off the vehicle and walks back toward the footprint. He sees more prints, and it looks like they were moving toward the wood-line.

He strolls in the direction the footsteps are leading and spots a broken stick and a wrapper from a granola bar.

"Littering's bad, Dee," he says to himself.

Turning back to the hunting party, he yells, "That way!"

Pointing toward a clearing where he believes Clifford would have traveled into the woods, he spies an area where the ATVs could get closer to sweep the area on foot.

Mose points toward the other vehicles and says, "Follow. This way!"

The three vehicles take off up the hill as fast as they can.

Barajas, with Mose seated pillion, speeds into the pass and hits a large lump.

Mose suddenly hears a whirring and whistle from behind him. He looks back to see something launch into the air.

"Shit!" he screams.

The spring mine that Clifford buried is a fraction of a second from exploding when Mose dives off the ATV.

Scolding-hot shrapnel sprays in all directions for yards, striking the ATV behind Mose.

The shrapnel also strikes the driver.

The ATV flips before the third one drives into it, launching the men from it into the air.

Mose's ears are ringing.

He stands up and sees Barajas hunched over, but still seated on his ATV.

"Are you okay?" he yells over.

Barajas shakes his head to clear the ringing in his own ears.

"Yeah, how's everyone else?" He finally answers with a groan.

Mose turns and heads back to the other vehicles to find two of his guys dead and several wounded.

In frustration, he shouts, "Where the *fuck* did he get a God-damned Bouncing Betty!?"

Clifford Dee hears the explosion. He stops in the middle of removing his wet clothes and listens.

He hears nothing but nature.

Pulling himself up onto a small boulder, he can see smoke billowing in the distance.

He knows they'll be busy, and he can afford to rest for a bit.

His attention returns to his wet clothing. He places the garments on sticks, and hovers them over the fire to dry. He wraps himself in a thermal blanket to stay warm overnight.

# Chapter Thirty-Four

**At one of JJ's safe houses** in Boulder. Sara, Dan, and Fabian are reviewing the information they have as Reese calls Bailey on speakerphone.

"Hey B, Reese here."

"Hey man, JJ told me you were the best out there. I'm glad you're with my people."

Reese replies, "Appreciate you. You've got a decent crew. Any leads from the information we sent you?"

Bailey continues, "I ran what I could on Anderson's phone. Found the towers his phone connected to and did some diggin'. There were over three hundred other numbers pinging off the same tower where he met his contact. Now when I moved to the next tower that Anderson's hit and cross-referenced the numbers, I could narrow it down to four of the same phones. By the third tower, only one other number popped."

Sara chimes in, "That's gotta be the guy who took Dee."

Bailey continues, "Yeah, but it's a burner phone. The FBI's looped in already. I don't have all my gear, so they can probably run further with this info."

Dan asks, "Hey, what else can you tell from the guy's burner phone?"

"I know he was traveling northwest. I lost the signal outside of Boise on Route 84."

"Idaho?!" Sara exclaims.

"Yeah. Going Northwest." Bailey confirms.

Sara asks, "Where do you think he was going?"

"I'm not sure. Oregon, maybe Washington. Could be headed up to Canada for all I know, but I doubt they would cross the border with Dee."

Dan chimes in, "So you think he's still in the US?"

Bailey replies, "Most likely. I know I wouldn't cross a border hiding a human."

"Unless they make it look like a medical transport? They *are* professionals." Sara suggests.

Dan nods, "Yeah, they relocate people for a living."

Fabian's eyes grow wide, and he looks to Reece.

"That's true. I almost forgot what we are dealing with," Bailey says. "I'll put a bug in Sims' ear about paying attention to anything like that on the border."

"At least we have a direction to go in." Sara says, looking at Dan.

"I have a few more tricks up my sleeve," Bailey says. "I'm gonna see if I can get a link to a credit card or something. This dude had to have stopped for gas."

Dan asks, "And if he paid in cash?"

"That would make things difficult, but not impossible," Bailey replied.

Reese chimes in and says, "I've got connections in Boise. I say we head up that way. Once you get more info, call your girl, Sara. Maybe we can spring on him before the authorities."

"Good idea!" Bailey says.

"Okay, keep digging and we will head northwest," Sara says just before ending the call.

***

A twig breaks. Clifford Dee's eyes spring open to see a giant moose directly in front of him. The majestic creature leans down, smelling the scent of the peanut butter and chili coming off of Clifford. The moonlight highlights the steam that rolls from the Moose's mouth and nose when he huffs at the scent. Clifford inches away, knowing how dangerous they can be. The moose huffs through its nose again and rises, asserting dominance.

They both know who's in charge.

Clifford reaches over and pulls the peanut butter tube from his bag and spreads some on a nearby pine cone. He lays it flat in his hand and raises it up to the moose. The moose leans back down and sniffs it. With his thick velvety lips and long tongue, he gathers the treat into his mouth and enjoys the offering.

Hearing footsteps in the wilderness, the moose travels toward the sounds.

Clifford notices his fire has cooled, the air is cold, and so is he.

He uses the distraction, slips out of his thermal blanket, trying not to make any sounds that would startle the majestic animal, and starts slipping on his drier clothing. The moose walks toward the sound, navigating the tricky rocks.

Clifford hears someone whistle for another's attention, more footsteps, and then talking.

"You see that big fucking moose up there?"

"What moose?"

"There!"

"Don't shoot it, you idiot!"

"Why not?"

"It's huge! You miss, that thing kills us. Leave it be. Its den's probably up there."

Clifford continues to listen intently to make out what they're saying.

"Hey, the boss wants us to head back to the trail."

"Why?"

"I dunno. I think he wants us to wait until first light. We can't find him in the dark."

"I can smell smoke. He must be close."

"Mose said to report back! Besides, we're not going anywhere near that moose."

"Fine. Let's go."

Clifford waits, keeping an eye on his new friend.

The moose watches as the men retreat down the mountain. He looks over toward Clifford as though he's returning the favor for his snack and steps away in the opposite direction. He waits and listens as the hoof-steps grow quiet.

In the silence, Clifford continues to dress, and press forward. He takes the opportunity and the cover of night to put distance between himself and Mose's men.

Continuing further up the hill, deeper into the wilderness, Clifford discovers it's becoming more and more difficult to walk. The trees become so thick that they're almost impassable.

Until it isn't.

He stumbles out of the thick onto a dirt path, seemingly a small trail for rangers and hikers to navigate the forest.

Clifford smiles and looks up at the night sky.

"Thank you!" he says to whoever's up there looking out for him.

Clifford adjusts his pack and starts hiking with ease down the trail.

A small clearing emerges, and Clifford steps out of the wood.

Creeping along the high grass and bushes. He looks around for any threat until he notices he's in a man-made clearing for power lines.

He follows the lines until he approaches a steep hill. A distant glow of light is on the other side of the hill. Clifford picks up his pace. He circumvents the hill to come up onto a small town. Day-break slowly adds more light as it peaks over the hills just behind the town. Clifford continues southeast toward the town, traveling into the sunrise.

***

All is quiet as Jessica makes her way out of the dense woods and onto a narrow dirt track. She looks around, focusing on the dirt and foliage near the track. After a few minutes, she spots a footprint with a round divot that looks like it was from a walking stick.

Jessica gazes in the direction as she takes a few extra steps. She smiles suddenly. "Mr. Dee goes to town," she says triumphantly.

# Chapter Thirty-Five

**About two hours** past dawn, Clifford finally makes it to the outskirts of a town, thinking Skyler's men should be stumbling upon his little sleeping den from last night. Now being on more even ground, he tests his bad knee. After a few slow bends, the knee pops. Clifford stands straight and lets out a satisfying groan. He tests it again, and can't get a full bend, but it feels stable and supporting. "There it is," he says, and tosses the mop handle on the ground.

Clifford continues down the road a little easier.

The town's quiet. A row of houses stands outside the main drag. Clifford makes his way to the first home with a light on inside. Making his way up the steps onto the porch, he knows he looks like death warmed over after spending time in the wilderness.

Spotting a much older woman through the window, he taps on it.

"Do you have a phone?" He asks.

The woman walks toward the window and pulls the shade.

Not blaming her, he mutters, "I'll try the town, thanks."

He continues further into the town until he sees a police station.

"Help - I need help!" He bellows as he walks into the small station in the quaint town.

A deputy circles a small group of desks, throws her arm around him, and guides him to a seat.

"Sir, I'm Deputy Byres. What's the problem?"

"I need you to call Agent Nathan Fulk of the Denver, Colorado Bureau of Investigation. My name's Clifford Dee. They're probably looking for me. I was in a car accident and abducted in Colorado."

Byres says, "Okay, just take it easy." She looks over to another deputy sitting at his desk and snaps her fingers. "Kissi, get Denver CBI on the line and ask for Fulk."

The younger deputy picks up the phone and starts calling.

A tall, older man with a neatly trimmed moustache walks out of his office.

"What's going on?" he asks with concern.

"Are you the sheriff?"

"Captain Wilson at your service."

"Sir, I just came from a compound. It's called SledgeHaven, I think. West of here, over the mountain."

Interrupting, Wilson asks, "You walked over the mountains?"

Clifford shakes his head. "I followed the stream mostly, but I had to go up into the mountains for a short bit when they started catching up to me."

"Foothills, son. You mean the foothills," the captain explains.

"Who's they?" Byers asks.

"Skyler Mose and his men. He made it clear that if I didn't join them, they'd kill me. They have a compound west of here. I know he's into shady shit, including human trafficking. Obviously, I declined his offer and escaped rather than wait around to be executed."

Captain Wilson scratches his brow. "Well, shit, son, that's a heck of a story."

"It's the truth, not a story. Call Agent Fulk in Denver. He'll vouch for me."

Clifford turns to Byers. "Could I trouble you for some water?" he asks her.

"Of course. I'm so sorry I didn't offer," Byers says as she rushes over toward a water cooler.

Clifford reaches for the small cup of cold water intending to sip it.

It's gone in one gulp.

"I'm so much thirstier than I thought."

Byers pulls another chair next to the water cooler.

"Sit here and refill your cup as much as you need to."

Clifford thanks her and sits next to the cooler.

Deputy Kissinger yells over with his hand over the mouthpiece of his phone.

"I have the Denver CBI on the line, Sir. They said they'll have to track Agent Fulk down. He's not in the office, but they know Clifford Dee. His story about the car accident tracks. Do you want to speak to them or wait for the agent to call back?"

"Have them give Fulk my cell," he says to Kissinger before turning to Byers.

"Let's get an official statement, and then you and I should take a drive to this compound."

After they leave, Kissinger asks Clifford if he'd like to sleep, offering the couch in Captain Wilson's office.

He shakes his head. "I know I'm exhausted, but I can't sleep right now. Can I make a phone call?"

Kissinger turns his desk phone around. "Be my guest."

Clifford dials Rox's cell number, but it goes straight to an automated voicemail.

"Damn," Clifford says in a worried whisper.

Kissinger notices he's starting to spiral mentally.

"Hey Clifford," he says, breaking his intrusive thoughts.

"Ca- Call me Dee," he says casually, realizing it's now become a reaction.

"You got a lot on your mind. How about we play some Mario Kart?"

Clifford chuckles at how much Kissinger reminds him of Dan.

"Sure, bud," he says.

***

Captain Wilson and Deputy Byers pull onto a long dirt road next to a sign that reads, "SledgeHaven - A Private Community."

Underneath it continues, "A small slice of heaven for your family."

Captain Wilson slows over the divots and small rocks on the road and pulls up to a closed gate.

A man emerges from a small building and says, "Hello Sheriff! What can I do for you?"

"I'm Captain Wilson from Summit Creek. We got a report that there was an incident here, yesterday."

The man shakes his head. "Sorry, Captain. There were no incidents yesterday, today, or any other day, for that matter. Are you sure it was here?"

"Yep, that's what he said."

"Who's that now?"

Wilson smiles. "Mind if we drive around a bit? It shouldn't take long."

"Sure, I just have to take down your vehicle information real quick."

He proceeds to the front of the cruiser and starts documenting the car number, license plate, and town.

"I would reach out to our Township Commissioner to escort you, but he's out of town on a supply run with a few others right now. But please, show yourself around if you like."

He heads over to the booth and presses a button to open the gates.

The man glares as Captain Wilson and Deputy Byers pass.

He calls over his radio, "Summit Creek Police coming through the front gate. Says a man showed up there and reported an incident from yesterday."

The broadcast goes to all the radios in the compound, including the one Mose and his men carry.

Byers looks into the distance, and her eyes trace a dirt road to a field where people are laboring. She turns her head and can see kids playing outside a small school and shakes her head.

Wilson loops around a building and heads down another road. He continues down the drive until he reaches the church and enters the small parking lot.

He stops the car and looks over at Byers. "What do you think?"

"I dunno, sir. It looks normal, I guess."

Wilson smooths his mustache.

"It feels itchy," he says.

"How so?" she asks.

"This place. Something's not feeling right. Where are the homes?"

Byers points and says, "It looks like everyone lives in those."

Captain Wilson looks over and sees the row houses she's pointing to.

He shakes his head in disagreement. "I think that might be one big house with different front doors. There are no cars except those over there, behind the church, and I don't see any police buildings or emergency services."

Captain Wilson sees a man wearing a clerical collar coming up to his side of the cruiser.

Captain Wilson rolls down his window.

"I'm Father Strickland. Part of the congregation here."

"Father, do you know of any incidents that happened here yesterday?"

"Oh Lord, no. If something had happened, everyone would have known about it. This is a very small community."

"Mind if I walk about a bit?"

"Of course! Mind if I walk with you?"

Captain Wilson and Byers step out of the car. The captain nods, clips his car keys to his belt-loop, and says, "Sure."

The three begin their walk around the church grounds as Father Strickland speaks.

"This community is only fifteen years old. We were first established by three former military chaplains. They were looking for a quiet and private area to raise their families and worship. They pulled their finances together, purchased this plot of land and created this wonderful, fully functional private community. It's the safest place on Earth. Our little slice of heaven!"

Captain Wilson nods and says, "Like the sign."

"I'm sorry?"

Captain Wilson elaborates, "The sign in the front. It says 'A Slice of Heaven' or something."

The Father chuckles. "Ah, yes, like the sign."

They continue to walk as Father Strickland tells them little brochure-style facts about the town.

Captain Wilson feels his foot graze on something that doesn't fit the terrain.

Father Strickland continues to walk until he realizes the captain is no longer next to him. Father Strickland turns to see the captain looking at something on the ground.

"Deputy, could you hand me an evidence bag, please?" Captain Wilson says.

Father Strickland's eyes narrow as he watches Wilson retrieve, and look closely at, a pair of bloodied handcuffs hovering just above the ground on the end of his pen.

"Gosh, I really wish you weren't the one to find those," Strickland says quietly enough for only Captain Wilson to hear. He pulls a gun, firing a bullet into the side of Wilson's head.

Deputy Byers draws her pistol from a few yards away, and fires a round into Father Strickland's chest.

A shot rings out in the distance. A bullet grazes Byers in the shoulder, and she falls to the cold, hard ground with a thud. Another round fires off in her direction, narrowly missing her head.

She scoots closer to Captain Wilson's body, through a pool of his blood, using him as a human shield.

Two more rounds hit Wilson, intended for her. She reaches down toward his belt to unclip his keys while several more shots hit the captain. "Shit, shit, shit," she says in panic.

Blood sprays across her face and neck. She's struck by a round that goes through his body first and lodges in her radio, knocking her backward onto her back. She scoots back, close to the body of her captain. Her fingers, slick with his blood, continue to slip on the keychain until finally, she's able to unclip the keys and hold them tightly.

She lies on the ground for a minute, counts to three, and jolts up from underneath the captain, making a mad-dash toward the police cruiser. Several rounds fire off, every one of them missing her as she zig-zags through the open area.

As she reaches the car, she dives across the hood, followed by bullets dancing across it behind her. Metal chips and paint spray as she hits the ground on the other side of the vehicle. She opens the door and climbs into the car and starts it.

Staying down, she uses her hand to apply the brake and uses her other hand to put the car into drive as bullets shatter the glass and spray debris across her back.

The car slowly rolls toward the broadside of the church.

The area is quiet as the tires crunch across the frosted grass and frozen dirt. She steers the cruiser behind the church to use it for cover and pops up into the seat.

Byers cries in pain.

"Fuck. Fuck. Fuck."

She grabs the radio in the car, but it's dead. The antenna, broken.

Feeling panicked, she tosses the useless radio transmitter.

Noting how quiet it is, she assumes that whoever was shooting at her is repositioning.

She needs to go. And fast.

Byers takes a deep breath as she scoots fully into the driver's seat and mashes the accelerator.

The cruiser lunges forward, and she bolts from behind the church. She finds the road as more bullets ring out. One strikes the back window, breaking it. She continues toward the front of the compound, noticing security bollards rising to prevent her from leaving via the road.

She cuts the wheel and sends the cruiser through the fence, down a small incline, and hops a small drainage ditch.

The cruiser lurches, and she loses control for a moment. The car tail-spins, but she quickly regains control, and speeds back to town.

# Chapter Thirty-Six

**Clifford** and Kissinger are playing video games when Clifford suddenly pauses the game. Kissinger perks up and looks over at Clifford, who's frozen.

"Sounds like Motorbikes or something," Kissinger suggests.

Clifford shakes his head and says, "ATVs."

"Oh yeah, good ear. Those are definitely four-wheel ATVs. You're good."

Clifford sets the game controller down.

"So, am I under arrest right now?"

Kissinger shakes his head. "I don't think so. Cap didn't say anything about holding you. Why?"

"Is there a back door in this place?"

"Yeah, down the hall to your right. Why?"

"I gotta go. You should probably go, too."

"I can't leave the station empty."

Clifford stands up and says, "They will kill me the second they see me," as he heads down the hall. The sounds of the ATVs grow loud.

Kissinger yells down the hall, "Hey, should I be worried?"

Clifford yells back, "Very!"

Kissinger stands up and heads over to the weapons room while Clifford continues toward the back exit.

Clifford opens the precinct parking lot door, and a tall woman immediately grabs him, holding a knife to his throat.

Wide-eyed and alert, but disheveled from her own trek in the woods, Jessica demands, "Are you Clifford Dee?"

"If I say yes, are you going to swipe left?"

Jessica's brow furrows. "What? I don't know what that means! Are you Dee or not?"

"Okay, yes," he says, as the sound of the ATV's get closer.

She holsters her knife.

"They're getting close. Come with me."

Jessica ushers Clifford back to the main road in front of the station. She can feel his hesitation.

"They haven't reached the bend in the road yet. They won't have visuals of us."

She tugs his arm before she darts across the road, and Clifford follows. They reach an alley next to an empty building with a commercial real estate sign in the front window.

Jessica kicks open the side entrance from the alley and pushes Clifford inside, closing the door behind her.

"Who the fuck even are you?" Clifford asks, confused.

"Name's Jessica. You met my husband, Saul."

"Saul?"

Jessica nods. "The one you chatted up before leaving the compound."

Clifford thinks. "Oh, right... hole in the perimeter fence."

Jessica huffs. "Because he didn't stop or kill you, Mose gouged out one of his eyes."

"Jesus!"

"Funny. Mose acts like he's the second fuckin' coming."

Clifford shakes his head. "You don't sound like you're under his spell."

Jessica looks out onto the street from a gap in a boarded-up window as a car drives by.

She turns to look at him.

"My father liked to call me 'The Observer'. I clocked Skyler Mose a mile away."

She looks back at the road as another car drives by, going the speed limit. "I am curious what Mose is going to do," she says. "I've never seen him this manic before. You've really fucked with his head, huh?"

Clifford joins Jessica at the window. "I never knew Mose to be religious. Well, to be fair, I actually don't know Skyler Mose. The man's name was Kyle Somers when I knew him."

"I'm sure he has a few more aliases with passports sitting in a lockbox," she says, shaking her head. "And he's not religious. Just uses religion and violence to keep his sheep compliant. He has his tentacles in a lot of shit the community isn't aware of."

"So," she glances at him. "You two have history? Is that why he's after you?"

Clifford smiles, "Our history has nothing to do with him trafficking children to the highest bidder."

"Fucking hell! I knew it," she replies.

"What do you mean?" Clifford asks

"He shows up in the community sporadically with new people and then poof, they're gone. Mose, too. It's mostly young women and children. Boys and girls. They blow in and blow out like the wind. We're not allowed to question and no one in town mentions them. It's like they never existed."

Jessica tenses up when she spots Mose's men riding into town. "He's here," she says through gritted teeth.

Clifford watches the ATVs, built more for utility than speed, slow down even further as they come into view on rugged MT tires not meant for asphalt.

"I feel bad for Kissinger."

"Who?"

"The Deputy, in the station; He's alone."

Jessica shrugs.

Clifford continues, "Young guy. Pictures of kids on his desk."

Jessica lets out an exasperated sigh and shoves her sidearm at Clifford.

Barajas hides the pain he's still feeling and the frustration of his impaired hearing from the landmine explosion as Mose gives him an order.

"Take a few men and do a loop around town. Don't waste too much gas," he says before snapping his fingers and pointing at one other. "Sean, keep an eye on the front. Eddie, you watch my back in here. Let's go."

Barajas orders two men to stay ahead of him and three others to pace behind him as he revs the engine.

Kissinger keeps his eyes on the men in front of the station as he walks from the holding cells back to his desk. He glances at the two rifles he propped against his desk earlier and places a Glock in his open desk drawer.

He continues watching through the front window as one of the ATVs breaks from the group, along with several individual men walking in pace in front and behind the utility vehicle.

"Hello officers!" Mose says as he enters the station with one of his men.

"It's just me. Deputy Kissinger. How can I help you?" Kissinger says warily.

"Just you, huh?" Mose smiles and moves across the room, angling toward the desks.

"Sir, I'm gonna need you to stay behind the desks, please."

Mose raises his hands to show he means no harm and takes a step back. He musters a smile.

"I'm looking for someone. You tell me which way he went... I'll be on my way."

Kissinger looks over at Eddie, the companion who walked in with Mose. He stays in the doorway, keeping the front door wide open.

He's laser-focused on every move Kissinger makes.

The Deputy keeps his eye on Eddie's hands as he slowly sits up and asks Mose, "Who're you lookin' for?"

Mose follows Kissinger's gaze. He signals his bodyguard to relax with a hand signal.

"A felon escaped our community," Mose says before pausing with a smirk. "Needs to finish out his sentence. You understand."

Kissinger places his fingers over his keyboard and asks, "Of course, what's his name?"

"He's, uh, a member of a *private* community. Different set of laws," Mose says, expressionless.

Fighting natural impulses, Kissinger remains stoic. He now understands Dee's parting words.

He forces a smile through the building fear. "What makes you think he's here?"

Mose's patience is paper thin. He closes his eyes and sighs.

"I don't have time for this," he mutters as he reaches for his gun hidden in the back of his waistband.

A rifle bullet hits Eddie from behind, and his chest explodes out inside the doorway.

"Hey, fuckface!" Dee yells, taking aim toward Mose from behind the door leading to the station's two holding cells. He fires a round at Mose to force him to scramble into a better angle so he can take him out once and for all.

Mose, instead, dives backward towards the back hallway.

Kissinger grabs one of the two rifles and fires toward Mose, barely missing him. Mose blindly returns fire as he sprints to the back entrance.

From her perch on the second floor of the empty building, Jessica observes Barajas turn right in his ATV as three of the men sent to walk alongside him stop at the sound of the gunfire coming from the station.

They run back, moving their rifles from their backs to the ready position as she takes aim. Jessica's next bullet passes through the neck of the man she knew as Ricky. She smiles as the wife-beater's blood spurts and pours out of him and his body crumples to the ground.

Mose exits the station back to meet with Sean, who'd taken cover behind a parked car since the first shot rang out on the main street.

"Where's the sniper?"

Sean, holding his rifle, points to a building across the street and to the right. Mose looks over and spies the sniper's position from a window on its second floor.

Plaster explodes near Jessica's head as Mose sends several rounds her way. She ducks for cover away from the window. Jessica moves quickly to the windows, on the other side of the room. Peering out, she sees Barajas still moving down the other street slowly, as he looks around, focusing in between buildings and windows.

Clifford runs over to Kissinger. "You okay?"

Kissinger nods, "Yeah. I'll be fine. Thanks for coming back."

Clifford notices the tremble in Kissinger's voice. He knows the young man has never been in a real gunfight like this before.

Kissinger reloads. "Who took the first shot?"

"A woman from Mose's compound. He pissed her off, and lucky for us, she's the vengeful type."

Jessica runs down the steps of the old building to the main floor. Billy, walking ahead of Barajas, ducks into the alleyway to make his way back to the main road.

Jessica wraps her scarf around her left hand while she waits for him to move past the same door she kicked open earlier.

With his focus ahead of him to what's unfolding at the station, and his gun held down at his right side, Jessica sneaks up behind the man who's a few inches shorter than herself.

As she plunges her ten-inch Bowie knife into Billy's liver, she brings her scarf-wrapped fist around the other side and shoves it into his mouth.

He drops the gun as his muffled scream barely makes it past the woolen fabric.

Despite the pressure of his teeth as his jaw tightens, Jessica pulls her bare hand out from the scarf shoved in his mouth and pivots. She twists and pulls the knife out of his back as his legs fail him. With one swift motion, she slits his throat.

Jessica drags his body by his hair back into the vacant building to give Mose something to find if he breaches it. She pulls the scarf out of Billy's mouth and gazes at the frozen expression on his face as she uses the scarf to clean her knife. She silently curses herself for getting so much blood on her coat sleeve.

The men still in the street in front of the station lay cover fire until Mose reaches them.

"Okay, boys, we got a sniper on the second floor over there," he yells, pointing to where he fired at Jessica.

He looks around. "Where the fuck is Barajas?!"

Chris returns, panting. "He's still patrolling the next street over. I don't think he can hear over his engine." He stops to look around. "Billy must still be with him."

Mose seethes. "Get Billy and the two of you better clear that fucking sniper. Whoever it is, I want them *eliminated*!"

Seeing at least two of his men dead on the street, Mose decides to make another sacrifice.

He squeezes the brake of one of the ATVs and then jams a stick on the accelerator. The back wheels start smoking as the rubber burns from sitting in place while spinning. He releases the brake and the ATV jolts forward, up the steps of the police station and through the front door.

The utility vehicle works like a battering ram to the opened front door and comes to a stop against a desk.

Clifford narrows his eyes and sniffs the air. "Gasoline!"

Kissinger points to the back of the building. "Go-Go!"

Mose tosses a lit road flare from his position to the stream of gas leading to the new destruction.

Another shot rings out from the street over and Mose feels confident Barajas is handling the surprise sniper as he watches the flames dance across the road, up the steps, and into the police station.

Kissinger pulls Clifford away from the building just as a small explosion rocks the town. "This way. Let's go!"

Mose smiles. With the sniper busy or contained and Dee with his young Deputy busy fleeing, he and his men make their way into the open street again.

The loud roar of an engine on his left side catches the group off guard.

Mose looks over to see a police cruiser quickly bearing down on their group.

"Move!" he shouts.

The men dive out of the way, but not before Byers strikes two of them. Mose hits the ground again and rolls out of the way. The cruiser slams into two other ATVs, destroying them.

She skids to a stop, cutting the wheel for the vehicle to be used for cover just past the burning station.

She leaps out of the side, pulls a shotgun, and starts laying suppressing fire, sending them scrambling for cover. Chris takes off between two buildings and attempts to flank Byers, when he runs into Jessica.

Kissinger cheers, "Byers! Fuck yeah!"

He and Clifford turn back and hurry over toward Byers' car while Mose and what's left of his men scramble from the street to take cover.

Jessica leaves Chris' body in the alley and joins Clifford and Kissinger with Byers behind her car. Barajas finally figures out that Mose's plan has gone sideways. He turns the ATV to go back.

Kissinger slides down beside Byers. Clifford joins them, but Jessica grabs him and points toward the mountainous tree line. "We should go!"

Clifford looks down at her bloodied sleeve as she, again, sheaths her knife, and then over at Byers and Kissinger. "We're not leaving them like this."

Mose leads his men into an alley. He follows a thick blood trail to a broken side door into the same building he knew the sniper had been.

He pushes the door open. "Found Billy," he says in exasperation.

Kissinger examines Byer's gunshot shoulder. "Cap?"

Byers shakes her head and raises her dried blood covered hands. "I barely got out of that shitty cult town."

Clifford feels remorse over Wilson's death. He eyes Jessica's soaked sleeve again. "How many did you take out?"

"Only four," she says with disappointment in her voice.

"Damn," Kissinger says as he shares a brief look with Clifford.

She points and asks, "Hey, who's that?"

***

"Holy shit! It's a fuckin' war zone!" Dan yells as they get closer.

"I see Dee!" Sara says, feeling relieved to see her friend still alive. Fabian races toward the carnage on the road ahead of them. He brakes and turns the wheel to offer more cover while Reece leans out of the window, laying suppressive fire.

Dan opens his door and rushes to Dee's side before Fabian comes to a complete stop.

Clifford has never been so relieved to see his friends.

Reese yells across, "Clifford Dee, JJ sends her regards!"

Jessica looks for movement through the smoke and dust. She spots Mose through a window on the first floor of the building across the street. She bolts from her secure position to get a better angle.

"Jess!" Clifford yells as she hurries off.

Sara positions herself with Fabian and Reece behind their car.

"Hey, Dee?" she yells over the car.

Clifford smiles at the sound of his friend's voice. "Yeah?"

"Missed ya, Bud. Love your girlfriend, by the way."

Dee nearly chokes. "Rox is alive?!"

Sara smiles to herself as she cocks her weapon. "Let's get you two crazy kids back together. Whadya say?"

The sudden stop of gunfire casts an eerie silence over the town. Dan lies flat under the police cruiser to get a better visual. He notices a carefully moving man focusing on something.

Dan sits up and looks over to see that Jessica has taken cover, and Barajas notices her movements. He turns back to see Barajas sling his gun over his shoulder as he climbs a fire escape for a higher position, attempting to get a view of the movement he spotted.

Dan makes his way to Sara.

"Cover me," he says, gripping one of the ninja stars he took from Fabian's trunk.

"Go!" she yells as she and Reece stand, securing the area.

Dan sprints to position himself behind Barajas in the alley.

Surrounded by the metal of the fire escape, Barajas sees a rifle barrel jetting out from behind a covered area. He waits for a clear shot. When it presents itself, he carefully takes aim, center mass. The throwing star bounces off the handrail and strikes Barajas in his forearm.

"Fuck!" he shouts as it pierces his arm. His last shot goes wide.

Jessica rolls out of the way and scurries back to Clifford and the Deputies.

Barajas curses loudly as he pulls the star from his flesh and tosses it on the ground before entering the building through a window he broke with the butt of his gun.

Flames from the burning police station reflect in Skyler's eyes as he seethes with anger.

Barajas approaches, gripping his wounded arm. "Mose!"

Mose snaps back to the present as the call breaks his gaze.

Barajas continues, "We need to go before we're completely surrounded. We should regroup."

Mose says through his teeth. "Surrounded implies comple- never mind, who's still alive?" he asks with an exasperated hiss.

Barajas looks at Sean and Wayne. "We're it."

# Chapter Thirty-Seven

**As the feds** show up, the Summit Creek fire department has the fires under control.

Reece shakes Dan's hand while Fabian surprises Sara with a big hug.

"Hope to see you guys again. This was actually kinda fun," Reece says, leaning in for his own hug from Sara.

"Stay in touch," she says. Reese smiles as he looks back. "You know I will, Badass!"

The group huddles in the library to go over everything.

Interim Captain Byers informs the FBI of her findings at the SledgeHaven Ranch while Deputy Kissinger gives his own statement.

Byers finishes her statement and walks up and waits as Clifford is in conference. Sara and Dan join her in waiting. Byers looks over at Sara.

"Where are the others that helped?" she asks.

"Well, those two guys were just our Uber," Sara says, with Dan nodding behind her.

"Uh-huh," Byers says.

Clifford scoots back from the table and stands up. He walks to the group and smiles.

She looks around and says, "Did Jessica leave with their Uber driver?"

Clifford shrugs. "No, I think she's got something else in mind."

***

Mose and his men walk until the sun sets across the mountain range. They decide to shelter in the hills, still a half-day's walk from SledgeHaven, and radio calls to the community go unanswered.

Mose cannot sleep, confounded by how Clifford Dee could make so much go wrong in such a short amount of time. He pulls first-watch and sits up, staring into the fire until Barajas wakes in the wee hours of the morning.

"Boss, why are you still up?" He asks.

Mose is silent.

Barajas moves closer.

"I have a terrible feeling, Barajas," Mose finally says somberly, looking back into the light of the fire. "We haven't been able to reach home base. We're still hours away, and we will need to move... again."

"What about Big Sky?" Barajas asks.

Mose nods. "Yes, but first I need to call in another favor."

"What's the favor?"

Mose grins. "*The* favor."

Barajas looks over toward the men sleeping and back at Mose. "Do we have enough resources to start over?"

"Not from scratch. I think we need to take a different approach. Top down. And I know just the person who can help."

Barajas says, "Well, shit, in that case, Happy Birthday, Boss."

Mose looks at him confused, so Barajas continues. "You're being reborn, so today's your birthday."

Mose smirks. "Would you look at that; I'm born in winter."

Night fades to morning, and they make their way back down the side of the mountain, heading toward the road when they hear a caravan of vehicles echo off the hillside.

Mose stops and takes a covered position to get a look.

After a minute, he spots several dark SUVs, armored cars, and US military troop carriers driving away from the direction of SledgeHaven. Mose hands Barajas his binoculars without a word.

Barajas takes a quick look and says, "I hope this doesn't mean what I think it does."

Mose stands up. "Let's take the scenic route instead of the road."

Hours later, Mose stands in a clearing on a hilltop looking miles away at the SledgeHaven church, billowing smoke. There are several National Guard troops inside, clearing the smaller buildings and detaining people. News vans and reporters stand near the perimeter, covering the story.

His attention turns toward the valley where the river splits the hills when he spots movement, and changes his position to get a better look.

He identifies several people from the community and says, "Let's move!"

They race down the hillside with haste to meet up with their people.

Brandon, walking with a bad limp and his arm bandaged from the injuries the bottle bomb caused, spots Mose and says, "Skyler! The feds attacked us!"

Mose walks up and throws his arms around him.

"Brandon! Come away from the river. They have choppers in the air looking. We must take cover in the trees."

"Skyler!" Doctor Lans shouts.

Mose turns to see him helping Saul navigate.

He pivots as he asks Barajas to help Brandon while he talks with Dr. Lans.

"You got it, boss," Barajas says, as he takes Brandon from his grasp and walks away.

Mose grabs onto Saul to help as Doctor Lans says, "Skyler, I must tell you something."

Mose can feel Saul tighten under his grip.

"What is it, Doc?"

Doctor Lans catches his breath as he adjusts his glasses. "As a doctor, I want to help people, but I am also loyal to you. I could have left him to the feds, but I brought Saul here to confess. Mrs. McKinley trashed the infirmary when she discovered her husband's condition. I'm sure they were plotting against you, but it was hard for me to hear. She locked me out of the infirmary, so I can't tell you what she said... but he can," he says with a nod toward Saul.

"Where is Mrs. McKinley?" Mose asks.

When Saul doesn't immediately answer, Dr. Lans speaks up.

"She left the compound not long after you did," he volunteers.

"Oh, she did, did she?" Mose says more to himself than anyone else. He quickly reflects on what he knows about Jessica McKinley, and the realization of who the sniper was in Summit Creek smacks him.

He scowls at her husband.

"What did she say, Saul?" he asks with feigned politeness through clenched teeth.

Saul stands quietly.

"Use your words, you fuckin' simp! What did she say!?"

Saul still doesn't speak. His defiance is clear, but so is his trembling.

Mose breathes in deeply and clenches his fists. He raises his left one, ready to punch an injured man with his weaker arm.

All of Mose's followers have noticed the confrontation and are watching.

He relaxes for a second as he whispers to himself, "No."

In a flash, Mose strikes Saul with his right fist into his left, empty, orbital socket. Saul stumbles backward and screams in pain.

"What did she say?!" he yells over Saul's scream.

"Skyler, please!" Doctor Lans pleads, surprised by the sudden violence of his patient.

Mose turns toward the doctor and says, "He and his big cunt of a wife caused us to lose our home."

"Jessica was right about you all along," Saul whimpers.

Mose smiles as Saul finally finds his words. He raises his gun as Saul continues, "You're a bully and a bad person. I shouldn't have trus-"

Mose fires a bullet directly into Saul's good eye.

"Shut the fuck up," he says calmly.

The followers he has left stare in awe.

"Dammit," Mose says under his breath as he walks to higher ground.

"People!" he says, projecting his voice while navigating a large rock.

The group looks at their leader, confused at what just happened, as Mose continues.

"Family. I am sorry you had to see that. I just learned that Saul and his wife Jessica have been plotting against us. *She* is the one who sent the Feds. And *she* is the reason we could not get Clifford Dee in time. They were all working together."

People in the group start looking around and nodding. Someone in the back yells out, "Fuck that bitch, Jessica!" and the rest of the group replies, "Yeah."

Another voice called out, "I never trusted her!"

Mose waves his arms. "Calm down. They tricked us. And we were the fools, but... I have a trick of my own."

The group moves closer, and Mose notices.

"No, not here. I can't tell you here. First, we need to split up and heal. Head into the trees and travel in groups, no more than four."

The group talks among themselves until one man asks, "Where do we go now?"

Mose nods. "Timothy? Is that right?" Tim nods as he continues. "Splitting up makes it harder for them to track us. Go East. In thirty days, we will regroup when it's safe."

Another man looks up from the crowd. "Meet up where?"

Mose looks sternly and says, "We're going to Big Sky!"

Tim asks, "What if they told them about that too?"

Mose nods and says, "We can't talk now. I just need your trust."

The people look around in agreement, and Tim says, "We trust you."

Mose jumps down from the rock to share the ground with Tim and takes him into his confidence. "Timothy, I have a special mission for you." Mose hands him the gun that he used to kill Saul.

# Chapter Thirty-Eight

**After staying overnight** in a Washington hospital, Clifford Dee flies for a scheduled meeting with Fulk and Sims at Denver's FBI Headquarters.

The FBI task leaders and the board of directors wait to listen to the details of Clifford's experience with Skyler Mose and his community at SledgeHaven.

The board hears from Clifford Dee, Sara, and Dan of BluTrace Investigations, as well as Special Agent Sims, who also reads a statement from Bailey about his attack. Agent Fulk and Captain Gates sent in reports as well.

They read victim impact statements that Grace and Hadley had prepared. Once the review is over, the board wants a private discussion, asking for the room.

In the hallway, Clifford sits alone and looks out the window, across the city of Denver.

Sara slowly approaches. "Hey."

Clifford looks up. "Hey."

"What do you think they're talking about in there?"

Clifford sits for a moment, looks away, and then back up at Sara.

"How to punish us. What to do with us. I dunno."

"Sims wouldn't let them-"

"I don't think Sims is really running this show," Clifford interrupts. "He might give his opinion, but he doesn't decide."

The doors to the conference room swing open, and Sims invites everyone back into the room.

They all file in, and Sims stands in the back near the door.

When the door shuts, the head of the board stands up.

"Clifford Dee, we've reviewed everything. The FBI acknowledges evidence of your abduction, and we believe you are a victim in this case. We also wanted to let you know we found very little usable evidence of human trafficking, as we don't see a strong link from your original case to this. We have very little evidence of weapons dealing, and no evidence of conspiracy against the United States of America.

"But because of their attack on a police precinct, we're going to continue to track Skyler Mose and the rest of his group to bring him to justice."

Clifford looks over toward Sara and Dan and then back at the director as they continue.

"As I said before, you were a victim, but also you and your team broke laws. With that said, we also decided that you acted on impulse, which helped discover missing children. You acted on impulse after your abduction, which directly led to what happened in the Washington State community of SledgeHaven. Because of this, we will not file any charges against you, and no charges to your team or company."

Clifford's chest lightens. The tension that was building evaporates into nothing, and a small smile grows on his face.

"However, we will place you on probation. An agent will be assigned to your team. They will be in charge of what cases you take and will send us all reports of these cases."

Clifford asks, "For how long?"

"One year. The start date will be determined later."

Clifford nods and says, "Understood."

"But it will not be Special Agent Sims."

Sims looks over in shock as he believed he would have been a shoo-in for the position.

The board director continues, "Sims has become too much of an ally to you. He made that perfectly clear during this investigation, and we feel it would be a conflict of interest to allow him to be the liaison. We've selected Agent Glen Arbor. He will report your activities directly to us. You must provide him with reports of all your clientele and anyone you partner with. When Agent Arbor makes his temporary duty arrangements, we can give you a better idea of the start date."

Clifford looks over at Sims and then back at the director. "Understood," Clifford says again.

The director gathers up the files on the table in front of her and stands after she straightens them. "Everyone's dismissed. Clifford, I need you in my office to sign some paperwork, and you can be on your way."

"Yes, Ma'am," Clifford says as he stands.

He looks over toward Sara and Dan, flashing a quick smile of relief.

Dan nods, and Sara smiles back.

# Chapter Thirty-Nine

**Dan** and Sara leave the boardroom and head downstairs ahead of Clifford and Sims.

Clifford walks out of the Board of Directors chambers and heads down the hallways of the FBI. Sims catches up to him.

Clifford turns and smiles when he sees him.

"Great meeting, huh?"

The smile on Clifford's face fades. "So, Agent Arbor, huh? Do you know him?"

"He's a good kid," Sims says, trying to ease Clifford's mind as they begin their ride down in the elevator. "Relatively new to the club here. It'll be a good assignment for him. I think he'll fit right in with you guys. Oh, and before I forget," Sims says as he hands him a brand new phone.

"From Bailey. All you need to do is log in."

A smirk grows on Clifford's face. "Cool, thanks," he says, unboxing it and placing it in his back pocket.

He'd gotten used to not having a leash, but knows his partner wouldn't tolerate a lack of communication with him any longer.

Sims smiles and hands him something else. A watch.

Clifford laughs. "Really?" he asks. The elevator doors open and he tosses the empty phone box into the trashcan just outside of them.

Sims chuckles and says, "Yeah, he said you'd like that one best."

As Clifford rounds the corner to the lobby, he spots Rox sitting next to Sara.

His heart leaps from his chest as he sees her in a neck brace. She has a faded bruise on her left eye and a few scrapes and cuts on her beautiful face.

"Rox!" escapes his lips. He rushes over at near full sprint.

"Bruised ribs, Dee!" Sara yells as she spots him coming up to them.

Rox shifts her body in the chair in time to see Dee slide on his knees up to her. He wraps his arms around her waist.

Rox smiles through the tears. The cervical collar keeps her from looking down. She cradles his head in her lap, raking her fingers through his hair. "There he is," she whispers.

He makes a guttural sound that's a mix between a laugh and a sob.

Sara covers her mouth as she stands up. Her own tears fall as she makes her way over to Daniel. She turns, leaning her back against him so they can both enjoy the reunion.

Dan puts his arm around his friend and whispers, "This is awesome."

Clifford sits up and gently cradles Rox's face. "Oh, honey. I'm so sorry. How do you feel?"

"Like I could fly," she says, laughing and wiping away tears.

Clifford presses his forehead to hers, trying to be mindful of her injuries. He fights the desire to pull her into him for a long overdue kiss.

"I'm so sorry," he whispers again.

"Yeah, how dare you get abducted," she gently teases.

Still on his knees, he sits back and places his hands on her legs as he searches her face.

"You've been in constant danger since we met."

Rox places her hands over his. "You've never put me in danger. That psycho and his minions did this; not you. You protected me."

"I still wouldn't blame you if you never wanted to see me again," Clifford says, gently touching her cheek on the edge of her bruise.

Rox holds his hand still as she presses her cheek into his palm. "A friend of mine visited me in the hospital, and I told her all about you," she says with a smile. "She helped me understand something."

Clifford tilts his head. "What's that?"

"That *you* are the greatest adventure of my life."

Clifford smiles. "I'd love to meet her."

"Well, you'd need a Ouija board," she says with a chuckle. "Kate passed away years ago, but she knew how to live."

Clifford shakes his head with a soft chuckle.

"Do you remember what we were talking about before we were... rudely interrupted?" Rox asks.

Clifford nods with a wry smile.

He sighs before the smile completely fades.

"I don't look forward to any day without you in it, but I can't promise you a calm life," he finally says.

Rox narrows her eyes. "I don't remember asking anyone for a calm life, Mr. Dee."

Clifford cradles her head in both of his hands and leans toward her. "I love you," he whispers.

She moves to wrap her arms around his neck when she suddenly says in frustration, "Fuck this thing!"

Rox grabs at her neck brace and pulls the Velcro apart. Before Clifford can protest, the brace falls onto the empty chair next to her.

"Help me stand up," she demands, and Clifford obliges.

Rox steps into his arms and buries her face in his chest. He holds her for a minute before taking a step back. She looks up at him carefully until she visibly winces.

"I'm going to kiss you, and then we're putting that thing back on," Clifford says just as he tilts his head and presses his lips to hers. He continues to cradle her head to keep her neck stable as he deepens the kiss.

The sound of Sims clearing his throat breaks the spell. Clifford and Rox acknowledge they had forgotten about their audience. Clifford holds her steady as he retrieves the foam brace.

"I won't fall," she says with a chuckle.

"I know. I just don't want to stop touching you right now."

"Well, that's gonna make going to the bathroom awkward," she quips.

"Marry me," Clifford says as he secures the Velcro straps under Rox's ponytail.

"Hmm, No. But, we can revisit that," Rox says softly.

"Can I convince you to make a cross-country move?"

"Easily, but I'm definitely getting a job, and you have to embrace being a cat dad."

"I love Baskets as though he were my own. You'll have to embrace self-defense and weapons training."

Sara walks over while Dan asks Sims about travel logistics.

"Ooh, I can teach her!" Sara interrupts when she reaches them. "You and Baskets can even bunk with me, too."

"Well, it appears my fur baby and I have some options, and a cross-country drive will give me plenty of time to think about it."

Clifford looks down at Rox. "You're not making this move by yourself."

"I can make the drive with her?" Sara offers.

"No, no, no, no," Clifford protests as he wraps his arms around Rox. "I'm not letting her out of my sight for a very long time."

"You'll get no argument from me," Rox says, leaning into him.

Sims walks over with Daniel. "The three of us will fly back today," he says, nodding towards Sara, who's looking at her phone.

Sara looks up from a text and over at Clifford. "Hey Dee, Bailey says to log into your phone. He wants to call you."

Clifford does as he's told. He gives Rox several more kisses on her head as he waits for the phone to load.

Several chimes and vibrating bursts of queued notifications come through on the new phone. He sees a text from Grace and opens it immediately.

*You will find extra funds in your account.*

*I'm taking Hadley out of the country for a while.*

*I'm forever indebted to you, Clifford. Thank you.*

"See you in a few days?" Sara asks

Clifford gives her a thumbs up. "A few days. Oh, and do me a favor."

Sara asks, "What's up?"

"Give this to Bailey. I don't want to lose it during the move."

Clifford hands her the folded-up note he took while in the church at the SledgeHaven community.

"What's this?" She asks.

"A phrase I saw on a painting. I thought it looked important."

Sims pulls out his phone.

"I'll meet you and Dan at the airport in an hour."

Sara says, "Aye aye, Captain!" and turns with Dan toward the door.

# Chapter Forty

**The drive** to Northern Virginia is uneventful.

As Clifford approaches the neighborhood and turns down his street, the mood changes. The sky grows dark. Clifford can see his team standing outside, waiting for them.

"Oh no, something's wrong!" he says with a tone of worry in his voice.

Rox looks over and sees everyone as well.

"Why are they outside?" he asks. His voice fills with worry as he feels fear building.

"Dee, relax, honey. I think they're the welcoming committee."

The car comes to a stop, and everyone has abnormal smiles on their faces and is strangely happy. Clifford can see Sara, Dan, Bailey, and Sims, but there's a dark cloud surrounding them. In the distance, a large sand squall approaches and covers the buildings, trees, road - everything.

The sandstorm parts and out walks Skyler Mose.

"I'm coming for you, Dee!" he says in a deep, ominous voice.

Behind Mose is every person Clifford killed. "We all are!" they say in unison.

Clifford looks at Rox. Her eyes roll to the back of her head, and she stops moving. Old, decayed flowers lay in her lap. Blood flows over her lips and runs down her chin. Her eyes disappear into her skull, and black sludge drips from her eye sockets. She groans in pain, and her skin withers before his eyes.

"Help!" he screams as he turns toward his friends, now all dead, decapitated, and lying on the ground.

"One-two-three-four-five, Clifford Dee is still alive. One-two-three-four-five, Clifford Dee is still alive. One-two-three-four-five, Clifford Dee is still alive."

Rox shakes Clifford awake.

"Dee! Oh my God! Are you okay?"

Clifford's eyes open. He's been talking in his sleep.

He focuses on catching his breath as he sits up.

"Yeah. It- It was just a dream..." he says as he squeezes his eyes shut. The cool air hits the sweat on his skin, and he shivers.

Clifford takes a few deep breaths and runs his fingers through his hair. He's still amazed by the reality of the nightmare.

Rox gets out of the bed and says, "I'll get you some water."

She heads into the kitchenette of the hotel suite.

She joins Clifford as he stands at the door to the balcony looking at the spectacular view of the Gateway Arch, the midpoint of their journey to Virginia.

"What's with the counting?" She asks, handing him the cup of water.

Clifford turns around and smiles. He takes the water from her and swallows a few gulps.

"It's a coping mechanism I used to remind myself that I'm not dead."

Rox's eyes widened with worry.

Clifford continues, "The dream - everyone was dead, including you, and I saw Kyle, or, Mose. He was threatening. I also saw all the people I-" Clifford paused. He didn't want to say it.

"All the people, you, what?" Rox asks, inviting him to tell her more.

Clifford takes a deeper breath and slowly releases it. "I've killed people, Rox. - It weighs on me."

Rox embraces him. "I think it'd be worse if it didn't weigh on you," she says as she presses her cheek against his bare chest.

Listening to his heartbeat regulate, Rox closes her eyes as she lightly glides her fingers up and down his back.

Clifford finishes the water and tosses the empty cup on the floor before wrapping his arms around Rox.

She leans up to place a warm kiss at the base of his neck. "You're my hero, Mr. Dee," she whispers. Baskets jumps from the chair he's using as a bed to inspect the cup Clifford discarded on the floor.

"How are the ribs?" Clifford asks as his body reacts to Rox's touch.

She smiles before nipping his neck. "Manageable," she says.

Clifford reaches down to pull her up against him, and she instinctively wraps her legs around his waist.

# Chapter Forty-One

**It's late** by the time they get home to Virginia. There's no welcoming party, and Clifford feels more at ease.

He parks the moving van and walks around to help Rox and Baskets out.

Dan jogs across the parking lot with Sara. "Can we help?" he asks.

Dee hugs them both. "Just travel bags for now. We can do the rest tomorrow after a good night's sleep."

Sara takes Baskets in his carrier from Rox and escorts them into Dee's home. Bailey rolls in after Sara.

"This must be the beautiful lady who pinged Dee's heart," he accuses with a large grin on his face.

Rox turns and laughs.

Bailey spots the carrier in Sara's hand. And gasps dramatically. "Is that a cat?"

Sara grins. "Uh-huh."

"Gimme!" Bailey says, reaching his hands out.

Sara places the carrier on Bailey's lap.

"Oh, my goodness," Bailey whispers in awe. "You're so cute."

Dee and Dan come in carrying bags in time to see Bailey react to Baskets.

"You okay, B?" Dan asks, confused.

"I always wanted a cat but was never allowed."

Baskets is still angry that he's in his prison, and the crowd gives a collective aww when he meows in protest.

Dee and Dan continue through to set the bags down, and Sara closes the door.

Bailey hands the carrier to Rox. He waits to talk shop until she takes the cat to set up in Dee's bedroom.

"Dee, I have news. I didn't think you'd want me to wait any longer to tell you... Kissinger, his entire family, and Captain Byers; they are all dead, man."

Sara gasps and sits down. Dan runs his fingers through his hair, hit suddenly with grief and anger.

"What happened?" Clifford asks in shock.

"Kissinger and his family succumbed to carbon monoxide poisoning in their sleep."

"Fucking hell," Sara breathes as her head falls into her hands.

Bailey continues. "They're claiming Byers killed herself."

Everyone shakes their heads.

"One hell of a coincidence, if you ask me. Dammit! They were good people," he says as he feels the need to sit down, too.

"Well, I have one more coincidence to add," Bailey says somberly.

Rox returns and sits with Clifford on his couch.

"Go ahead," he says to Bailey, giving him permission to speak in front of Rox.

"Grace's home was burned down. There were fatalities."

Rox gasps, "Oh no!"

Dan makes his way over to a chair of his own.

Clifford's brow furrows. "Grace told me she was taking Hadley out of the country."

Bailey nods. "Right now, there's only a few bodies identified, but none during prelim exams appear to be of females of Grace or Hadley's approximate ages."

"Spencer," Clifford blurts out. "She had an employee named Spencer."

Again, Bailey nods. "One of the confirmed dead is Spencer Rollins. Shorter side, fifty-seven years old. Sound like him?" he asks.

Clifford rubs his face. "Yeah."

"Dillon?" Clifford asks, suddenly remembering the attendant in the garage.

Bailey shrugs, "Could still be one of the unidentified. No mention of a Dillon with any spelling variation."

Bailey looks at Sara and Dan.

"Dee, you two've had a long day, and I just laid this heavy shit on you. We're gonna go. We can plan a meeting to pick up on this shit later."

***

Clifford kisses Rox's head as she lies against him, propped on pillows. "He's got access to his food and nothing's blocking him from his potty. Our boy's set when he leaves his hiding place."

Rox chuckles. "I'll treat him with a Churu tomorrow."

"Maybe Bailey should."

Rox sits and turns to look at him. "The look on his face was so sweet. He looked like a little boy; he was so happy."

Clifford gazes at Rox's smile as she talks about his friend and nods in agreement. He gently pulls her into him.

She lays her hand on his chest as she leans in for a deep kiss.

"As much as I want to christen your first night in my bed properly, we've put your body through a lot lately," he says gruffly as she tucks her head under his chin.

Rox listens to Clifford's heartbeat and steady breathing until it becomes Basket's scratching in his litter box, and she realizes Clifford's no longer in the bed. It's also morning. Late morning.

She rises as Baskets walks out of the bathroom. Rox smiles and praises him when she sees the note on Dee's pillow.

*You needed sleep. I went to the grocery store for some basics.*

*Breakfast is on the island. Fresh pot of coffee is ready - Just push the brew button.*

*I'm at Bailey's. Knock on his door when you're ready to start the day.*

*Take your time, Love.*

She leaves Baskets in Dee's room and walks downstairs to discover pastries sitting in a large pink box. As she eats a flaky cheese Danish, she acquaints herself with his kitchen. The nearly empty fridge from the night before now carries essentials. Rox reaches for the coffee creamer, deciding to leave the orange juice for another time.

She takes her coffee back to the bedroom to shower. After dressing, she hears a soft knock at the front door and runs downstairs to look through the peephole.

"Hey, beautiful!" Sara says when Rox swings the door open.

Rox steps to the side to let Sara in. "Good morning, Dee's at Bailey's," Rox says, assuming that's who Sara's looking for.

"I know."

Rox smiles. "Did he send you to check on me?"

Sara plops down on an oversized chair. "Actually, I came over to see you. Dee told me You've lived in the same area of Colorado all your life. This must all be a little... intense?"

Rox settles into the corner of Clifford's couch and takes a deep breath.

"It's a little overwhelming. I mean, I've only been here for about fifteen hours, so it hasn't fully hit. At least, I don't think it has."

"It takes time. This area is a bit more," Sara searches for the right word. "Chaotic."

"I've been a bartender in a tourist-trap town. I've seen chaos. Excluding this past month, of course."

Sara chuckles and says, "You've also been on your own for a long time."

Rox stares at her lap, nodding absent-mindedly.

Sara shifts in her seat. "I was born, raised, fell in love, and settled down in Kentucky. I had my routine. I knew my way around town with my eyes closed," she chuckles again. "Moving anywhere else never occurred to me, much less near the Capitol of Corruption."

The two women share a laugh.

"Dee brought me with him. He brought all of us, and now we're a family."

"A family doing dangerous work," Rox interjects with a hint of concern.

"It is dangerous. I'm not gonna lie to you. It's also important work. My point is that I know what it's like to find yourself in the middle of something you no longer recognize. There was no plan to start over in a new state. This shit just happens because... Life. My journey before was safe, and it suited who I was then. Now, it's an adventure."

Rox recalls her dream in the hospital. Kate's voice echoes in her head.

*"Sounds like he's going to be the greatest adventure of your life..."*

Rox knows being here feels right, but anxiety always has a way of grabbing onto the reins.

"I've always liked living on my own, but maybe that suited who I was in Colorado. In case you haven't guessed, I haven't decided where I want to live yet," Rox admits.

"Now, did you really think you'd have that figured out in the two days it took to get here?"

They share another laugh.

"Look, whatever you decide, Dee's gonna support you. I mean, we all know he wants to lock you down, and who can blame him? But he shows patience better than any man I've ever met."

"Ya know, if I take you up on your offer, we could each double our wardrobe," Rox suggests.

"Let's just do that anyway," Sara says.


The ladies make their way across to Bailey's newly renovated place. Dee answers the door. His smile widens when he sees Rox behind Sara.

They enter in time to overhear Dan going on about his new parkour and free movement training.

"You need to join me next time. I think you'd like it," he says to Sara, who's already heard the story he was relaying to the other guys.

His friends become background noise as Clifford takes Rox's hand and leads her back outside.

He kisses her and pulls her in for a hug.

"This is your first Virginia morning. How'd you sleep?"

"So good. The boy used his potty, too," Rox says with pride.

"The boy slept between my legs again."

"Aww, he has a favorite sleeping spot," Rox says against his chest, and Clifford chuckles.

"I'm glad he came out from under the bed. He may get used to his new place before I do."

Clifford lifts her chin so her eyes meet his. "There's no rush. You've been through a lot lately."

"I've never not had a job, but I *really* don't want to go back to bartending," she explains.

Clifford kisses her head. "We'll figure it out. In the meantime, you and Baskets will be taken care of."

Rox takes a step back and lays her hands in his. "I don't want to be a burden-"

"That's not a word in my vocabulary. Not with you. *Never* with you," he says, bringing her hands up to kiss one at a time.

"I wonder sometimes if I was actually killed that evening at Wild Willie's, and all of this only exists in my dying brain."

Clifford feels the weight of her words. He keeps his grip on one of her hands, and they walk towards one of the nature trails nestled throughout the town.

"What would you like to do today? We can go anywhere you want."

"Honestly, I just wanna stick close to home. Get to know my new friends better. Maybe we can have dinner with everyone later?"

Clifford places her hand in the crook of his arm as he continues to escort her down the trail. "Touristy shit doesn't appeal to you at all, does it?"

"You're figuring me out quickly, Mr. Dee."

# Chapter Forty-Two

**The walks** on the trails become a daily routine for the two of them. A standing date that they both make time for.

A week after the routine's established, they're forced to cut one short after Clifford receives a text from Bailey to get to his place.

As they reach Bailey's, Dan and Sara meet them by the door. Dan says, "Lunch meeting. We're heading over to Paisano's to get some pizza."

Rox says, "Ooh, I could totally crush some pepperoni pizza right now."

"Say less," Sara interjects.

Clifford pulls a hundred from his wallet. "You fly, I buy. Them's the rules, right?"

"I likes them rules," Dan says as he snatches the money from Clifford's hand, and continues toward the car with Sara.

Clifford heads inside Bailey's with Rox. He plops down on a small sofa-chair next to Bailey's desk and asks, "Any *pings* on Mose?" with a smile, wink, and nod to Rox.

Bailey lets out a slight chuckle. "Well, I've been running scans for anything related to Skyler Mose or Kyle Somers. I'm even searching for Barajas. I figure they'd stick together."

Clifford nods as Bailey continues.

"I got a few hits, but none were him," Bailey says with a hint of frustration.

"Cool, does it flag you for new stuff or just archived?"

"Both. If he pops up anywhere, I'll find him."

Clifford smiles, "Sounds good. I'd like to get a head start before Agent Arbor gets here and we have to start reporting everything."

"Smart. Oh, and Sims sent me a text. Arbor reports on the first Monday of next month, so we have another week," Bailey says.

Rox looks at the information gathered and focuses on the two names written out. Kyle Somers and Skyler Mose.

"The name's not even creative," she mutters to no one in particular.

Bailey leans back to look at her. "The name's not what now?"

"Well, his name *was* Kyle Somers. Skyler Mose is an anagram," she explains, pointing at the board.

Bailey huffs and starts typing furiously on his keyboard as Clifford walks over to her.

"Did I say something wrong?" She asks, looking past him at Bailey.

"Not at all. You just highlighted something we didn't notice."

Bailey yells out, "You just gave me an idea to run a scan on names with any combination of the same letters. The chances of him doing it again are slim, but it's another avenue. Thanks!"

Rox's interest piques, and she inquiries about Bailey's proprietary software. He's all happy to explain it to her, even if she doesn't fully understand.

Sara and Dan eventually get back with the pizzas, and Rox rushes to the kitchen to grab a slice.

"Hey Dee? You want me to bring you any?" she yells out around the others.

When he doesn't answer, she looks around the wall to see Clifford and Bailey's attention are on the television. She carries her plate over to see news coverage of Skyler Mose's death.

*...international terrorist known as Skyler Mose was confirmed dead by members of his community when they were tracked to a compound in Big Sky, Montana...*

"That's not him. That's not Mose!" Clifford yells at the television.

Sara and Dan join the others to watch the story the media is running with unfold.

The news shows surveillance photos of a man; one with a bandage over one eye and another without the wound. The name on the banner underneath the photos reads, Skyler Mose.

"That's Jessica's husband, Saul!" he says, exasperated.

*...the FBI released this video confession of one loyalist claiming to have shot him...*

The video shows Timothy in handcuffs at an FBI detention center with Special Agent in Charge, Mark Tanner, questioning him.

Tim shakes his head as he says, "Skylar lost his eye during the fight at the police station. We saw him by the river, and we all knew at that point who he was. We didn't want to believe it, but when I saw him, I was so angry. I felt so betrayed by him... I shot him. I shot him in his other eye."

Rox gasps as she reaches for her phone. "That guy! He was one of the ones who ambushed you at the hotel!"

She scrolls through pictures of Clifford and Baskets until she finds the one she took that evening of the two guys at the front desk.

Clifford can make out the scab still on Timothy's Adam's apple and nods. "Tim," Clifford says.

The screen changes to a surveillance photo of a robust woman

*Authorities say Skyler Mose's accomplice is this woman: Jessica McKinley.*

*It's believed she fled the compound well before the federal raid.*

Another video clip with a community member airs.

A bald, slender-faced man in his sixties and wearing glasses, emotionally says, "She trashed our infirmary the day before leaving. She made sure none of us would get the medical care we'd need. She left us vulnerable!"

The anchor returns on screen to finish the breaking story.

*Jessica McKinley has now been placed on the FBI's Ten Most Wanted.*

*Ironically, replacing Skylar Mose.*

The anchor then announces a commercial break, and Bailey mutes the television.

Dan snarls. "That fucker put a target on her back!"

"Bailey, we need to find Jess first," Clifford says to an already nodding partner.

The commercial abruptly switches to a live news broadcast with a reporter talking in front of a gathered crowd. The automatic closed-caption quickly reveal the words:

"Unmute!" Clifford, uncharacteristically, demands.

His eyes transfixed on the man in a tailored gray suit with two small butterfly bandages on his left cheek standing next to the Governor of Montana.

The FBI Director, Martin Rafini, is firm in his televised speech as he gives credit for the organized raid on Big Sky and, subsequently, Mose's demise to -

*CIA Agent Jack Hayden.*

The name rattles Clifford.

"Kyle!" he growls, as the clean-shaven man in the grey suit with the fresh scar and a third name shakes the Director's hand and steps up to face the cameras. A feigned humble smile firmly in place.

"That sonofabitch looks awfully comfortable at a podium," Sara says spitefully.

Rox asks, "Bailey, did you know about that alias?"

Scrambling back to his computer, "No, but why does that name feel familiar to me?" he says, typing the name into his search.

Rox looks over at Clifford. "Dee? You okay?"

Clifford can feel her hand on his back, but Fred's voice is in his head... from that very first morning in Colorado...

*"His name's Jack Hayden. I met him about six years ago or so. I was still on the force. A confidential informant in a case I was working on."*

An alert comes across Bailey's computer.

"Shit!" Bailey exclaims before explaining. "I gotta hit on a name from Hadley's file!"

Before anyone can ask, Bailey yells, "Dee! Fred's Guy! Jack Hayden!"

Words and links scroll fast with images scattered in on Bailey's main monitor for all to see.

"He's! He's..." Bailey's voice trails off as he turns to the group. "He's everywhere... and every time..."

Clifford looks over at him. "What do you mean, every *time*?"

"Archived hits - some going back decades. Those would've been easy searches for my program the first time."

"Should we alert Sims?" Dan asks.

Clifford shakes his head. "What's he gonna do? Look into it? They never had a description of Mose until they ID'd Saul as him. Basically, it's our word against his. And besides, who'd you believe? The problematic team on probation? Or the country's newest hero?"

Sara chimes in. "They even made sure Byers and Kissinger couldn't help us," Sara says. "Would've been nice to call in a favor for street cam footage of what happened to their town."

"Favor!" Clifford says aloud.

*'I asked for a favor, and he was happy to help.'*

"Fred asked for a favor!"

Sara asks, "Like muddy boots guy?"

Clifford grabs his phone from the table next to Bailey's desk.

He opens it and scrolls through his text messages, finding one from Fred. He opens it and clicks the 'contacts' icon. It brings up his phone number.

"Bailey, got another spare phone?"

Bailey opens a drawer stocked with burners and grabs one. "What's your idea?" He asks.

"Could you log into one with just a phone number? Like with Hadley's phone?"

Bailey shakes his head. "Well, no. I'd need a passcode or his fingerprint. Remember, Grace gave you her password."

Clifford smiles.

"What is it?"

"I'll be right back."

Sara looks at Rox with a quizzical look, and Rox can only shrug.

After a few minutes, Clifford returns with a coin inside a baggie.

"Fred told me he had never been in the military. When Fulk and I were looking in his office, after he was killed, I saw this 2nd Cav coin on his desk and thought it was strange he'd have one. So, I snagged it. It might have his prints. Can you lift it?"

Bailey says, "It's possible, but I don't know if it's usable. I'm trackin' you so far, but I still don't know where you're goin' with this."

Clifford says, "Fred asked Jack Hayden for a *favor*. Anderson had to download an app to communicate with him to *return* a favor. What if Fred has the same app?"

Bailey smiles. "Dee, that's genius. But... lifting a print and then using said print? It really is a long shot."

Clifford sighs. "Can you try?"

Bailey nods. "Of course. But it'll take time, and I'll need a few items."

Clifford says, "Text me a list and I'll run out to get whatever you need."

He turns to Rox. "I may move quicker without you. Are you good to stay here?"

"Mm-hmm," she manages with her mouth full as she raises what's left of her second slice, and moves to sit with Sara

The sun is set by the time Clifford returns from gathering the items Bailey needed.

Sara and Daniel are already setting up an investigation board with all the information they have, and Rox is taking her own notes.

The top of the board reads: 'Redivivus'

Clifford stops to marvel at his team, working perfectly as a unit before taking everything over to Bailey.

Clifford walks over to Rox as he continues to look at the board.

"You're naming the case Redivivus?" he asks Sara.

"It was on that note you told me to give Bailey. I thought it was fitting."

Clifford nods. "I like it."

"It's working!" Bailey says.

Clifford looks back over and asks, "Are you in the phone?"

"Oh God, no! Step *one* is working," he says before going on a technical rant.

"Basically, I'm using the laser to scan the coin for fingerprints. Luckily, this coin was maintained really well while on display. There is a solid print on it, and the laser's picking it up."

Clifford says, "Nice! Then what?"

"Next, it'll load the print onto the computer. I'll see if I can print it on a latex glove you can wear."

"Will that work?" Clifford asks.

"Dunno. I told you it was a long shot."

Clifford shakes his head and says, "Okay, keep at it."

He walks over to the board and starts reading and makes a few suggestions as they brainstorm.

After several minutes, Bailey says, "It's done."

They all walk over and watch as Bailey puts the glove on and tries to unlock the phone.

It was successful but asks for a four-digit pin.

Bailey scoffs, "I'll run my 'passcracker' app on it. This'll take hours."

Clifford says, "Try one, nine, eight, four."

Bailey types it in and the phone unlocks.

"How did you know that?"

Clifford says, "Fred graduated from the Police Academy that year. It was on his plaque in his office. He seems the type to keep it as his pin."

Bailey plugs Fred's phone into the computer and starts downloading all the apps and files.

An app flashes across the screen, named "Manus Manum Lavat." Rox spots it and says, "What's that?"

Bailey asks back, "What?"

"Go back. I saw something."

Bailey scrolls back, and Rox sees it again. "There."

Clifford asks, "What does Manus Manum Lavat mean?"

Rox says, "One hand washes the other. It's Latin for doing a favor. I scratch your back, yadda, yadda, yadda."

Everyone looks over toward her, and she says with a smile, "I studied Latin."

Bailey clicks the app, and it's a blank screen with a blinking cursor.

"So, should we type something?" Clifford asks.

Bailey cautiously shakes his head. "I don't know if that's a good idea. It could have keylogging technology. I'll run a scan."

Seconds later, a message types across: *"Hello Dee…"*

# Clifford's War: Redivivus
# Epilogue

**The sun** finally sets over the mountain peaks, and a woman sits scraping a bit of pine resin onto a small piece of wood. She removes a cotton ball from her med-pack and lays it across the wood and rolls it across it, coating the cotton with the resin. Setting it into her tiny, boxed firepit, she takes a Bushcraft fire starter and strikes the steel onto the flint to create a spark. The cotton catches a spark, lights, and the resin sustains the burn long enough to allow her to place twigs and cones onto the flames to start a cooking fire.

Minutes later, the sound of a spoon clanking on a small cast-iron skillet echo across the rocks. Inside is a small amount of snow, melting over the pit. It will be a few more moments before the snow-melted water will be warm enough to soak her frost-nipped fingers.

The small, one-person tent positioned strategically blocks the wind rolling off the picturesque snow-covered hills. The dense ponderosa pines provide cover from the only road cutting through the wilderness, following a mountain ridge.

A quaint frozen over pond lay in an opening further down the landscape, where a herd of buffalo are plowing the snow in search of food, as they slowly make their way closer to her camp.

After her fingers are warmed and dried, Jessica slaps the side of a portable satellite television. She only watches for an hour a night to keep up on current events as she continues to track.

She returns focus to her meal on the fire. She was successful in trapping, skinning, and now cooking her first weasel. She takes a bite and instantly begins to gag. The gamey taste is much worse than the muskrats she was able to trap earlier in the week.

Losing the satellite signal again, Jessica fiddles with her hand-held device to try to reacquire the signal. When she does, it's in the middle of repeating breaking news from earlier in the day.

…"NO!"